WHITE LIES

JO GATFORD

Legend Press Ltd, The Old Fire Station,
140 Tabernacle Street, London, EC2A 4SD
info@legend-paperbooks.co.uk | www.legendpress.co.uk

Contents © Jo Gatford 2014
The right of the above author to be identified as the author of this work has
been asserted in accordance with the Copyright, Designs and Patent Act
1988. British Library Cataloguing in Publication Data available.

Print ISBN 978-1-9101620-4-0
Ebook ISBN 978-1-9101620-5-7
Set in Times. Printed in the United Kingdom by TJ International.
Cover design by Simon Levy www.simonlevyassociates.co.uk

Legend ▌Press

Jo Gatford is a writer from Brighton. She was the winner of the 2013 Luke Bitmead Bursary and longlisted for the 2013 Tibor Jones Pageturner Prize.

She has, at one time or another, been: a till-monkey in a book shop, a circus performer, a childminder, a cleaner of expensive Hovian houses, a baby massage teacher, a graveyard-shift hotel waitress, an antenatal yoga teacher, and musician. Her flash fiction and short stories have been published in various UK and US literary magazines, including *Litro*, *PANK*, and *SmokeLong Quarterly*.

Visit Jo at
jogatford.com
or on Twitter
@jmgatford

For my boys.

Chapter One

There's a head-shaped hole in the plasterboard of my living room wall. A cracked depression, clumsily slathered with Polyfilla. I've learned how to ignore it, to unfocus my vision when I pass. I've acclimatised to the discomfort of it, like a lump I can't swallow. I thought it might be easier once I'd cleaned the blood away. There was only a smear from where he'd lurched up, after the impact. A smear and the echo of a little internal voice that said, "I'm never getting my deposit back now," instead of, "Is he okay?"

Because, at the time, I couldn't give a shit. That's the sum of it. And they all know it. My fault. Blame me. Even though the autopsy report said it was inevitable, even though the police poked unenthusiastically at the crumbling dent in the wall and offered shrugged condolences instead of handcuffs. I know. I killed my brother.

"Half-brother," I corrected the policeman as he wrote in his little notebook. Let's get that right at least.

I don't believe in ghosts but he's haunting me all the same, like an absence of noise you hadn't noticed was there - the unsettling feeling of pausing a song on the inhale. I sleep on the sofa, the muted TV for a campfire - to keep the wild things at bay. Except it doesn't. The moment I slip away, the nightmares creep through the cracks in the plaster and my half-brother's stupid head leers out at me. A reminder of my purgatory, every Sunday, bowing at the altar of my father's armchair, mumbling the same answers to the same questions:

"When's Alex coming?"

"Where's Alex?"

"Why doesn't he visit me?"

"Why doesn't he come?"

And I have to take in a slow, dry breath, as though the air is full of sand, and it starts all over again: "Dad... Alex died."

Today the news slips out with no preamble, no parachute to lessen the gut-wrenching drop. It's been three weeks. Sometimes it's better just to say it straight away. Sometimes, these days, he doesn't even reply. Dad's responses have cycled through distress, hatred, obliviousness, ambivalence and, most recently, a sneering disdain - like he doesn't even believe me. Practice doesn't make it any easier. In fact, I'm more bored than sick of the whole fucking thing. Maybe tragedy becomes dull when it's inevitable.

My father sits there in his floral armchair, three feet away from me, pretending I don't exist. He stares at the door, occasionally dropping his chin to his chest, clearing his throat of fifty years' worth of tobacco-tinged phlegm, glancing nervously at the drawers beneath his bed.

"Dad? Did you hear me?"

He looks up, nods absently, and pats down the left arm of his chair in a vague attempt to find the remote control. It's on his lap, next to the stump of his right arm, where his hand used to be. I don't point it out to him, don't want to show him how slow and stupid he has become.

His world has been reduced to a single room in the third-nicest dementia nursing home in the South East and his mind is downsizing along with it – making heavy-handed attempts at erasing itself, like trying to cover footprints with dynamite. I'm the last one he reliably recognises, and I'm probably the last person he wants to see.

I cast around for something to say, some reminder that might yank him back from fairyland for a minute or two. He sits like he's in a waiting room, imposing on someone else's home, sitting in someone else's seat. He'll spend the day that way, anxiously anticipating something he can't remember, too proud or polite to ask where he is, or when he's going home.

I can't sit here anymore. The bed twangs and undulates as I stand. We watch it come to a lazy stop. A slice of afternoon sunlight, full of dead skin, highlights a single square on the silky quilted eiderdown. The type of bedding Nana Alice thought was classy and luxurious but would fuse to skin like molten plastic if ever it saw a naked flame. It's not the same as hers; the wrong shade of dirty pink, the wrong pattern of roses. Not familiar enough, though it has that same musty scent of sandalwood and sweat. I used to lie belly-down on her bed and press the cool satin against my temple, a crackle of static in my ear. But these are my memories, not Dad's. I carry around the same questions for him as I did when I was small, when Nana Alice's house was home and he was just a visitor. Thirty-something years and I still can't bring myself to ask him plainly. And now it's too late. He's too weak to interrogate. Instead, I worry about health and safety and wonder if I should tell the staff about the fire hazard combination of my chain-smoking dad and his highly flammable eiderdown.

His few remaining possessions are laid out on top of the chest of drawers like a shrine: a stack of books, photos in heavy silver frames, a radio, his prosthetic hand. It looks obscenely false sitting there, like a prop in a comedy sketch. I pick up each photo, hardly seeing them, replacing them as softly as I can. Even movement is slow in this thick air. Angela with a red-eyed baby Clare, Alex and me in an apple tree, my step-mum Lydia's teasing smile. None of me before Alex was born. None of my mother. I took the last remaining one of her with me when we cleared out his flat. The one that used to sit on his mantelpiece. He never asked for it back. A charity Christmas card sits next to the radio - a robin in snow, a generic Merry Christmas from all the staff at The Farm House and an extra kiss from Angela, his step-daughter, my step-sister, destined to watch him fall to pieces in her workplace. Poor fuckers, the lot of them.

He watches me out of his peripheral vision while I pick through his belongings, reluctantly searching for a conversation starter. Something not to do with Alex.

He used to ask where he was, why he was here, what we had done with his glasses. Before that, the questions were more innocuous but it was his questions that brought him here.

"Where do I keep the beans?" he'd asked, when I brought his shopping up to the flat. And according to Angela and the doctor and the nursing home, knowing which cupboard you store your baked beans in – unchanged for fifteen years – is the hinge upon which independent living hangs.

He didn't ask any more questions when I explained how Angela could get him a place at The Farm House at a subsidised rate, and that by selling his flat he could afford to pay the rent at the nursing home until… And then I didn't know how to phrase "until you die".

I took his silence for reluctant agreement.

No, I didn't.

I took his silence for miserable defeat, but I pretended it was reluctant agreement while we packed up his things and sold off his furniture, putting the rest of his stuff in storage until… "In case you want them sometime, Dad."

I swallow, reaching limply for small talk, turning the cheap Christmas card in my hands. "Angie said she wanted to take you to The Boatman for Christmas lunch, maybe."

No response. I force words out of myself like splinters, trying to trigger a memory. "Remember when Nana Alice picked a fight with the chef there? About the scampi?" I say. Nana Alice is a safe choice. The memory of his mother-in-law might revive him if only to bitch about her. "She said it tasted like gristle wrapped in bits of cardboard."

Deep, glutinous memories. A squat, thatched bungalow perched on an island of green, bypass all around, the rumbling white noise of traffic topped with *Sounds of the Sixties* on repeat. Walking the perimeter of the dining area, tapping on wood-panelled walls, hoping to discover hidden secret passages to smuggler caves. Reaching skinny arms into snooker table pockets, trying to guess the colour of each ball before it emerged, the thud against soft green felt, the sluggish trajectory, the mesmeric roll. Once you let go there is no way of influencing the journey. Studded leather benches in muffled little booths, all three kids to a side, Dad and Lydia on the other, Nana Alice on the corner, next to me. Every public holiday: a phone call from my mother's mother that made Dad squeeze his eyes into a wince, or provoked a catty, overenthusiastic, "Wonderful!" from Lydia. The Boatman, for lunch. Something with chips and peas. Orange and lemonade. Steamed pudding with a custard moat. Bellyache, holding seatbelts away from anguished stomachs and full bladders on the ride home.

Dad lifts his eyes from the floor but his expression doesn't change.

"You were mortified, I think," I say. "She demanded to look round the kitchen to see if they were really deep-frying cardboard back there. They ended up giving us all free ice cream sundaes and - " And all memories come circling back to the same resolution. I toss the card back onto the chest of drawers. "And Alex knocked mine over and I cried."

Dad looks back at his knees, notices the remote control, tries out a few buttons, receiving the reward of a high-pitched squeal as the ancient set buzzes to life and the screen fills with electronic snow.

I raise my voice to match the weather report coming through the static. "He said we should feed it to the fish in the pond, and you and Lydia laughed."

" - *brisk easterly wind with persistent snow for parts of East Anglia -* "

"And I couldn't stop crying, and you slapped me on the leg to make me shut up, and then you all ate your fucking ice cream while I watched, until Angie gave me half of hers.

Remember that, Dad?"

He's looking at me now, eyes moist and jerky with uncertainty.

" - *remaining dull and cold, with light sleet across the South for most of the morning -* "

"You remember who I am?" I ask.

A dip of the head, "Matthew."

"And Angela?"

Another nod.

"And Alex?"

"When is he coming to see me?"

Fuck. I can't say it again. "I don't know."

Dad knows, I know he does, he just won't let himself remember. The agony is there in his eyes, in the twitching of his Adam's apple, in the unconscious clench of his arthritic fist. We're similar for the first time - all the physical symptoms of grief with none of the emotion. It's not that I don't care, it's not that it doesn't hurt, but I just haven't worked out how to mourn for someone I hated.

I wasn't with my brother when he died, but I can see it happen every time I try to sleep. And if I sleep, when I sleep, he's there, cursing my name. Of course he fucking is. Screaming ancient, nameless, binding curses as he stumbles down the concrete steps from my flat to the frost-dusted street outside, cursing me right up until the moment something inside his head implodes.

He collapses as though he is folding into three pieces – at the knees and waist – landing sideways onto gravel and glass and fag ends and rain. His head bounces off the tarmac. His brain is bleeding and his body doesn't know what to do with itself. Pulses of steaming blood silence him, deafen him with soft pink swollen tissue. I see him from above, lying there. I hear him whispering, even after the scene ends and I know he's dead. He never passed up a chance to cause me pain when he was alive. Why shouldn't he do it from the grave, too?

The nurse comes early today and sing-songs the little

magic spell that rouses us from our mutual silence and allows me to leave.

"Lunch time, Peter!" As if Dad's been waiting for this bland, overcooked meal his whole life. She apologises, tells me I'll have to get going, and I feign reluctance with a sad smile - for her sake, not his. Or maybe for my sake, so I don't seem like a total bastard. No, please, let me stay and atrophy with these walking corpses while they drool gravy down their hairy chins.

I pat him on the shoulder as I pass. He's not quite one of them yet. He looks up at me, showing his teeth in a tentative smile, as if he can't remember if I'm here to fix a tap or rob him. He could be a poster boy for gum disease with that mouth. I resolve to floss twice daily, hit genetics where it hurts.

"Time to go, Dad. I'll see you next week."

He scratches his right nostril and turns to the window, back into the foggy depths of his head. The nurse is all rosy-cheeked sympathy but she stinks of cigarettes and bleach.

I'm almost at reception when Angela appears out of nowhere and grabs me, perpetuating my fear that one day I will look behind me as I walk through the nursing home's gaudily wallpapered corridors to see a horde of growling, crawling zombies, eager for flesh. A cold flush of sweat ripples down my back.

"Jumpy," she says.

"Zombie," I mutter.

"How's your dad?"

"The same."

"He's having a good day today," she claims, though I can see she doesn't believe it either. She lances me with a significant look. "Did you tell him about Alex?"

"I tried. He didn't cry today. And I told him about your little Christmas day trip, which you know he's not going to give a shit about. He's getting worse, Angie."

She deflects the negativity with a tight smile, slipping her arm through mine as we walk. "Familiar places are good for his memory." She lowers her tone a few notches when we pass her supervisor and the receptionist, "He needs to get out of this place now and then. Otherwise he's just going to get more and more confused."

"He's already confused." The same question, over and over again. Where's Alex? Where's Alex? Where the fuck is Alex? Even the inflection is the same. Telling him his favourite son is dead was hard enough the first time; by the fiftieth the words don't even make sense. I shake my head. "He doesn't know who you are any more, does he?"

She jerks her arm like I've burned her. "Sometimes he does," she says, "Sometimes he thinks I'm Alma."

"Who's Alma?"

"His Greek dentist."

"He never had a Greek dentist."

"In his head he did."

"Have you seen his teeth? He never went to the fucking dentist."

"Language, Matthew," Angela stage whispers.

An old lady with toothpaste stains down the front of her cardigan glares at me and purses thin lips into a wrinkled cat's arse. I smile back charmingly and she spits something yellow into a tissue. Bile rushes up my throat.

Angela pushes me towards the door with a long sigh, brushing down her uniform and turning back to face the legions of withering, floundering patients who snarl and snap and dribble and shit themselves and call her a bitch and a prostitute and try to pinch her arse and weep silently as they clutch at her hands, because they have no idea where they are any more. Angela is beyond human, beyond the zombies. And in amongst the daily miracles she performs, she still manages to smile and love the man who raised her like a daughter but for some reason now thinks she's here to give him a root canal.

She pauses at the door and attempts a nonchalant expression, "Is Clare okay?"

My middle name should be 'uncomfortable mediator'.

14

No-one's talking to Angela, not Dad, not even her own daughter. Clare, my niece, has been sleeping at my flat since Alex died. "I don't know," I say, "I mean, yeah, she's fine." I press my fingertips into the hollows under my eyes. Tiredness beyond talking. Too many faces that can't seem to smile any more. And they're all looking to me. "I've been trying to get her to call you, I promise."

A slow, stoic nod from Angie and she turns away, waving once over her shoulder as the double doors swing shut behind her.

Across the car park I see Dad's empty armchair through his bedroom window on the ground floor. One more week until the next weighing of my heart. The same chair, the same sagged face, uneven with stubble. Since his last stroke, one jowl hangs a few millimetres lower than the other, one eye sits deeper inside its discoloured hood. Another week closer to losing the answers he's always refused to give me. Because I'm not just here for Angela, for whatever I owe Alex. I'm here because I don't want him to die without telling me the truth: what really happened to my mother.

Chapter Two   Peter

My mind does not simply play tricks on me, it tucks me into bed, sneaks out on tiptoes and runs naked through the streets while I sleep soundly, unaware of the damage it causes and the horrors it commits and the humiliations it leaves laid out neatly for me when I awake.

It's becoming harder to distinguish the spaces in between. My bed has been made but I don't remember lying in it. The only hint that I did not pass a silent night is the splintering ache in my limbs, the heaviness of my joints, a flaring of pain behind my eyes with each pulse of my over-stimulated heart.

The nurses describe my nightly exploits in the same tone Ingrid next door talks about the latest soap storyline: lip-lickingly plump little portions of can-you-believe-its, wrapped in quasi-professional restraint. Last night they found me hysterically sorting socks, searching for something in my top drawer that clearly wasn't there. And I woke wondering if there would be croissants for breakfast.

They say it's a benign symptom, harmless to the one who experiences it, but it's not. The not-knowing is like chloroform, stuffed into my nostrils, shoved deep down into my lungs - like a strap stretched tight across my sunken chest. The dread in knowing there will come a day when I blithely give away all the things that should never be known, without even noticing. My brain melts, my tongue loosens, and secrets could slip out of me as easily as sighs. The only way I know they haven't already done so is the fact that my children are still speaking to me.

Matthew sits there, not three feet away from me, watching the clock until he's spent his requisite hour and feels justified in leaving. He does it kindly, I suppose, or perhaps it's contrived. He times his visits exactly an hour before lunch so that it will be one of the nurses who asks him to leave and not his own decision to go. He breathes through his mouth so he won't have to smell the sweetness of the phlegm and decomposing flesh that permeates the very walls of this death camp. He's given up trying to uphold a conversation with me, never knowing whether he will find a relevant response, a stammering idiot or a silent rebuttal. An hour of stifling quiet in between, "Anything you need, Dad?" and "Nurse says it's time to go, Dad. I'll see you next week."

He must think I'm not speaking to him, but what is there left to say? You really don't have to sit here and watch me disintegrate.

He looks tired. A petulant anger that must surely be directed at me. I worry about the hidden things when he's here. I can't concentrate. He's saying something but I can't decipher it. It's hard enough trying to keep my eyes from fixing on what I don't want him to find. The eyes in the shadows beneath the bed.

The room is too small and the walls lean in. A divan, a chair, drawers, a window, two doors. One leads to a bathroom that could fit inside a cupboard. The other leads into the leafy-carpeted corridor, to notice boards and dado rails twisted with tinsel, a multitude of comfortable chairs and staff rooms locked tight. Two doors, but not always a bathroom and a corridor. Those are just two possibilities within the labyrinth. Sometimes the doorways lead to my kitchen, my aunt's greenhouse, the plumbing aisle of Warton's building merchants', the passenger seat of Lydia's car, a clifftop.

The clifftop is the worst. There are fingernails on the edge, elongated footprints that slide from mud to sky, waves rising up to block out the sun. There is no way of returning from where you've been, but there is always another door. The only door on the clifftop is the telephone box and I can never bring myself to step inside.

The dementia is vascular, sniping at me with little strokes, a descending staircase, pushing me deeper within myself. Each one blunts another corner, cutting off the link between fingers and buttonholes, spoon and teacup, time and movement, nurse and step-daughter. I wonder if it will turn me inside out, eventually. The universe has become finite, composed entirely of doorways, shrinking ever smaller, closing down the open spaces. I move from door to door, from this gentle prison and weathered body to standing at a bay window, swaying a warm baby in my arms; to dragon-breath steam in a morning garden, turning potatoes out of the soil with a fork; to a dark, vanilla-scented bedroom, tracing Lydia's waist with hot palms, back when I had two of them. Some days I look down to find my right hand sawn off with no recollection of the bite, the gangrene, the surgery.

I always return, though I don't always know I've been away. And there is always another door.

I watch the doorway to the hallway now, keeping an eye on the predator, tensing for the pounce. It is waiting for Matthew to leave, urging me to slip through its wavering threshold.

"Dad?" he asks.

I nod.

"You remember who I am?"

When I am here, when I walk amongst the other residents, I see them slipping. Each day less coherence, fewer smiles, more confusion, fear, frustration. I feel them dragging me along with them, though I won't know it when I'm pulled under. Am I getting worse? And would they tell me if I were? Matthew looks into my eyes as though there is less of me there to be found. He watches for the day when there is no recognition at all. Today, I remember. I know my own son. I say, "Matthew."

"And Angela?"

I nod. Step-daughter. Lydia's eldest, Alex's half-sister, Matthew's step-sister. Poor Angela, siphoned in between the pieces of a badly-fitted family jigsaw.

"And Alex?"

A chill hits my guts, rising up, crushing my oesophagus until I can't swallow without wincing. Alex. My baby boy, always, even though he stands at my height, even though his breath smells of tobacco and he talks about base-rate tracking mortgages and doesn't let me pay for drinks. I miss him. I don't know how long he's been away but it feels like too long. Angela comes less frequently these days, too. I would be angry but I can't access it - it falls limp in the place of a sadness I can't justify. The real reason they haven't visited lurks behind yet another door – this one locked and bolted and impenetrable – and Matthew won't tell me.

"When is he coming to see me?" I ask him.

He shakes his head. Disappointment. I should know why. But I cannot have all things at all times. It's enough that I know where I am, know this musty, gloomy room and the cause of my imprisonment. I know my eldest son. Tomorrow it could all fade behind a discoloured film of the past - he could be a stranger like the rest.

#

Matthew is gone, and the nurse attempts to coax me into the common room for lunch. I offer mild-mannered refusal and she eventually leaves me with the contemptible cliché of a tartan blanket draped across my knees. I cannot move, not when the doorway beckons with promises of elsewhere, the possibility of a brief hiatus from the inexorable nursing home days.

The home's brochure describes lunch as 'a sociable affair', which translates into 'sandwiches on side tables and laps, wherever we happen to be sitting'. Sandwiches and tea, the never-ending supply that might as well be administered intravenously. Testing each chair for dampness before sitting becomes second nature once you witness the sheer volume of warm liquid consumed daily. Then, the choice between Battenburg or Victoria sponge. On Sundays there is chocolate log and mint Vienetta. When Ingrid's sister bakes, there is fruit cake you could use to sink dead bodies.

Dinner is a tightly orchestrated 'sit down affair' in the dining room - meat and two veg boiled to oblivion so as to disintegrate harmlessly when pressed against the roof of one's mouth. It coincides with the shift change, so must be served and eaten by six precisely. Actually, it's beside the point whether it's eaten or not. As soon as the clock in the foyer starts its hollow pinging, plates are whisked out from under chins, forks snatched from hands, napkins yanked out of shirt collars and the very tablecloth pulled away like a magic trick. Except all that's left is a sad collection of trembling, stained leftovers, cowering in their wheelchairs, blinking like confused, surfacing moles.

When I step through a new door they disappear back underground, all of them. They cannot intrude on things that have already happened, or into echoing misty landscapes that even I do not recognise. I am lost here, but through the warren of doorways I have years ahead of me, and the torturous illusion that I could do things differently. It shows me things I didn't even know I'd done wrong. It shows me Lydia, before the hospice. And it shows me Heather, before she vanished. Before Matthew.

Back here, with the rest of them, the pull of gravity is a thousand times more urgent. We are the most fragile of fruit, rotting from the inside out while our skin puckers and our orifices slacken, bruising like two-week-old plums. We are reduced to mucus-ridden, barking turkeys upon contracting a simple cold. Our eyes dim milky yellow, our ears grow ever larger but ever more useless, our teeth crumble in our mouths and our brain cells – having long stopped reproducing themselves – die lonely deaths, jettisoning random memories as the ship goes down.

The doorway calls. I need to move. Before I can gather the right connections between intent and muscle contraction to raise myself out of the armchair, a woman who looks remarkably like my dentist lays a tray on my lap. She smiles for longer than seems necessary, asks if there's anything else she can get me. I shake my head at my knees, uncomfortable with the over-familiarity, hoping I did not misunderstand the question. She leans forward and gives me a light hugging around the shoulders before she leaves. A waft of shampoo scent hangs in the air behind her. She has the same hair as Lydia, all frizz and unruly wonder, standing out from her skull like balloon static, conker-brown and squirrel-red in the light. Windy autumn hair. You'd expect it to smell like damp grass and bonfires but it doesn't. It smells like almonds and chemicals. I watch her go. If I squint my eyes I can imagine that she is my Lydia, just off out to get some milk, and I am sitting in my leather recliner, about to watch the tennis.

Next door, the incessant bing-bong of the nurse-call button harmonises with the rabid yelling of my neighbour, Ingrid, who is apparently in need of some new sheets. No matter how hard I squint my eyes, there is no way of squinting my ears.

It is time. The doorway glows, expanding at the sides as though an enormous bubble is pushing its way through, distorting the physical space within the architrave. There are answers inside, and faces. Alex's face, impatient and irritated that I have taken so long to find him.

My knees obey, finally. The contents of my tray hit the carpet with a muted clatter of plastic and melamine, blanketed in tartan. Flakes of tuna and kernels of sweetcorn stick to my slipper soles. A slice of cucumber, carefully whittled into the shape of a leaf, lies sneakily camouflaged against the patterned carpet. The doorway beats a blood-gushing heartbeat into the air around it, sound waves almost visible, sucking the air out of the room like an airlock on a spaceship. Step through or die. Follow or stop breathing.

There's something the other side – something more vivid than tuna mayonnaise and salad vegetables and white sliced bread, something that is long dead but still more animated than this place. It knows I will always step through. She knows. I have been following her for thirty-five years.

Chapter Three

Alex died on my birthday, almost as if he'd timed it on purpose. Like he was making sure I wouldn't ever forget.

Angela had booked a table at a cheap Italian, picked up Dad from the nursing home, and insisted everyone order three courses, even though I knew she couldn't afford it, and I didn't want to celebrate anyway.

"It'll be good for your dad, too," she'd said. "A chance to get him out for an evening, to get the whole family together - how often does that happen?" What she meant was: Alex had decided to come down for the weekend and my birthday was a convenient excuse to get him to see Dad, to salve his state of mind with the presence of his favourite son.

But Alex hadn't turned up, as I suspected he wouldn't. We filled up on garlic bread and wine and he eventually sent a text to say he was on his way but traffic was a bitch and that he'd join us for dessert. I laid bets on a second text within twenty minutes saying he wasn't feeling up to it and maybe he'd see us tomorrow, and that everyone would be okay with this. Disappointed, but not surprised, though somehow it was never his fault.

"You're paranoid," Sabine said. She was still my girlfriend back then, with a weird affection for my dysfunctional past.

"One day," I'd said, "you'll lose your blinkered optimism about my family all getting along and see what a manipulative bunch of fuckers we really are."

She used to laugh at my snarling, jaded rants. This time she just scowled. "Oh, I know exactly what you are. But you're becoming worse than any of them."

My second glass of red wine set alight a glowing in my chest. The tea lights on the tables reflected double in the French doors at the back of the restaurant, transforming the £13.99 set meal into something more festive. Even the way my dad ate with his mouth half open didn't seem to be quite as annoying as it usually was, until he said, "The one time Heather made meatballs, even the cat got ill."

Angela looked from my face to Dad's with a frantic expression, as though reality would cease to exist if someone didn't respond quickly enough.

"Really? She... Heather was a bad cook?" Angela said. The rest of us stopped breathing for a second. Dad poked at his pasta.

I felt Sabine's hand slide into the crook of my elbow, heard her breath catch at the top of her throat. Clare gaped at her grandfather, disbelief cornered with the hint of a smirk - the prospect of a scandal.

The acoustics in the restaurant were off-balance, somehow - too much glass in the aspirational modernist architecture that turned the clatter of crockery and echoes of speech into pressurised white noise.

"Peter?" Angela prompted, "You were telling us about Heather's meatballs."

Clare sniggered and Angela slapped her on the thigh in a reflexive movement, then breathed out a hushed apology.

"Hmm?" Dad murmured.

Sabine's fingers clasped around my forearm with anticipation and I fought the urge to shake her off. This was not meant to be dinner and a show. I slammed my fork onto the glass table and everyone startled. Dad laughed around a mouthful of spaghetti as if we were all mad for gawping. "If you like your meat raw, eat at Heather and Peter's. That's what our friends said. Your nan was no better, you should remember that, Matthew. God almighty, 'Beef Stew Thursdays' at Alice's used to give me chronic gut-ache."

The silence finally reached him and he looked around the table for a response. "You remember, Matt?"

I suddenly wished Alex was there, knew exactly what he would say if he were: "If your mum was such a shit cook, why was she so fat?" Except it would have been a whisper in my ear, never within range of Dad. A lifetime of yo-mama-so-fat jokes to justify Alex's angst that Dad might have loved my mum more than his.

Sabine squeezed my arm to bring me back. "Matt?"

A quiet rage sapped the blood away from my face and fingers, leaving them tingling. I almost asked Alex's question myself, just to see Dad's face change. See it melt.

"Thirty-five years today," I said, instead.

Dad gave me a nod. Angela exhaled, as if suddenly aware she had been holding her breath. Sabine removed her hand from my arm and folded her napkin in her lap. Clare raised her glass of Coke with a toneless, "Happy birthday, Uncle Matt."

I let them relax for a second before clarifying: "Since my mum disappeared. Thirty-five years today." I kept my eyes on my dad, and the relieved atmosphere promptly dissolved.

"That's thirty-five birthdays she's missed then," Dad said. "Well counted, Matthew."

"You had us though, Matt," Angela said quietly.

"And Lydia," Sabine added. And by invoking her name, just like that, I lost my chance to reply. Alex would have had a field day.

I could have pointed out that Lydia wasn't my real mother, and they would have replied: but wasn't I grateful that she raised me since I was three?

I could have complained that my birthday was forever shadowed by my mother's disappearance, and they would have replied: but you're thirty-five now. Do birthdays really matter anymore?

I could have asked why my dad never told me anything about my mother, and they would have replied softly: but couldn't I see the man was still mourning, too? Couldn't I just give him a break?

My dad had returned to his spaghetti with new purpose, spinning his fork into the centre of his plate, creating a pasta vortex too large for a single mouthful, until flecks of tomato sauce began to slop over the edges and splatter against Angela's cardigan.

I took a breath to say something but Angela's phone buzzed on the glass-top table. I raised my eyebrows to Sabine, waiting for the confirmation that Alex had stood us up.

"He's not going to make it," Angela said, and I laughed and drummed a victorious rhythm on the table but no-one else thought it was funny. "He's around all weekend though," she continued, brushing the tomatoey specks from her sleeve.

"Is he?" I said. "Is he really?"

Sabine glared at me and Angela set her jaw. The waitress arrived and bounced on the balls of her feet behind my chair and said, "How's everything for you all? Okay? All done?" She glanced at Dad but did not falter at the sight of his unwavering focus on his rotating food, or the plastic hand that clattered clumsily against his plate.

"It's fine, thank you," Sabine replied, when it was obvious no-one else was going to.

The waitress ceased her bobbing and stooped to retrieve a fallen napkin, catching sight of a silver-wrapped present poking out of Angela's bag. "Ooh, someone's birthday?" she asked, shrilly.

I pulled my mouth into a brief smile and raised a guilty hand. Clare sank several inches lower in her seat.

"Would you like to order some dessert, birthday boy?" The waitress grinned, and started stacking plates and wiping the tabletop. As she leaned across me, her blouse brushed my cheek and I blushed like an adolescent, then winced, feeling the coldness of Sabine's sneer beside me.

I passed the waitress my plate. "No. Shall we get the bill?"

"I'll have a coffee, please," Sabine said mildly, though her ambivalent expression was a poor mask for what I knew lay beneath.

Angela's attention shifted from her stepfather to her daughter, who was chewing ice cubes noisily and kicking the central leg of the table.

"You've hardly eaten anything."

Clare shrugged jerkily, "I'm not hungry."

Angela lowered her voice while the waitress jutted out a hip and fixed her smile, hand hovering above Clare's barely touched plate. "What was the point of ordering if you're not going to eat it?"

"I've eaten breadsticks."

Angela sighed in exasperation. The waitress moved round to Dad's side of the table and loitered uncertainly, waiting for him to notice her and put down his utensils.

"Take it home then," Angela said, "we can ask for a doggy bag."

"Jesus, Mum. Stop trying to force-feed me. I don't want it. I'm sorry. I didn't even want to come." She flicked her eyes momentarily up to mine in apology. I smiled my first genuine smile of the evening back at her.

I could feel the ache of my niece's embarrassment as she shrank in her seat under the scrutiny of the entire table. Angela had adopted Dad's hardness rather than her mum's laissez-faire approach to parenting. Clare's bland 'kill-me-now' expression felt so familiar, as if there weren't sixteen years between us. The reverberating noises of the other diners seemed to close in even more tightly as Angela watched her face for submission and tried to ignore Dad's incessant fork-turning. A meatball rolled off his plate, across the table and into her handbag. The waitress stifled a squeak and fished it out with seamless professionalism.

"Let me just take that, shall I?" she said to Dad, sweeping his plate onto the carefully balanced arrangement on her arm and leaving him with a redundant fork, dangling with cold noodles.

"What's wrong with you?" Angela hissed at Clare.

"How about some ice cream?" the waitress suggested enthusiastically, as though Clare was a decade younger.

"No. Thank you," Clare said politely. Then, to her mother, a vicious whisper: "I feel sick, okay?"

"Leave her alone, Angie!" Dad boomed, and the conversation in the restaurant fell into a sudden curious lull. "She's not bloody hungry." As the noise gradually and uncertainly returned to half its previous level, he reached for the wine bottle and filled his empty water glass.

"Peter, you shouldn't, not with your medication - " Angela said, and the waitress' smile fell a few millimetres, her eyes fixed on the fork still in Dad's fist.

Dad knocked back the wine like it was a shot and ceremoniously tossed his fork into the empty glass. The waitress swiped it away and quickly retreated to the kitchen. Peter raised a finger, as if we were all still mid-conversation: "And I'm not the only one who had the decency to keep quiet about things that don't need to be discussed in the middle of a bloody restaurant." He jabbed the finger into the table in front of Angela, "*Your* mother could keep a secret, I'll tell you that now."

"Fucking hell," I said.

"She might not have been honest, but she kept her mouth shut."

"Okay, we're going home," Angela said, face flushed and downturned, aware that the people at the tables around us had stopped talking.

"You mean, *you're* going home. *I'm* going back to that nuthouse."

"Peter!"

Clare lurched forward in her seat, the skin of her face almost translucent with a sudden draining of blood, "I'm going to be sick," she said, and bolted for the bathroom.

"I'll go with her," Sabine offered, but the screeching of Angela's chair on the tile floor stopped her.

"No," Angela snapped, "I'll go. You two get him outside."

"Cart the old man off, that's right," Dad said, shoving his chair backwards and steadying himself on the table. "Where's Alex?" he asked – the first of what was to be innumerable times – not that we knew it then. "I thought Alex was coming."

"Dad, shut up," I said, as I scooped up coats and bags and tried to head him off before he toppled into the diners next to them.

"Don't tell your dad to shut up," Sabine said. And that was the moment, I reflected later, that it was probably all over for us.

We weaved Dad through the maze of tables to the front door, no time for embarrassment as we focused solely on avoiding knocking over any glasses or bumping into passing waiters, while my dad grumbled and protested at our treatment. As we passed the door to the toilets we could hear Clare's voice, high and strained, calling her mum a bitch, asking why couldn't she just let her make her own fucking decisions. And Angela losing it, slamming a palm against a cubicle door, saying for God's sake, Clare, you're acting like a child.

The waitress, waiting at the front desk, didn't even attempt a smile as we pushed Dad through the door, yanking his arms into his coat like an overtired toddler.

The cold air struck us into silence. We gathered ourselves for a moment on the pavement outside, eyes adjusting to the streetlight glare and the flashing of headlamps on the wet road, wrapping scarves around our throats and shoving hands into pockets.

"Where did Angie park?" I said, but Sabine ignored me and Dad shrugged. A laugh curled up and died in my throat.

I shook Angela's handbag until I was able to follow the sound of jingling keys to an exterior pocket. I aimed the remote at the dark lines of parked cars on the street, eventually saw the blink of her car's indicators down to the right, and herded my unwilling companions towards it.

By the time we reached the car, Dad seemed to have deflated to half his previous size inside his coat, eyes no longer full of the righteous anger that so effectively destroyed my right to reply. He let me help him into the back seat of Angela's Fiesta and folded his hands into his lap.

I slammed the door harder than I needed to and leaned against the side of the car. Sabine was looking at her phone, and I had no chance to say anything apologetic before Angela came jogging up.

"Where is he? Is he okay?"

I nodded to the car. "Where's Clare?"

"Still in the toilets. How much do I owe you?"

"What? Oh. Shit."

"You didn't pay? Oh my God, Matthew."

Angela snatched her bag out of my hands and ran back round the corner to the restaurant, returning a few minutes later, still alone, with a voice that said there was a lump high up in her throat.

"Well, we're not going there again. Clare's not inside. Did you see her come out?"

We shook our heads.

"She's driving me mad. She hates me at the moment. She - " Angela sighed, decided against explaining. Asking for help seemed to almost cause her physical pain. "She's probably gone to Becca's. And I need to get Peter home. Back, I mean."

I wanted to hug her but I waited too long to carry out the thought and she began scrambling in her bag, trying to hide her reddening face. I hated Sabine, then, for her lack of womanly solidarity. She should have been the one to be patting Angela's arm and telling her it would all be okay, but she stood there, scrolling with one finger on her phone's screen, as though she couldn't hear us at all.

"I'll take him," I said, but Angela emerged from her handbag and thrust a gift-wrapped rectangle at me.

30

"Happy birthday. Sorry, Matt. I'll talk to you later. If you hear from Clare, let me know, okay?"

When her car had disappeared over the hill, Sabine and I found ourselves still standing apart from each other, looking in different directions - too much distance for us to be a couple.

My phone rang and I answered it without seeing who it was, regretting it the moment I heard the response to my hello.

"Matty," Alex said. "Are you home? I'm coming over."

Chapter Four

The doorway calls. The belt of my dressing gown slithers along the carpet as I step through and leave my bedroom behind, a breadcrumb trail back to the present. For a moment, in the space within the portal, there is unadulterated silence, full of the promises of death. Onward. Onward to go backward, following the scent of a time long gone but never forgotten. How could I forget this night? I emerge the other side, wavering with the shift of gravity. It takes time to adjust to the change in the spinning of the earth, but then I solidify, feet rooting into the ground like bindweed.

Home. Standing in the perfect trapezium of light cast by the streetlamp outside the living room, a week-old baby in my arms.

And alone.

I thought it wouldn't be for long. I thought she'd come back. I thought then that this terror would last no longer than a few days.

The night I took Matthew home from the hospital was longer than a night had any right to be. The house was all at once unfamiliar, as though Heather had taken with her the essence of what had made it mine.

I drop into this young, uncertain body and begin to sway without realising it - a pendulous movement that doesn't need to be learned. I avoid looking at the baby as I walk slow circles around the living room, trying to find something that truly belongs to me, trying to find an anchor.

Windows filmed with condensation. A fat sponge on the sill, waiting for its morning work. Heather's work. I would leave the glass unwiped until black blossoming mould began to creep across the panes. The curtains hang open, unlined, because Heather loathed her sewing machine and told it so whenever she hauled it onto the kitchen table. Above the mantelpiece the sunburst clock that I can't stand glows bronze in the low light, an instrument of auditory torture. Heather's choice, or was it a gift from her mother? A blanket embroidered with Matthew's initials lies rumpled on the sofa in the shape of a mountain range. The house is full of baby things. They conspire against me and pile into corners – I do not recognise any of it, not the booties, the bottles, the bibs, the bassinette – Heather's choice, Heather's choice, Heather's choice. I wonder if she had started to systematically remove me from the house long before Matthew arrived.

He stirs in my arms, heavy with awkwardness. I do not want to put him down in case he breaks. I do not want him to cry again because that was worse than any stroke, any heart attack - electricity running through his lungs into my nervous system. He had wailed without warning, an acute note of outrage at crossing the threshold from the front step to the hallway. There was no-one to consult, no-one to look to, no-one to take half of the knifing noise into their ears. The house rang with the sound and I felt nothing but pity for myself.

My aged self slips quietly into my younger body and forces my eyes downwards, to the little face turned away from the street light, turned in, to the valley between my chest and my arm. I am struck by how much the baby Matthew looks like the man, how I didn't know then how he would look when he was grown. Now, it is just so obvious. There's the eye, the lip, the hairline, the ear. The fluency of handling a child sweeps through me and I adjust him so that he lies across my arm, legs dangling, cheek squashing his mouth into a questioning

O. He settles once more, a dead weight.

I walk through the house from front to back, something I didn't do the first time I was here. I squint into the darkness of the kitchen windows, wondering if his mother is out there, if she came to see him this night, crouching behind the garden hedge, peering into the lighted rooms while we paced. Or whether she was already far from here.

Matthew slept for five hours, woke at three to nuzzle a bottle of milk and went back to sleep. Thirty-five years ago I managed, eventually, to put him down - clumsily swaddled in the Moses basket Heather had taken forty minutes to choose over the other almost identical option in the shop. I had only touched him to feed him, supporting his swollen head like I was told to, wiping the white tracks that flowed from the corners of his mouth and burping him until he threw most of it back up on my shoulder. This time my young hands are made strong with the gift of being possessed by my elderly self. Two hands, intact and steady. I nestle him into my chest, breathe a soft Edelweiss into his ear, humming when I don't know the words, rhyming bright with light, white, night. New lyrics about hearts rising and falling, fall and rise forever. He doesn't mind. Alice knew the right words and he'd learn them from her in time.

But I can feel the link fading, my ghost losing weight, drawn by the magnetism of the door to the hall. Another door. Another time left behind. I know what happens next and I must move onwards, ever on. The new father's fear begins to take hold again, a nauseous twist, a collapsing tunnel. He will be alright. I promise him that as I close the door behind me.

#

Heather's mother came by at six in the morning and I knew that she hadn't slept either, watching the clock until it was an almost acceptable time to come over, until the milkman had been, at least, until commuters were leaving houses and trains running sleepily from their bunkers.

"Where's the little soldier?" Alice shouted as she came through the door that first morning, flinging off gloves and layers, dumping bags of yet more baby things across the hallway. I pointed to the living room where he still slept and made a cup of tea. Matthew woke for Alice and squinted indifferently at her as she made all the appropriate noises and her skin shone, flushed, as though she had just run a mile.

"Wait 'til your mama gets home, little man," I heard her whisper, over the boiling of the kettle, "It'll be love at first sight." I didn't point out that Heather had already missed that opportunity.

I put up with that kind of talk for three weeks. Constant reassurance starts to grate after a while. "When your mama sees how *big* you've got, little one," and "Won't your mama be proud of you, drinking up all your milk?" I put up with it until the police told me the negative correlation between the time a person is missing and the chance of finding them alive. They told Alice too but she snapped her head to the side like a toddler refusing a spoon. "You don't know my daughter," she'd said to them. For a second I thought she was talking to me.

By the time he was a month old we had become used to our awkward routine. Alice finished the decoration of his little bedroom - not much more than a glorified cupboard, strung up with a sheep mobile and an alphabet cross-stitch wall hanging. It smelled of Alice even when she wasn't there, soft and clean and warm and motherly. He struggled in my arms, as though I was coarse all over. He threw himself away from me, coiling backwards like he was in pain. I stood in the doorway of my bedroom and watched as she changed him, dressing him up for a walk to the shop, cooing: wouldn't his mama love to see him looking so smart in his dungarees? Her hands moved with surety, anticipating each involuntary movement with practised ease in a way mine wouldn't learn until I was able to try again with Alex.

35

Matthew had begun to watch everything with dark, unblinking, gullible eyes – finally acclimatised to this bright, loud world – as though he knew something was not quite right and had decided to start taking stock.

"You look like a little sailor boy," Alice told him. "Oh… the big ship sails on the ally-ally-oh… " She thought he had started to smile but I read in one of Heather's baby books that it was probably just wind. The boy stood with her assistance, legs a year away from supporting his own weight, chin doubling – tripling – into his chest as his head flopped forward. He threw himself backwards so he could look at me. Alice made him dance and laughed at her little puppet.

"Your mama used to love that one too. She'll sing it to you when she gets back."

I stumbled then, even though I had been standing still. There was the limit. Once I reached beyond it, I never found a way back to the silence of before. The quiet of denial. And if I couldn't have that falsified peace then I could make sure no-one else could either. My yell made them both startle: "Stop telling him she'll come home!"

Matthew wailed. Alice looked away.

"Don't promise him things that you can't make true," I said, quieter. "Don't do it to yourself, or me either. It's not fair."

She gathered him up and held his head against her bosom, covering his ears. When she turned back to me, her face and her tone were gentler than I'd expected. "I'll tell you what's not fair, Peter. Pretending she never existed."

She took the baby downstairs, placed him in the pram and tucked a blanket around his chest like a corset. Alice was the type of woman who would chase the milkman down the street for leaving a silver top instead of a gold top, which is why the worst thing she could have done was not deafen me with self-righteousness. She finished packing up the pram and wheeled him out onto the street.

"Alice… " I couldn't mobilise myself to follow her. A lawnmower moaned outside. I managed to make it to the front door. She reached the end of the path. The lawnmower stopped.

"Morning!" Graham from next door raised a slow hand in a wave, stalling as he saw our expressions.

Alice ignored him along with me. The lawnmower started up again, slightly more vehemently than before. Heather's mother took a ninety-degree turn and marched the pram towards the sun. And under the cover of the lawnmower's growl, I closed the front door and screamed at the radiator.

#

The next doorway leads through to the nursing home conservatory. The windows are blue-black, a timeless tiredness has muffled the other residents into rough-edged statues. I blink at the room, counting the hours I must have lost within that other place, my baby son's milky breath still warm on my neck. A nurse takes my elbow and moves herself into my eyeline.

"Peter? Are you okay, love?"

I nod. They must know that yes means no when they ask that kind of question. She accepts my answer though, and brings tension to her grip, subtly pulling me forward until I follow like a pony.

"Here you are," she says, guiding me down into a chair by a viewless window. "Tea'll be round in a minute. Can I get you anything, Pete? One of your books?"

No-one has ever called me Pete. I want to go back to my room but I can't find the words to tell her, and I know that once I got back there I would wish to be anywhere else. She takes my forward-facing stare to be a 'no' and moves on to the next abandoned mannequin. As soon as she has gone I laboriously get back to my feet and make an uneducated decision about which corridor to take. "Onwards," I say out loud, though I didn't mean to.

The nights are the worst. They are neither peaceful nor

quiet. Angela bought me a radio that plays 'the sounds of nature', supposedly to help me fall asleep: rain, rivers, storms, the sea and so forth. I don't see the point unless you are unable to urinate. No amount of rain can drown out 'the sounds of the nursing home': howling, grunting, coughing, dying and so forth. I failed to hide my unimpressed reaction when I unwrapped it and she called me a grumpy bastard. What's wrong with a normal radio? One that I can actually listen to? One with longwave so I can pick up the cricket now and then? I don't mean to offend her but I invariably do.

Whenever a purple-uniformed staff member passes me I pause, checking to see if their face belongs to Angela. I've lost track of her shift pattern and don't want to have to ask. I consult a list tucked behind my eyelids: pointed chin, skin tight and shiny over her forehead, hair that curls and spirals into helices on her shoulders, eyes that grow harder by the week. The image of her dissolves whenever I try to grip hold of it. I will recognise her when I see her. I know her when I see her through a doorway.

When she was ten and Alex had just been born, I asked if she wanted to call me Dad. She looked at me kindly and said, "Peter's fine." I don't know why I suggested it. I wouldn't have felt comfortable with it either, and was glad she refused. It must have been the thrill of a new baby, the idea of a family, cementing us together. I felt a grizzled, primal pain in my chest when I saw Alex for the first time. I can't remember when I first felt that for Matthew, but it was there just now, revisiting that empty house, that longest night.

Matthew's birth, his birthday, every instance of small talk that leads back to his heritage - each one is shadowed with Heather's disappearance. She is a black hole into which conversation is sucked, compressed and blinked out of existence.

I come to a double doorway at the end of a corridor but I know it will not take me anywhere new. It is an earthly thing, a man-made slab of fire-resistant timber and safety glass, nothing special about it at all. I step through into the next

38

corridor. The same synthetic carpeting, although I recognise this hallway - it will bring me back to the semblance of home they managed to cram into my room.

Angela must not be working today. She would have come to see me if she had been. She will keep up her mask of stoicism until I am dead. I ought to tell her to stop, tell her that it's okay for her not to be okay. I'm not her father but I have been her Peter for most of her life. I ought not to have let them put me in this place. She should be allowed to be a visitor and not my nurse. But perhaps that's what she's always been.

I turn left into the little cul-de-sac that contains my room and three others. Both my door, and the one opposite, are open. I stand between them and try to remember why I came back here. Something about Angela.

The sound of artificial breathing swishes into the corridor like a tide. In the room across the hall resides a skeletal being who has been kept silently but barely alive since I arrived here. She may actually be stuffed for all I can tell. Her door is permanently ajar. She sits there, propped up on her bed, unmoving and stern-faced, like Mother Whistler. At some point every day a machine next to her deathbed emits a beeping of ever-increasing pitch and volume until a nurse comes scuttling down the hall to switch it off. They will readjust a pillow or two, open or shut the curtains, pull the covers up a few inches, neaten a crease, and leave her to the oceanic rhythm of her ventilator.

I saw her move, once. The machine beeped but no-one came. I saw Whistler turn her head my way, then further, like an owl, and further still, until she looked almost one-hundred-and-eighty degrees behind her to stare yearningly at the glass of water on her bedside table. Then she fell right out of bed like a bag of kindling. She broke her collar bone and was in the hospital for two weeks before she returned, plastered, but no different. She doesn't have any visitors. Maybe that's the way to be. Quiet and patient and waiting for the end. I wonder if that would make Angela happy, to let her think that I'm taking this live deconstruction with some sort of grace. I want to shield her from my corrosion but I've never been able to lie to her. She's the only one who can cope with what is going to happen to me. The boys can't do this. Matthew resents every visit and Alex has stopped coming. Angela has always been the strongest of all of us - she takes appraisal of a situation in seconds before coming up with some sort of certainty. A direction. A way forward.

When she came to tell me she was pregnant, at twenty-one, with no husband, boyfriend or even a vague acquaintance to raise it with, she had no fear of my reaction. I, however, broke into a sweat.

"Okay," I said.

"I'm fine," she said.

"You want to keep it, don't you?"

She nodded. Smiled, even.

I didn't know why she needed approval from me, she knew I would have agreed, whatever she'd said. I had to say something, though. "Then, why don't you move back in with us?"

We celebrated with more nodding and standing around awkwardly. I have always been too scared of inappropriate repercussions to instigate a full hug, and she has always been happy with just resting her hand on top of mine.

She was due in the summer. She and I sat one afternoon in the garden, radio on, papers divided between us, discarded sections splayed on the grass. She couldn't seem to concentrate on reading, her belly conspicuously taking up her view. During an ad break on the radio she turned to me and said, "Do you think Heather disappeared because she was afraid?"

I didn't have to tell her. I didn't have to tell her anything at all, let alone the truth. I didn't lie, at least. "Yes," I said.

"It's a scary thing," she said, pressing her bellybutton down and watching it ping back out again.

"Yes. It is."

"Did she seem happy? When Matt was born?"

40

I shrugged, sighed. "Not really, no. She was in shock, I think."

"In shock. For all these years?"

I lifted my eyes to hers, just to warn her that she was getting close to the limit of her questions. She stared innocently back, newspaper face down on her enormous bump, toes scrunching grass.

"I think she was too embarrassed to come back," I said.

Angela nodded and turned back to her reading, twisting the radio volume up as music resumed. I was sweating, despite being in the shade. What is it about that girl that makes me sweat? I flicked the paper upright, feeling cautiously safe that her curiosity had been sated, but then:

"Peter?"

"Yes?"

"Do you think Matt knows why his mum disappeared?"

"No."

"But you do?"

I paused. She would have known if I'd lied. "Yes."

"Are you ever going to tell him?"

She didn't look at me when she asked, which made it easier to tell the truth.

"No."

A painful beeping sound that doesn't belong in the garden with Angela. Mother Whistler's machine is alive with lights. The door to my room sits half-open and it makes me feel sick. I need to see Angela's face, to remind myself what she looks like. If I walk the halls for long enough I'll find her. I'll find her and I'll admit I'm losing her, I'll admit that I can't remember why Alex won't see me, I'll ask her what I've done to make him stay away. I can't lie to her. Sometimes I think she has more of me in her than my sons do.

Chapter Five   Matthew

I've been sleeping on the sofa since Sabine left me. Frost edges itself through the gap under the living room window and crawls across the inside of the pane. The sun goes down before the day is really over and the birds screech because they think it is the end of the world.

Actually, I don't know if that's true.

It's something Alex told me, so there's a good chance it's a lie. When the sun goes down, the birds think that's the end of it, he said - the end of the world. So they sit there, silent, terrified, coming to terms with an imminent eternity in nothingness, eventually falling asleep out of pure exhaustion. And that's exactly how I get to sleep now he's dead - a cocktail of terror and guilt rising up until my brain has to reboot, just as those first rosy tendrils come creeping over the horizon like a sick fucking joke. Dawn's fingers are not gentle, they're clawed, scraping away at my eyelids like a drawn-out headache, a balloon skin stretched tight, about to snap.

And just like the rest of the nights since Alex died I will still be awake when the sun shows its face again. The birds though, well, they rejoice, go fucking mental, like hollow-eyed refugees in a bunker hearing the shelling stop. "It's over, we're alive, there's a tomorrow!" Well, the birds can fuck themselves because I don't know how much longer I can do any of this without sleep.

After he died, after the first week of coasting on the sheer what-the-fuckery of it all, Sabine made the break. My girlfriend of four years peered at the broken purple lines that surrounded my sunken eyes and said, "I love you," as if it was my fault. Then she left, like they all do: mother, step-mother, brother. The only one I can't get rid of is Dad, like a scab I can't stop picking.

Sabine said that I had enough to deal with at the moment and I didn't need to have to deal with her – with us – on top of that. What she meant, I think, was that she had given up waiting for me to act like a human being and grieve for my dead brother. He was the catalyst, giving her one final opportunity to see if it was worth putting any effort into redeeming me. To see if a little chink of humanity might peek through my flabby exterior. She was disappointed. She left.

It's something past one in the morning. Three floors below my flat a little scrappy dog has been shut out on a balcony and it barks like a cheap hacksaw stuck in a piece of metal, jarring back and forth, twice at a time, one, two, one, two. The TV is muted but the light waves flicker through the dusty air into the kitchen and turn the fridge blue, yellow, green - a flash of red in an action movie explosion then dark again. This is my routine: waiting for two a.m. to come and go.

Next door's phone rings. A call like that means tragic news or a drunken misdial. My bald neighbour and I share the uninsulated wall between his bedroom and my living room. He knocks in the same two-by-two rhythm as the barking dog when my TV volume is too high and I glow quietly with shame, imagining the scathing judgement of my programme choices. I don't knock when I overhear him masturbating to his own shitty band's EP, but I allow myself to thumb the volume button on the remote a few notches higher. Through the wall I hear a slammed receiver and muttered swearing. Just a wrong number. Carl or Greg or whatever his name is will turn over and go back to sleep.

On my birthday I had the other kind of phone call, the

middle-of-the-night call that has replaced the solemn policeman on the doorstep, his hat in his hands. Instead of a policeman I got Jamie, Alex's best and most irritating friend, the little weasel-bastard-moron who has plagued my life almost as much as my brother did. My call came at two-twenty-two a.m. Three little twos all in a row, red digits blossoming into the darkness. A wavering line of ducks waiting to be shot down. "You don't see that every day," I'd observed to Sabine, and laughed to myself for being so witty at such short notice as I rolled over to pick up the phone.

"Al's dead."

Before I'd even said hello.

"Hello?"

"Al's dead. Matt? Are you there?"

"Fuck off, Jamie."

"Did you hear me? Your brother - "

This was no time to be flippant but it was two-twenty-two in the morning and our usual conversation consisted of jokes about my personal appearance and sadistic wind-ups. "*Half*-brother," I said.

He was silent for too long. An echo that didn't exist began to zigzag around the inside of my skull, words that didn't belong together fused into misshapen lumps - little spasms of reality waiting to be acknowledged. "Okay," he said quietly, "your half-brother is dead. Happy?" And then he hung up.

#

The night of my birthday, after Sabine and I had returned to my flat, still hungry after our half-finished meal, she shut herself in the bedroom and pretended she had a migraine.

I made a bowl of instant noodles just to piss her off. She thinks they smell like dog food – and they do – but then again they are also an excellent passive-aggressive tactic. I wanted her to come stomping out to shout at me. I wanted to argue. It would have been better than the quiet indifference she pummelled me with, until she finally snapped, stole half my DVD collection and fucked off to some rich uni-mate's second home in Greenwich.

I could sleep back then. A few repeat episodes of a crappy '90s sitcom combined with the couple of extra stones I was carrying around and I was content to commit to a symbiotic relationship with the sofa. I had no qualms about sleeping in the living room, if only to prompt a "Why didn't you come to bed last night?" discussion with Sabine in the morning. At least there was sleep. There was no hole in the wall, then.

But there was a noise like a wall falling down.

"Matt! Let me in, you fuckhead!"

My adrenaline spike died away but the hammering on the front door didn't stop.

"Who the hell is that?" Sabine yelled from the bedroom.

My fear subsided into dread. "Alex."

Against screaming better judgement, I opened the door to a clout of winter air and the face of something far worse. "Matty."

"You're drunk."

"You're ugly. Oh, hello little one!" Alex leered around the door to wave at Sabine, who had appeared behind me in a t-shirt and a pair of my boxer shorts. He smiled at her in a way that made me want to slam the door shut on his head, but instead I let him hang off my shoulder as he leaned too far forward to keep his balance. Behind him stood Jamie, considerably more sober but no less unwelcome. "You alright?" Alex asked, making it very clear that he didn't care if I was.

"Are you?" Sabine said.

"No, I'm fucking not." He aimed an index finger in the vicinity of my face. "Get me a drink." I fought an urge to let him drop to the floor, propped him up against the wall, and went to put the kettle on.

"A drink, you moron, not a cup of fucking tea!" he said.

"We don't have anything. It's juice or tea."

45

"There's vodka on top of the cupboard," Sabine said, and I glowered at her, miming for her to put on a fucking dressing gown or something that would stop my brother's eyes from blinking slowly at her figure.

"Vodka. Yeah, great idea," I said. Alex let out a low giggle and weaved his way into the living room, sliding onto the sofa sideways and draping an arm across his face. I made him a vodka and orange with not much vodka in it, and hoped he wouldn't stay for a second one. Sabine and Jamie stood at either end of the sofa, mirroring each other: arms crossed, eyes on my brother.

"What are you doing here?" I asked.

"I told you I was coming. Happy birthday."

"Yeah. Thanks. Couldn't make it to the meal? I can see you've been really busy."

"I need your car."

And there it was, the real reason. "No," I said.

"Okay, I need you to drive me somewhere."

"No."

"Don't you even want to know where?"

I sighed, in the most impatiently-condescending-older-brother way I could muster. "Where?"

Alex squinted meaningfully. "Dad."

"It's what, half eleven? They're not going to let you visit now."

"Fuck you, I've got *the letter!*" He brandished a crumpled piece of paper to prove his unexplained point.

"Right, well, get a taxi. Good luck, good night - " I made a futile gesture towards the door but Alex climbed onto the back of the sofa like a Neanderthal man staking a claim on higher ground, holding the letter out of reach even though no-one was trying to take it from him. Sabine winced as orange juice sluiced across the cushions.

"Alex, go home," I said.

He shook his head so hard I expected his eyeballs to roll from side to side. "The old solici-fucking-tor died… " he said.

"Who?"

"My mum gave him the letter, for me, for eighteen - for when I was eighteen. To read. But then he died."

"What?"

The red eyes that I had first dismissed as abused, drunken blood vessels now looked more like they were swollen from crying. Really? Alex, crying? "A letter from your mum?" I repeated, "Why wasn't it with the will?"

"Exactly! It was sep-at-ated... Sepit-Separate. Just for me. But the solici-fucker went and died and it got filed and his daughter took over the firm and... " He took a slug of his drink and had to sit down. "And... forgotten about. For thirteen years."

Sabine said, "Oh my God."

Alex pointed his glass at her earnestly. "Yes."

"So, what does it say?" I asked, nodding to the scrunched up paper, wondering how much of the shaking of Alex's hands could be attributed to drink, and how much to the letter.

"*Wait* for it, Matty. I'm not there yet. The only reason they found it at all was 'cause they moved office and were re-filing or some... ing. Bastards!"

He was getting louder. I flinched and apologised to my neighbour under my breath.

"Alex, what does the letter say?" Sabine asked softly, and Alex smoothed out the paper on his knees, took a breath as if to read, then screwed it up again.

"Dad," he said, "is not," he laughed, "my dad."

#

It was two-twenty-two in the morning. I threw Jamie's phone call, and my phone with it, at the wall and woke up Sabine.

"What's the matter with you?" she whined in a high-pitched whisper and I wanted to throttle her.

"Give me your phone."

"Not if you're going to throw it at the wall."

"Please, Bina."

She heaved one arm out of bed and groped on the floor for the jeans she had been wearing the day before in an exaggerated display of outraged inconvenience. I leant over her, crushing her legs, swiping the trousers out of her hands. "For fuck's sake, I'll get it."

I fished out the phone and stabbed a finger at Alex's name. "The number you are calling is currently unavailable," an automated voice told me.

I lurched out of bed and crouched cold and naked in the centre of my room as though that might somehow make a difference. I redialled the number Jamie had called from. A beep after each ring meant a payphone. No answer. I tried again.

"What're you doing?" Sabine asked, just as someone picked up. I shushed her with a hand in her face. She grunted and rolled over, pulling the covers over her head.

"Hello? Hello? Jamie?"

"No," said a female voice. "This is the Hannigan ward."

Shit. Oh my God. "*Hospital* ward?" I asked, like a remedial echo.

"Yes. Who are you trying to reach?"

"Someone just - his name's Jamie. I mean, I'm trying to get hold of Alex, my brother, my half-brother. Shit."

"Look, you need to call the hospital switchboard, this is just a payphone. Sorry."

"Okay. Thanks. Sorry. Thank you. Bye."

Sabine's muffled voice drawled through the duvet, "What's he done now?"

The hand holding the phone was cold. I couldn't seem to blink. My mouth went dry then flooded with saliva. I swallowed. It hurt. "He died."

Chapter Six

I saw my dentist, Alma, again today. I think she might be following me.

She gave me some painkillers and said she'd be back later. I can't remember what dental work I have scheduled, if any. I have a suspicion that she isn't a dentist at all - her fingers aren't slender enough. They lack the precision of a skilled practitioner and fumble over pouring the tablets from their child-locked pot. Needless to say I smiled compliantly and hid the tablets in the shoebox under my bed when she had gone.

I agreed to take a Tai Chi class this afternoon, in the low-ceilinged, green-carpeted dining hall that smells of chips and disappointment, just so I could escape the conversational efforts of Paul, the idiot in the room next to Whistler's. Paul is deep in the throes of stage one - the first step to acceptance that there will be no escape from this place but the inevitable exit route.

It is painfully clear who is new here. In a fluster of shock and denial at suddenly finding themselves in care, they talk constantly about their children, their grandchildren, anyone who is still living their life on the outside: the births, the marriages, the divorces, the moves, the holidays to the Algarve, the GCSEs, A Levels, degrees, the new kitten, the new car, the new Xbox. No-one actively listens to these anecdotes, they simply serve as background noise while we are quietly assimilated into institution.

"Let's begin with *Wuji*," says the Tai Chi instructor, an outrageously tall man with glasses so narrow they must be functionally useless. He talks about the breath and the flow, and we continue to stand or sit in varying degrees of hunchbacked apathy.

In the early days, we try to fill our time with minor interests: a film night or seminar, a book, a walk, a visit. Later, anything that breaks up the day becomes vaguely appealing, despite being otherwise intolerable: bible readings, Indian head massage, school choirs and recorder recitals. In the end, we go where we are told, because it is good for us, they say, because it will do us good.

"Tucking your tailbone under and floating the spine," the instructor says. I cannot tell if anyone has changed their posture but someone farts and this is no longer a source of humour, but simply the sad punctuation of weakening sphincters.

Paul's harmless small talk will eventually metastasise into the putrid growth of dissatisfaction - an endless griping and grousing about day-to-day pains and ailments. Irritation will begin to creep in whenever he mentions his previously beloved family, the nurses, the staff, the management, the government, the foreign, the young. His audience will listen but no-one will offer sympathy. A knowing, callous nodding will accompany the monologues instead, as though we are wound up in perpetual motion. Humility and tact will be tossed aside for frank discussions about bowel and bladder, prolapse and prostate.

"Relax the shoulders and sink the elbows."

A woman at the back has fallen asleep in her chair. Another next to her is attempting to adopt the correct posture with a cup of tea in her hand. Something in my shoulder grinds and when I look down I see that my left arm is in a cast. I don't know how it got there but the sweating skin itches underneath. The plaster taps against the buttons of my shirt with the trembling of my hand, stretching my arms forward in slow motion supplication just like the instructor does.

Once Paul is rid of his pride, next will come the pacing, the checking on others, the checking on whether it's tea time, the checking of the minute personal details of the other residents, the nurses: "How did your Jack do in his driving test on Wednesday? Did you remember Ahmed's laxative this morning? Make sure you wish Lorraine a happy birthday when you see her." We sit because we cannot bring ourselves to move. We walk because we cannot bring ourselves to stop.

By the end, no-one speaks of their family; the darling grandkids are unimportant, milestones provoke only a passing flutter of acknowledgement. By the end, no-one bothers to mention the pain or the discomfort. Daylight and moonlight illuminate the same blank stare, the same shadowed face, the same absence of being.

And after that? I truly hope there's nothing.

"Touch the tongue to the roof of the mouth and connect the meridian channels of Governing and Conception," the instructor says, with an absolutely straight face. "Now integrate the whole body."

I sidestep until I have left the room. Even listening to Paul is better than this. But when I reach our little end-of-the-line corridor I find his room empty. He must be leeching out the will to live from some other recipient of his latest thrilling piece of news. The man will not be dissuaded from telling me details of his family that I could not value any less if it were a list of out-of-date train times for a place I will never visit. He tells me about his daughter, Sharon, her partially deaf husband, Harry, their curly-haired brat, Franklin, their recent trip to the Isle of Man and, repeatedly, the time Franklin hilariously decided that he wanted to ride a cow. At no point have I led him to believe that I am interested in anything that comes out of his mouth, yet most afternoons he finds his way to my doorway and updates me on some pointless piece of information or other. A lost green sock. A magazine subscription. The chance of snow later in the week. I could spit in his face and he would no doubt launch into some amusing tale regarding the cuteness of his grandchild's dribble. I hate him for reasons that have nothing to do with him. I hate him because I remember everything he tells me and yet my own memories have been flushed away.

My redundant brain has apparently decided that it is imperative for me to recall an inane collection of things which serve no purpose, while anything immediate and relevant slips inconspicuously out of my ears. I remember Eric Stafford at school telling me he'd once seen his mother plucking her pubic hair; the time I found a decapitated pigeon jammed up beneath the back bumper of my car; the phone number of Angela's sleazy supervisor at the Bowlplex, the way he slung his arm around her when she arrived at work, the way he gave her shoulder a little squeeze and told her to hurry off and get into her uniform, and how I wanted to put his head in the ball polisher. I remember the recipe for fishcakes that I used to make for Lydia, the ones I never really liked and haven't made since she died. I still remember Heather's fourth-finger ring size.

The things I need to remember lie just out of reach, up in the top-right corner of my vision, driven to the edges of my consciousness by the useless drivel I can't get rid of. If I sit perfectly still, the unwanted memories crowd in like radio babble. They keep me awake, jostling for attention, hoping to be the one that I choose, hoping they'll be the one to cause an epiphany. It's not really their fault; the problem's in the processing. My brain can no longer distinguish between the relevance of being able to recite the third verse of *Away in a Manger* or knowing if it's Tuesday or April. Walking helps, sometimes, coaxing an elusive memory down low enough for me to swing on. I should walk. I should try to find another doorway. I realise I am standing with none of the poise of Tai Chi in front of my other neighbour's room and the woman inside it cranes forward in her bed to catch my eye.

"Hey, Mr Solemn!" Ingrid says.

I try to start walking again, but the synaptic orders fail at the first post and I remain helplessly frozen outside her open door.

"Come here, will ya?"

I stare straight ahead, waiting for my limbs to regain function. Hurry, she's going to want to talk and -

"Do you need a bible?"

I shake my head.

"Do you need a packet of Turkish Delight?"

Chin left, chin right.

"Do you need... " she pauses, glances down at her lap, "... an audio book box set of *The Lord of the Rings* on CD, read by Rob Ingles?"

I turn my head a few inches to the left. She's smiling. "I don't need any of this silly crap anymore," she says. "Come here, Mr Solemn."

My legs obey her voice. I'm rather surprised, and frankly quite annoyed with them.

She props herself up on an elbow and considers me as I shuffle-stop inside her doorway. "Well, you, you're a scrawny little thing, aren't you? If you're not eating your puddings you can send them over to me."

I roll my eyes. I've seen the nurses do it to her face and she doesn't seem to notice.

"I know," she says, "I'm ridiculous. Just ignore me like you usually do."

I blush. I should be turning, leaving, but I cannot move.

She considers me for a moment. "Are you stuck?"

I nod.

"Right. Well. While you're here, you might as well fill me in on your bits and bobs then. Normally I only get the snippets from the nurses and my sister, Yvonne. Not gossip, Mr Solemn, just the goings-on."

My eyes plead for her to let me go but her expression is immovable.

"So, what did you do?" she asks, when it's clear that I'm

not about to offer up any information voluntarily.

I glance behind me at the empty corridor and take a subtle micro-step backwards towards it. The doorway is heating up like a jet engine. I can feel the hot air swirling, the particles getting excited, the lightning beginning to build. She's waiting for an answer to a question I didn't understand. I shrug.

"What did you do to get dumped here?" she says, within a single sigh. "You must have let something slip. Forgotten where you live or fed raw eggs to the cat? Something like that."

It's about this point I realise, by the rapidly filling catheter bag hanging from her bed, that while she is talking she is also casually urinating.

She fills the silence with: "Fine, I'll go first. Well. I kissed my own brother."

The catheter tube sways gently and bounces off the bedside.

"By that I mean *kissed* him, kissed on the lips. Like a lover."

I nod, then stop. I can hear her mouth moistly twisting in a grin but I can't take my eyes off the yellowing tube.

"So they tell me, anyway. I didn't know who he was, or at least, I knew that I knew him, and I knew that I loved him, very much, so I assumed he was my husband. He'd come to meet me and my daughter for a pub lunch at the Harvester, and when he walked in I took him by the face and kissed him. I might have squeezed his bum a bit too. He's quite handsome, even at his age."

She stops pissing and the tube stills and drains. I look up at her. She's laughing but she doesn't seem to find it all that amusing.

"My husband died eighteen years ago, if you can believe it. How could I forget something like that?"

I try to ask her a question but it flails out of me in a grunt, instead. Since the last stroke, it's been harder to push the words forward. By the time I get around to getting them in the right order the conversation has usually moved on. The doorway is almost ready, has almost reached terminal velocity. It vibrates around me now, so violently, so loudly that I can't believe Ingrid hasn't noticed, can't believe that there aren't paint chips and splinters flying across the room.

"They didn't see the funny side, let's put it that way," she says. "But you should have seen his face." She laughs in a lazy way: Ahah, ahah. Ha. "So, what about you?"

I want to answer her but I don't know what I did to deserve this place. It's bizarre to be told you can no longer look after yourself, like living with someone you never see; an annoying and intrusive character who leaves his shoes in the fridge. It reminded me of living with Heather, a compulsive but distracted tidier who would abandon small objects halfway through putting them away, having spotted something else that needed sorting. My watch would end up in the pestle and mortar, her cheque book in the fruit bowl, loose change in the craters of half-burned candles.

Before the doctors confirmed that my brain was shrivelling like a forgotten apple core, whenever things in the flat became misplaced, I wanted to blame Heather out of habit, even though she was thirty-odd years gone. She might well be invisible now, creeping in to sneak away with my glasses and the can opener.

Ingrid is still talking but the warmth of the doorway has reached my skin - the panicked flush of taking a wrong turn, missing a step, realising that you are about to drive onto the wrong side of the motorway. I know this feeling. It means I am reeling in a lost memory, albeit consciously out of reach. My body reacts to the recollection, but my mind isn't in on the joke. I wonder what it is. It feels like a nasty one. I don't really want to know, but I step backwards through the doorway anyway.

#

My foot lands on the cream kitchen tile of the house my children grew up in. Baked beans quiver in a pan on the hob, at the cusp of boiling. It was winter in the nursing home but here I stand in a short-sleeved shirt, irritable about cooking in the heat. Two plastic plates sit on the worktop: plain blue for Angela and Peter Rabbit in watery pastels for Matthew. My focus fixes on the miniature carrots and cabbages dotted around the rim. Not that Matthew ever ate his vegetables. He will be sitting next door, cross-legged, six inches away from the telly. Angela with him, in the armchair, in a book. The space above my diaphragm becomes a weightless vacuum of anticipation. I will bring them their tea and they will be four and ten again, and they will not know I have travelled here from so far.

The toaster pops. I butter the warm white slices and pour on the beans. Steam dampens my face and I know – even before I hear the clang of the plumbing in the bathroom above, even before the knocking begins – that this is the night that Alex is born.

Alex came early, which I suppose in a way Lydia must have been grateful for. All the panic and fuss meant her mathematical skills were never called into question. It wasn't a case of her thinking I was stupid, I'm fairly sure. It was more that she didn't want to push the ease of my acceptance. She chose me. She stayed. She loved her baby boy. Three ticks in a ledger against her name. I worried I wouldn't want him when he arrived but then there he was and it was like a childhood Christmas and people visited and brought casseroles and knitted little cardigans and sent cards of congratulations instead of condolences. Lydia and Alex were living, present, irrefutable proof that I was not completely abhorrent.

It's a Wednesday. Lydia and I had argued in the afternoon about the fact that she hadn't locked the car. Someone had stolen the stereo and my driving glasses but she maintained somehow that it wasn't really her fault because pregnancy makes you scatter-brained and she didn't know *why on earth* I was getting so worked up about bloody driving glasses and anyway, we had insurance. And my throat closed up around the responses I wouldn't say to her: "for God's sake" and "how hard is it to remember to lock a door?" and "what if it had been the front door you'd left open?" and "why don't these things bother you in the same way they bother me?"

So she said she was going to have a bath and I put on Matthew and Angela's tea. Ten minutes later she'd knocked a panicked rhythm on the floor and I went up to find her sitting in a red bath with a white face.

All they seemed to do at the hospital was check his heartbeat, over and over, never telling us if it was good or bad or non-existent. I left the room while they examined her and the next thing I knew she was being wheeled past me at high speed on her way to the operating theatre.

Alex was pulled backwards out of the hole in her stomach at ten to eight that evening. Grey, squirming, and smaller than a loaf of bread. Lydia wouldn't stop smiling, even when they took him to the special care unit and told us he might be brain damaged from the lack of oxygen.

The next morning I picked up Matthew and Angela from Alice's and took them to meet their brother.

"He smells like toilet cleaner," was Matthew's first observation, his nose pulling upwards like a concertina at the sanitary stink of the ward. He stared for a long time at the tubes going in and out of Alex's little face, and the little chest fluttering up and down, and the little dark mouth which gaped and contorted in silent cries, and the little claws which served as hands, clasping at something in the air that none of us could see. Matthew wriggled out of my arms and went to sit on a chair by the wall. Angela took his place and drummed her fingers on the plastic of the cot, a slow, wise frown on her face. "He looks angry," she said.

"I don't think he wanted to be born yet," I said.

"I don't think he likes the tubes," she said.

Alex spent two weeks in that room, fed by a dropper and a drip, cared for by a rotation of six nurses and two doctors and watched ever-smilingly by his mother, who was only allowed to hold his hand through the little hatch door. Adamant that he would be fine, she reassured the doctors when they twice came to tell her that he might not make it through the night. "You're doing a good job," she'd said gently. "He'll be okay, don't worry." Little white lies are the most painful of all. They told me that she would almost certainly need psychiatric help if he died.

I am still in the kitchen, waiting for the beans to cool. I won't make it as far as the hospital, I can tell. Time is viscous here, and not every doorway is active. Ingrid's door led only to this moment, and when I walk through to the sitting room I will find myself somewhere, sometime else. I've learnt to accept it, to appreciate my younger form with its ten fingers and toes, before the accident, before age took its pound of flesh.

In the last few minutes before Lydia starts to knock I hear Matthew jump from the footstool to the sofa with a thumping creak that used to make me bark with irritation. By the time Alex was his age, we'd given up trying to implement common sense rules like no jumping on the furniture. If they fell, they would learn. The rules were different for Matthew back then. At least from me. Lydia never minded anything much at all.

Matthew and Lydia were never closer than during her recovery in the hospital, a closeness that dissipated as soon as the demands of a newborn Alex came fully into play. But there on the postnatal ward, Matthew was the only one who wasn't bothered by her denial. He spent his visiting time curled up next to her, amazed by the stitches in her stomach, incredulous and delighted that she would let him pour himself glass after glass of water from the little plastic jug on her bedside table - drinking so much one day that he wet her bed.

I don't think he had thought far enough ahead to realise that we would be taking Alex home. I don't think I had thought ahead enough to think that Alex would even survive. But two weeks to the day he was born we took a shell-shocked car journey back to the house. And then there were five.

Chapter Seven

The night Alex died, the night he found out that Dad wasn't his dad, I almost had an urge to hug him. But maybe it was just the novelty of feeling sorry for him.

Alex looked at me – well, two inches to the right of me, while the rest of him swayed to the left – and grimaced, as if waiting for the fraternal sympathy he knew would never come.

I took a step away from him. It didn't make sense. I was the one who didn't fit. I was the one with the mysterious parentage. I'd dreamt of discovering the same thing – that I didn't belong to Dad after all – of claiming some sort of freedom, some other life waiting for me far away from him. It made no fucking sense at all. If Alex wasn't his son then why did Dad love him more than me?

Everyone was looking at me for some sort of reaction. Alex's expression was triumphant in a miserable, tired sort of way. I took in a breath and blew it out again when I couldn't think of any decent words to say. Then another, and a perfunctory follow-up question: "So, who is?"

"Who's who?"

"Your dad."

"I don't fucking know! Are you gonna drive me there or not?"

"No."

No fucking way. Dad never had any problem shouting at me, but whenever Alex confronted him all he could manage was a horrifying wounded silence. I was not about to invite myself to that bombshell explosion, even if I was sort of perversely intrigued to know whether Dad had any clue that Lydia had kept him as a cuckold all these years. And on this thought I must have accidentally blown a snort of a laugh out of my nose, because everyone looked at me with the same disgusted face.

"You're loving this, aren't you?" Alex said quietly. Sabine and Jamie shifted their gazes over to Alex and back to me.

"Loving what?"

"You can have Dad all to yourself now."

"Oh for God's sake, are you fucking mental?"

All three of them were waiting for my poker face to slip. I got lost somewhere between a shrug and a sigh. "Just go home," I said, as calmly as I could. Alex didn't move.

"Maybe you should talk to your sister first," Sabine suggested mildly.

"Yeah, talk to Angie. Maybe she'll take you tomorrow," I said, inching myself around as if I could subtly herd him back toward the door.

"What's she got to do with it?" he snapped.

"Well, what have I got to do with it?" I snapped back. It was late. It was Sunday. I had work in the morning. I'm not proud of it.

"He's *your* dad!"

"What? You think this is some kind of conspiracy? He was probably as oblivious as you. If you tell him… Alex, you're going to destroy him."

"So what? What about me? Am I supposed to just ignore this?" He shook the letter so hard his fingers tore through it.

"He brought you up!"

"So what?"

"*So what?* You're his fucking little golden boy. And I'll bet you anything he hasn't got a clue that you're not his."

I could picture Dad's face as he read Alex's letter, how his hands would tremble and his lips would struggle to stay still, how his eyes would close, the tears that would escape from behind the lids, the long exhalation through his nose, the attempt at a smile. What was the point in a painful truth? Why did Alex want to wound him for a secret Lydia kept? And why did I care if he hurt him at all?

"You'd want to tell him, if it was you," Alex said.

"No, I wouldn't. I'd keep my fucking mouth shut." I didn't need another reason for Dad to resent me. "You had two parents who loved you, isn't that enough?"

"So did you," Alex shot back. "Didn't stop you trying to find out about your mum, did it?"

"It's not the same."

"It's pretty fucking similar."

I stood over him, finger jabbing towards his face, while he sank back into the sofa cushions as if I was nothing more than a yappy little puppy. My voice was rising to a squeal while his switched down to a quiet, calm rumble, but I couldn't stop the heat from rising in my face, couldn't stop wanting to close my fingers around his windpipe to make him stop talking. "The difference is," I said, "they *wanted* you."

And Alex's response was a smile. And that's what killed him.

I snatched his vodka away. He propelled himself to his feet and slapped the glass out of my hand. There was a pause while we watched it spin and come to rest under the coffee table. Orange juice blotted into the carpet.

"This is not about you," Alex said.

"No, no its not. It's about my dad," I said. I mirrored him with a smile, an awful clenched thing that hurt the muscles in my face. "My dad. Mine. Not yours. How fucking ironic."

Alex swayed onto the tips of his toes and back on his heels and forward again. Then he tried to hit me.

He tried to hit me and he fell.

He fell and he hit his head.

It was an accident.

There's a great big dent in the plaster.

I'm never going to get my deposit back now.

He wasn't bleeding. Sabine and I tried to help him up but he pushed us away and stormed out like a drunken tornado with Jamie trailing after. I picked up the glass and chucked a tea towel over the damp patch, rolling my eyes at Sabine.

She looked back with distate. "What's wrong with you? He's your brother."

#

He was four and I was eight. I can remember the warmth of his little bony body pressed up against my back, skinny arms wrapped around my shoulders, chest going in and out like a foot pump, his hot breath on the back of my ear. We were at the open-air swimming pool, as cold as corpses, our dad and his mum, Lydia, watching us from the grass, imagining we were having fun. I waded round the shallow end with Alex like a leech on my back, legs numb, lungs constricted from the cold. When I reached the side I laid my arms on the warm stone and let the sun dry my face.

"Don't stop," he ordered.

"I'm tired."

"Keep going!"

"No, get off. I'm getting out."

"I don't want to get out!"

"Then learn to swim." It was cruel. I know that. I unhooked his arms from around my neck, uncrossed his ankles from around my stomach and launched him backwards into the icy water.

I turned as slowly as I dared to save my brother from his ten-second drowning, pulled him out of the water by his armpits and sat him on the side. He started crying in the same hyperventilating, screechy tone that he used when he would still occasionally shit himself. Rage and humiliation. He spat water in my face and attempted a few weak slaps which were ignored by Lydia and Dad as they marched over furiously.

His mum swept him up into a ready towel and shushed and placated and sweet-nothinged him quiet. Dad loomed over, casting me in shadow. "You will *never* do that again," he said, deadly quiet. No finger pointing, no rough grabbing of my upper arm, no spank. He just turned away and went to buy Alex an ice cream.

I swam all the way to the deep end and stayed there until it was time to go home, even though I was afraid that the shark that lived beneath the filter grates at the dark bottom of the pool was going to burst free and bite my legs off. At that moment, I would have chosen a watery, sharky death over having to sit on the damp grass with my dad and his other family.

#

It was two-thirty in the morning. We dressed hastily, clumsily, haphazardly, as if there was a rush. "I should call someone," I said. "Angela. Clare. Dad… Oh Jesus, Dad."

Sabine passed me a pair of socks and shook her head, "Worry about him later." She'd stared like a gutted fish when I told her what Jamie had told me, but shock gave way to uncertainty at the fact that I wasn't crying because my brother was dead. The pressure to cry was almost worse than trying to process the information.

"Are you sure?" she kept repeating, as if I'd heard him wrong, as if I were an idiot. Every "yes" I was forced to say made me feel less and less, until I was so numb I couldn't even put on my own shoes.

Sabine knelt on the floor and tied my shoelaces for me. Then she dialled Angela's number and put the phone in my hand. I couldn't remember if she was on a shift or not. I left some sort of vague message on her answer machine that didn't say what had happened but must have scared the shit out of her nonetheless. Sabine went into the living room and started taking quick, squeaky intakes of breath.

At the hospital she led me by the hand through rubber floored corridors as if I were blind. We squeezed into a lift full of glazed middle-of-the-night visitors and mourners and worriers. An automated announcement repeatedly told us to use the sanitiser gel to minimise infection and I couldn't tell if we were moving up to a ward or down to a morgue. My fists clenched around the hem of my coat until my nails began to burn. There could be no worse vision than Alex's body on a slab.

He was always into all of that shit - gore and horror and those gruesome bits at the back of lads' magazines about people managing to mutilate themselves or break bones in disgusting ways, or those programmes about teenagers riding their BMXs down flights of concrete steps and smashing their faces in, or skaters shattering their kneecaps, or dumb DIYers nail-gunning their feet to the floor, or a kid who shot himself in the head with his dad's shotgun and survived with half a skull. Alex laughed and I cringed. He boasted a wrist-to-elbow scar from trying to jump between the roof of the bike shelter and the prefab toilet block when he was thirteen. Maybe I could identify him from that jagged mark, without having to look at his face. They'd called me into the school office to stay with him until the ambulance arrived and his eyes seemed full of the blood that had drained out of his face. Splintered and unblinking. He wouldn't look at me but the moment I sat next to him he clutched onto my arm with his good hand and wouldn't let go until the sirens were turning and the paramedics sent me back to class.

He counted his stitches like a miser hoarding pennies, tortured me with descriptions of the way the skin was starting to fuse back together. He took pictures of the wound so he could recreate it with face paint to turn himself into a zombie for Halloween. He'd borrowed *Night of the Living Dead* off Jamie's cousin when he was eight and I was twelve, persuaded me to watch it with him one Sunday night while Dad and Lydia slept.

We sat six inches from the screen with the volume on the lowest notch, eating cold roast chicken from the fridge, straining to hear every groan and scream. I cried silent tears behind his back, unable to move my cramping, shivering legs; my buttocks riddled with pins and needles, my veins thrilling with terror and exhilaration.

When the tape rewound itself we watched black static until an unspoken, unheard signal sent us running for our room. I lay awake until the morning, snivelling into the dark because I'd never realised how easy it would be for zombies to unlatch the garden gate and force open the dodgy window in the back porch. They could have been making their shuffling, moaning way up the stairs at that very moment and every creak and ding of the plumbing confirmed it.

The undead forged a brief truce between us. We devised a plan for zombie-proofing, an escape plan and Armageddon survival strategy that we would continue to develop in intense detail over the following few months. The only time we didn't want to kill each other was when there were zombies to kill instead.

Now it's his reanimated body that chases me through our old house in my nightmares. These days I let him bite me, just to get it over with. I know I won't wake up. I need to feel the bite; canines glancing off bone, hot saliva mixed with blood dribbling down my skin, rabid eyes inches away from mine.

"Matt… "

My eyes were closed. A palm came to rest against my cheek, the vinegar sting of hand sanitiser seeping into my pores. Someone coughed.

"Matt, this is our floor," Sabine said. "There are people waiting."

It was safe in the lift. Leaving meant seeing my brother. I looked down at my shoes, tied in a double bow, too tight, not the right kind at all for running from the undead. The lift went bong and the doors tried to close but Sabine stuck out an arm to stop them. "Please," she said. Her voice broke like rotted wood, jagged and weak. She looked scared, and Sabine is never scared. She had shrunk – pale and sickly and aged and skinnier than she should be – shivering in her pyjamas with only a coat on top. She made me wonder what my face looked like, to make her face look like that.

Chapter Eight

I follow Angela up to the outpatients building, dragging my toes with each step. My lethargic brain is intrigued by the scraping noise it creates and I can't help but enjoy the subtle irritation it provokes in my stepdaughter.

We've been coming to the memory clinic since before The Farm House and with a wash of irony I can remember exactly what happened at each appointment. It used to be a way to assuage Angela's anxiety after my first stroke, a distraction from her forceful attentiveness - the visits and spot checks and medicine deliveries and unannounced drive-bys, hoping to catch me combing my hair with a fork or trying to water the plastic plant in the hall or talking to the doorbell. But now, with three little strokes under my belt and an inmate's blank eyes, it is all pointlessly detestable. There is no recovery.

A receptionist greets us unenthusiastically and directs us to wait in a room with soft, rounded edges and a vile pink carpet stained with grey. A low coffee table covered with leaflets divides two lines of screwed-down chairs. I can't focus well enough to read the titles. *How to Deal with Your Demented Stepfather,* possibly. Angela plucks one up, opens out the folds and tosses it back on the pile. She looks sideways at me with a smile, that all-enduring flat grin that shows just how hard it is to pretend I'm not going insane.

The receptionist picks her nose behind a glass screen that

she perhaps believes to be opaque. Perhaps she just doesn't care, liberated by an audience who won't remember her.

Angela wears Lydia's rings. She sits looking at the backs of her hands as if she has just realised they are turning into her mother's. Her nails have hardened and grooved with the years, and she has even begun to file them into the same shape as Lydia's - rounded points of a sensible length. The only sensible thing about Lydia was her fingernails, I suppose.

No wedding band for Angela. She took her mother's advice, even though Lydia ignored it herself, twice. We were each other's second spouse and happy never to discuss Matthew's mother or Angie's dad. I was an exception, Lydia said.

"We were made to make babies, not to make families. You were better off without a dad like him," I heard her tell her daughter once. "And Alex, too."

Instead, Lydia said, she had chosen me. I hoped Angela hadn't bothered to study me as an example of a father. I was always tired. I couldn't help with maths homework. I never apologised when I shouted. And I was shouting, scarlet-faced and sweating, the first time she saw me, calling her mum a silly cow for crashing her car into mine at the crossroads outside Matthew's nursery. I yanked Matthew out of his seat, crushed him to my chest, yelling, "You bloody fool woman!" as I ran round to Lydia's car but she was clutching her own child, sobbing sorry, sorry, sorry. Angela and Matthew looked at each other and then up at us, and it was as if they knew.

Lydia used to ask men for directions to places she knew how to get to, just so she could flirt in gratitude. She'd leave her purse on the counter in the newsagent's so that the long-haired, dark-eyed salesman would run down the street to return it to her, and she would blush and gabble and he would touch her arm and say it was no problem. He would look nervously to me but there was nothing I could do. Flirting was her default form of communication. I often wondered if Angela's mother had spotted me long before she drove her car into the side of mine. And a little less than nine months later,

Alex was born.

An echo of a song flaps through the door as it closes behind an old woman and her nurse; someone singing louder than is socially acceptable in a corridor that rolls the sound back in thrumming resonance. The nurse nods to Angela in some sort of carer's solidarity, or perhaps it's a secret signal. The old woman pauses when the nurse stops her, walks when the nurse gently nudges her forward. They sit to the right of us and the woman closes down; chin to chest, hands in lap, knees falling open. The nurse fishes in her handbag for gum. Angela shuffles closer to me, lays her hand on my thigh and quickly removes it again. We are so very bad at affection. One thing we have in common.

At three, Matthew was a little watery-eyed silent thing who liked to sit as close as humanly possible to Angela on the sofa - hip bones sticking into her thighs, his arm squashed up against her side, head a few bare inches away from resting on her shoulder. He never made it that far, though he seemed to long to do so.

Lydia would roll her eyes and pull us into rough hugs, kissing our ears, leaving bells ringing inside. Alex would climb up legs and onto laps and throttle us with love, his open-mouthed kisses full of teeth. I patted heads and nodded solemnly, the sort of expression to be adopted when confronted with something I don't know how to react to. I can feel the frown clamping at my muscles now as the doctor leans around her doorway and asks us to come through. But her doorway has no magic, I can tell, and I don't move until Angela prods me in the fat underneath my arm.

My doctor is younger than Angela, with deep brown skin and eyes whose irises are almost as dark as her pupils. I may be no good at physical contact but something about her manner makes me want to crawl into a ball on her lap. I'm fairly sure she would be too polite and professional to mind. Doctor Samyal consults her notes, smiling every so often, trying to divide her attention between me and my chaperone.

It's a careful balance, and one she negotiates well: don't make the patient feel like a child, but ensure that any important information is retained by the one with a properly working brain. I watch her and nod without listening, trying to keep my expression as neutral as possible because after our last appointment Angela said I looked at the doctor like I wanted to kiss her.

My straight-faced response has always failed with Angela, ever since she discovered brown blood in her knickers and rushed to tell me because her mother was at work, and she didn't seem to think it mattered that I didn't share her body parts. The pain must have shown clearly on my face as I rummaged through the basket in the bathroom that contained Lydia's products and creams for things I didn't normally investigate.

Angela took Lydia's stance on embarrassment: it's something that only applies to other people. "We talked about it at school," she told me. "They gave us free tampons but I don't have any left because we threw them all at the boys."

I nodded, not trusting myself to answer. I passed her a pad and a tampon of every colour I could find. "You know what to do?"

"Mmm hmm. They gave us a booklet too. Thanks, Peter."

Nod. "And you know what it all means? Uh… *It?*"

"It means I can have babies now."

"You're twelve, you're not having babies yet."

"Yes, but it means that I *can*." She laughed at me gently, elated – part of the great women's club at last – blushing with the happy knowledge that tampons were no longer just surplus missiles to be launched at the sniggering boys in her class, to make them squirm with the same uncertainty and discomfort I felt fifty-odd years on.

It didn't get easier. I reacted in much the same way when she did, in fact, have a baby ten years later. I was the first to know then, too. Lydia was dead and I was alone again, navigating the terrifyingly familiar territory of being responsible for

70

children I wasn't prepared for.

I studied the rays of sunshine on the ultrasound and gave an emphatic nod.

I took Clare in my arms the day she was born and pressed my face against her blanket to blot away the tears I pretended I wasn't crying.

I walked her up and down the hall while she wailed out her colic.

I watched her cobalt-blue eyes roll ecstatically as she breastfed, the little dimples of her inverted knuckles pawing at her mother's necklace, a lazy smile on her lips.

I remember this. I remember all of it, in blossoming, flaring Technicolour, and yet there are times when I don't recognise Angela's face.

I have a pencil in my hand, a blank notepad on the desk between me and the doctor and I cannot recall what has just been said.

She asks me to copy a picture of interlocking shapes, and I fail, just like last time. She asks me to remember three words: chair, blue and blackbird, which I am to repeat back to her at the end of the consultation and I am able to do so. I am told that there is a difference between two apparently identical pictures and asked to spot it but I can't. I am not embarrassed. I am not upset. I am filled up with a vacancy that is not unpleasant, because it is not anything at all.

Angela is troubled. She's spent too much time around people losing their minds, I know. She can anticipate how it's going to go, how it's going to end, except this time she's the relative and not the nurse. Or she's both, which is twice as awful. I cannot comfort her and I don't want to try.

The doctor writes out an appointment card, explaining to Angela about a new set of exercises which will help to maintain as much memory function as possible, intermittently blinking kindly and regretfully at me. I jerk to my feet. By the time they react with echoing repetitions of "Peter? Peter?" I am already out the door and down the corridor, and even though Angela catches up with me at the foyer I don't let her slow me down. I know exactly where I'm going. She follows me unobtrusively out of the clinic and all the way to the high street shoe shop that used to be a travel agency where Heather once worked. I sit on one of the chairs with my feet on a foot-measuring stool and ask the shop assistant if she knew, if she was even aware that this place used to be a travel agency. If she knew that Heather worked here. A bit of accounting, that's what she did. And some secretarial duties. She hated it. She hated everything, by the end. The shop assistant didn't know, and she shakes her head with a slow, patient, painfully tolerant expression. Angela sits down next to me and waits quietly until I allow her to persuade me to go back to the home.

#

I don't remember dinner, or getting into my pyjamas, or taking my medication, but when the resonance of Heather's workplace finally leaves me I find myself sitting up in my bed, steeped in the catnip stink of my room, with the ocean-sounds radio set to some sort of waterfall. It is as if I have been dug up and replanted, like a sickly tree. Perhaps if you put it in the shade at the back by the fence it will survive, and if it dies you won't notice, it won't be missed.

I may be falling asleep or I may be falling through some sort of horizontal doorway, but all I can keep hold of is the image of a woman I thought I once knew. Perhaps I saw her in the shoe shop, or out of the window of the car, or in the conservatory back at The Farm House - a woman, a witch, a figment of an untethered imagination. She remains when I close my eyes, threading a voice through the hair inside my ears, telling a story that I've heard before, to the rhythm of a bleating heartbeat:

A prince. Waiting for his execution. And a bell, ringing a hole in his head as he sat in his stone cell and swore instead of prayed at the dirt under his feet.

A woman. Standing the wrong side of the locked door. Brown toothed, swarthy, and twisted like willow. A witch, almost certainly.

"Evening," she said, with a voice like a broken back.

There were no windows in his cell but the chill of the sunset had reached him hours before. He raised a princely eyebrow at her but she said nothing more until he asked, "What is it you want from me?"

"Your fear," she replied.

He did not understand. The incessant bell tolled reason and thought out of his brain with each sweet-toned peal.

"I'm not afraid," he muttered, not even believing it himself.

"Don't you want to know how they'll do it?" she asked coquettishly.

The prince forced himself to sit up straight, to the fullest height he could manage while shackled to the wall. He had a proud chin - his portraits, now pulled down from the walls of the palace and replaced with his usurper, had always captured it well.

The woman had magic. In the earthen floor she drew visions of his end: the desperate silence of a hanging, the heated knife disembowelling and castrating, the bubble and pitch of burning alive. He kicked the images away like a drowning man jerking his last.

She watched his bloodless face, the battering pattern of his heart. "No fear?" she said.

The prince shook his head once each side.

"Well then," she sniffed, "I'll leave you to your death."

As she turned away, he wondered how she would leave – how indeed she got inside – with no keys, with no sign that the guard outside his cell had any idea she was even there. "Wait," he said. He didn't feel strong enough to witness a woman walking through a solid door.

"Yes?"

"I am," he said slowly. "Afraid. I'm terrified."

She smiled.

"I can make it all disappear."

And she did. And it did.

#

The beeping won't stop. I am standing at the foot of Mother Whistler's bed and though her lips aren't moving I can hear her voice as clear as the bells of the prison tower.

"Is this what you wanted?" she asks.

I shake my head once each side. One, two. No. No.

She doesn't smile. Her machines are furious. Red and green lights illuminate the pitted and sunken flesh of her cheeks in stuttering flashes. "You still have to pay," she says, without saying anything out loud.

I can hear the nurses coming to turn off the noise, to return the technology to a placid hum, to tuck her up and chase me away. "How much?" I ask, just as silently.

"Two."

"Two what?"

"Sons, Peter. Two of your finest boys."

"But I don't have any children."

I can hear her laughter above the bleeping. For a second the corner of her mouth twitches upwards. "Oh Peter."

"What if I say no?" I ask her. The darkness cloys at my skin, seeping between my pyjamas and my nakedness like a coating of cement, turning me to stone with every second her eyes fix on mine.

"You won't," she says.

Chapter Nine

The first time I told him I thought it would be the only time. Angie and Sabine came with me and we lined up like dominoes outside Dad's bedroom, waiting for the catalyst, for a giant finger to flick us over. We stood in height order, tallest to smallest - a space missing for Alex who would have stood at the end of the line, ahead of me, his bony shoulder blades poking out like bird beaks, the three moles on the back of his neck forming a triangle, his hair protruding at odd angles around his double crown. But if he were still here then we wouldn't have any reason to deliver any news.

We hadn't rehearsed this ridiculous line-up. We'd simply come to a gentle, otherworldly, swaying stop at Dad's door. We stood there for at least three minutes in silence while I picked at the inside seam of my jeans pocket and Angie cleared her throat of phlegm that wasn't there and Sabine shrank into herself like a retreating snail. The woman in the room next to Dad's hummed along to David Bowie on the radio, muttering crossword clues and shaking out her newspaper.

A nurse walked past and nodded to Angela. As if it was some sort of prearranged signal, Angela took a loud intake of breath and put a hand on my back. "Right," she said. "Let's… " But she never finished the suggestion.

Sabine let out a sigh like a landslide. There was a lump in my throat that was not from tears or nausea but almost as if my body had decided it would rather not breathe than do what it was about to do. Angela had stalled. Her fingers contracted around the back of my jumper. It had to be me. I had to lead the way. I felt my entire weight fall into my shoes and pushed open the door to my father's room.

Inside was the kind of quiet that made skin prickle, the kind that creates an inexplicable urge to cough. We filed in like naughty schoolchildren and stood in front of him, blocking his view of the television.

"Hi Dad," I said.

He looked up, not bothering to smile, then returned his attention to the TV where a celebrity chef was making hollandaise against a timer. I wonder if Dad guessed - if he mentally ticked off the various possibilities and worked out the reason why Alex wasn't there.

"Hi Dad," I said again.

"Hmm?" he said.

I stood between Sabine and Angela. They squeezed my hands simultaneously. I tongued my ulcers and tried to remember the series of sentences I had prepared for the occasion, stock stuff from soaps and films and dramas, like: "There's been an accident," or "Something terrible has happened." Or maybe: "I know he was your favourite son but at least you still have me, Dad."

"You alright?" he asked, leaning around to keep his eyes on the telly, reaching unconsciously for his tobacco packet and flicking out a Rizla.

Angela squeezed harder. My knuckles jarred against each other. "No," I said, "no, we're not alright."

"Oh?" Dad said, mildly amused. "What have I done now? What are you all doing here?" He eyed Sabine, in particular, suspiciously.

"Peter," Angela began, but I crushed her fingers in mine and she stopped, water pooling in her lower eyelids.

"Alex had something to tell you," I said.

"Matt," Sabine said under her breath, "don't."

"He came to see me last night."

"Matthew… " Angela this time.

Even I'm not that much of an arsehole. My dad calmly rolled himself a cigarette and pretended he wasn't still watching the chef whisking manically. I couldn't tell him that his prodigal son had not sprung from his loins. He'd have found a way to blame me. I shook my head sharply, like a bull about to charge, trying to throw off the rage.

"Well, where is he then?" Dad asked.

Words started coming out of me in a voice that was a few millimetres above a whisper. They should have been soft but they came out completely devoid of feeling:

"Alex had a brain aneurysm. Probably been there for years. It ruptured. He died last night on the street outside my flat."

All three of them watched my straight face, waiting for more. I shrugged.

"And that's it."

It was an echo of the detached doctor who gave the news to me – more guilt than sorrow – although at least the doctor managed a kind of numb empathy. I missed by a mile. I was a human fucking telegram. No sobbing, no breaking down. I was not bereft, destroyed, hysterical. There was no keening or beating of my man boobs while I told a man his son was dead. It just wasn't normal and I could tell they all found it utterly repugnant.

Dad looked across our expressions, moving along the line and back again, measuring something that I couldn't gauge. Then he stood, hoisting his cigarette in my face. "'Scuse me. Going to have this outside," he said, and shuffled past us into the corridor.

"Peter!" Angela's voice squealed unpleasantly.

Sabine turned and punched me as hard as she could on the shoulder, though I didn't really feel it. "Are you completely dead inside?"

"What the fuck did I do?" I yelled back at her.

Angela had fallen into a crouch and was pushing her palms

into her eye sockets as if she could erase her own face by sheer force. She hardly ever cries, but when she does she sounds like a walrus in heat.

"What's going on in there?" the woman next door hollered. "Some of us are trying to bloody read."

#

They tried to give Angela compassionate leave but she wouldn't take it. She was back at the home within a week, perhaps thinking no-one else would be able to look after Dad as well as she could. But he didn't need looking after. He was still refusing to acknowledge the news of Alex's death; he was completely unbothered by a situation he was blind to, albeit confused as to why Angie burst into tears whenever she tried to speak to him. She told me she couldn't face telling him again. She said she felt like she was drowning whenever she looked at him.

"You're going to make yourself ill," I said. But really I was just jealous of how easily her emotions poured out of her. I hadn't even told my boss. I was still thinking about practical things like picking up milk and butter on the way home, and where Alex's funeral should be, and forgetting to record the final episode of that documentary series on all the different ways global warming is going to fuck up the world, and whether I had to ring the utilities companies to stop the gas and water and electricity at Alex's empty flat. It didn't matter how many times I said it out loud – *my brother is dead* – it was just four little words in a line. Subject, verb. This thing is that. I pretended I was being strong for Angie but they knew. They knew.

Angela wouldn't stop asking: "How did it happen? How did he fall?" Tell me again, how he hit the wall, at what angle, was he knocked unconscious, did he cry out, did he bleed? Never the ones she wanted to ask: "Did you push him? Did you hit him? Did you kill him?" I had to rely on the fact that she trusted what Sabine and Jamie had seen, trusted the police, trusted my witnesses.

"He tried to hit me and he fell. He fell and hit his head." Sentences with the simplicity of a child learning to read. Lies are straightforward. The truth is complicated. The police were less concerned about the details than she was. Once the post-mortem results came back they stopped asking anything.

A bubble. In his head. That's all it took. Here one second, screaming in my face, gone the next, dying a hundred feet from where I knelt blotting up orange juice from my carpet. I didn't even hear the ambulance. Jamie didn't think to come back up to the flat to tell me, even then. No, a payphone call was all I deserved. He took those last moments, he took the time of death announcement, he took Alex's last words. He was there. He stole my brother's death away.

The first time I told my Dad about Alex wasn't the hardest. It got worse over the next few visits as he folded the information away into a deep inner pocket and I was lulled into expecting a reaction of intense denial. But the fourth time was the charm. He heard it all. Took it all in, swallowed it down like crushed glass. He got hung up about the fighting part, even though it could hardly have been called that. Dad's eyes stopped blinking until they were so full of water he couldn't possibly have been able to see.

"Why were you arguing?" he whispered.

"He was drunk."

"And he fell."

There's the tone of disbelief. The same as Angela. They need a villain.

"He lost his balance," I said. "They said the aneurysm could have ruptured at any time, it might not have been caused by the blow to the head." *I'm* not even comforted by the word-for-word recitation of the doctor's assurances but I have to say it. It's my only defence. "It was a time bomb." And now all I can think is thank God Dad wasn't Alex's dad and there's no secret hereditary risk of exploding brain death in my blood, too.

It was the second time I've ever seen my dad cry - a terrible silent weeping that cements just how far apart we are, have always been. I did the same thing I did when Lydia died and I walked into the bathroom to find him sitting on the edge of the bath with her toothbrush in his hand. I sat opposite him and I watched as tears and snot became indistinguishable on his upper lip and he licked them away. I watched until I couldn't look any more and then I stared into my lap. Eventually he stopped and I said, "I'm sorry," because it was the only thing I could give him. My guilt.

I gave it to Angela, too, as she tried to work out which was less painful: telling Dad his son was dead or worrying about where Clare was. None of us had heard from her since the night of my birthday and Angela shifted between reassuring anger and uncharacteristic panic. Clare must have missed a hundred calls but neither of us wanted to leave a message saying her uncle was dead.

"She's just pissed off with me," Angie said on the second day. "She'll be at Becca's. I think she snuck into the flat when I was at work to get some clean clothes." On the third day she called the police. I was glad then, that my dad had retreated into his safe little coward's denial. I imagined him officially reporting my mother missing when I was three days old. I tried to picture his face superimposed over Angela's sleep-deprived eyes, grainy and sore, over the wrinkles that sprang into life around her mouth overnight. Three days makes you a missing person. Thirty-five years makes you a ghost.

On the fourth night, I answered a knock at my door at a quarter to midnight and there Clare stood, looking like she wanted to fall down and sleep in the doorway. "Clare, what the fuck?"

"Can I come in? It's freezing."

"It's November and you're not wearing a coat. Of course you're freezing. Are you okay? Have you talked to your mum? Where the fuck have you been?"

She edged past me and folded herself up like a praying

80

mantis on the armchair, knees up to her chin, arms twisted around her ankles. She frowned up at the hole in the plasterboard. "What happened to your wall?"

#

I let her stay. I don't know what she and Angela argued about in that restaurant, but Clare refused to have any contact with her mum and begged me to let her sleep at mine. I couldn't say no. I could barely follow my own conscience, let alone tell a teenager what to do.

She set up camp on the sofa and only left it to prowl the kitchen. Alex had been dead six days. I sat with my back to the dented wall and stared bleakly at my niece while she made a brief circuit of the kitchen cupboards before turning to face me accusingly.

"There's no food in this fucking place."

I nodded to the coffee table and the bowl of sad-looking fruit upon it. Every few weeks I attempted to ease my pizza-guilt by filling the end compartment of the trolley with fruit, which proceeded to turn white, then green, then static with fur, before melting quietly into the bowl.

She cast me a loathing look and picked out a clean satsuma, studying it with deep distrust. I watched in dread as she began to peel it. She struggled to flick a strip of pith from her fingernail and her sigh came out gritty.

"There's too much fucking white stuff on it."

I considered my reply, anticipated her reaction, and said it anyway, "You've got to work for your food, that's the fun of fruit."

Scorn rose from her skin like steam - distilled abhorrence concentrated entirely upon my face. "You think you're so fucking funny, don't you?"

I tried to smile, as if I wasn't terrified of her. "It used to be easy to make you laugh."

I still think of her as the three-year-old who dissolved into hysterics at even the suggestion of a wiggly-fingered tickle. For a fraction of a second I considered leaning over and blowing a raspberry on her stomach. I actually jolted in my seat to stop myself. She looked at me as if I had just vomited on her shoes.

Keys scraped in the lock and my shoulders fell back in relief as Sabine walked in, a couple of Tesco bags in each hand. She dumped them on the counter and stood back as Clare descended, lobbing the satsuma, half-peeled, in the bin. Sabine shot me a look full of sharp and pointy objects and extracted a bottle of wine from the decimated shopping.

"What's for dinner?" Clare asked her.

"I'm not your mother," Sabine said.

"No, but you *are* my host."

"Oh, you're a guest are you? I was under the impression this was some kind of tactical occupation." Sabine poured two glasses to the brim and passed one to me before going straight to the bedroom and shutting herself in. Clare distributed an entire packet of cheese spread onto four pieces of toast.

"Have you talked to your mum?" I asked.

"No."

"Why won't you tell me what happened?"

"She's a bitch."

"She's not a bitch. Clare, her brother just died, give her a break." Funny thing: it sounded sadder when it was happening to someone else.

Clare stuffed half a piece of toast into her mouth and blinked furiously at the ceiling, forcing away the water in her eyes as she tried to swallow. "I know. I just can't face having to talk about… stuff."

I took two deep gulps of my wine and winced before I managed to say it. "Clare, you can't stay here forever."

She put down the toast and turned away from me, sniffing loudly and wiping her eyes with the heels of her hands. I let my head drop back against the back of the armchair. "Clare… "

"No, I know, I know," she said, in a little voice high up in her throat. "I'm sorry. I know *she* doesn't want me here." She jerked her head towards the closed bedroom door at Sabine.

"No, it's not that. I mean, why here? Why aren't you staying with friends or… Do you have a boyfriend?" And I realised I had no idea what my niece's life was like. I didn't even know what she was studying.

Clare brought her plate over and sat on the armrest next to me. She stuck her hand deep inside her bag and brought out something covered in tissue, cupped gently in her hands. "I thought you'd be the nicest to me," she said.

I leaned backwards slightly, watching the thing in her hands closely in case it was about to jump up and attach itself to my face. "What's that?"

She unwrapped the tissue and showed me.

"Shit," I said.

#

Seven days after my birthday and Alex's deathday, we gathered in a cold crematorium that smelled oppressively of lavender and saltwater. Music piped out of the walls almost beyond the range of human hearing, producing an effect of uncertainty - a paranoia that perhaps some sort of odourless sedative was being vented into the room along with the music.

The guests unconsciously segregated themselves either side of the aisle into family and friends invited by me and Angela on the right, and friends known only to Jamie, rounded up and scraped into suits on the left. The room's muffled quiet was punctuated by the brief exchange of sympathetic smiles and surreptitious stares directed at us, the immediate family, checking for signs of devastation.

I stood with Sabine, Angela and Clare in the front row, enjoying the feel of the carved wooden handrail in front of me. I had no uncertainty where my perceptions came from, I was one hundred per cent sure they were born of the quarter of a bottle of malt whiskey I had sipped my way through an hour before. Angela and Clare had gone on ahead to the crematorium while a funeral car with a silent driver took me to pick up my father from the home. We'd waited in the car park while I drank for twenty minutes before calling the reception from my mobile – ten metres away – to ask them to bring Dad out.

My mouth was dry, bitter, and one of my eyes wanted – in an amiable sort of way – to veer slightly to the right and peruse the fake marble pillar there, while the other fixed adamantly on the velvet curtains in front of me.

Clare started crying even before the music got loud enough to provoke the tragic effect it had been composed to convey. A woman in a badly-tailored suit and hair too short for her square face came to stand at the lectern and told us all to sit down. I sighed a full-body sigh and fidgeted on the pew, finding my breathing heavier and noisier than it should be. Someone shut the big double doors at the back of the room, which had somehow been engineered to close in the most respectful way possible: a single modest click. Angela leaned towards my ear, gestured to the empty space next to me and whispered worriedly, "Where's your dad?"

I swivelled round and swung my eyes over to where my father's fake hand rested on the very back pew, the rest of him obviously there too, standing as far away from the action as possible and grimacing at the backs of everybody's heads.

I nodded at him, Angela sent him a supportive smile and we turned back to listen to the service, which was cut short in its prime by someone noticing the fact that the father of the deceased had collapsed, suffering his fourth stroke of the year. Unconsciousness spared him the crunch of his wrist fracturing as he hit the ground.

The two strokes before this one had been so miniscule that he'd gone about his day as normal, albeit with a headache and some blurred vision. Both had occurred in the nursing home – a little less mobility, a little more moodiness, a little further into confusion – bit by bit, each one pushing his brain one notch higher on the stairlift to uselessness.

The first had left him on the kitchen floor of his flat, covered in milk. He must have watched the spilled bottle fill the grout lines of the tiles as he lay there, listening to Angela stack his answer machine with messages.

Later, we watched the CT scanner rings rotate slowly around him and listened to the feedback of a tannoy somewhere in the hospital. The doctors chicken-and-egged the dementia and the stroke, agreeing eventually that they had most likely conspired hand in hand to floor him; to take away coherent speech for a week and a half; to insert a tremor into his knees when he stood alone. Over the next seven months he got worse at hiding the anomalies and mistakes, and eagle-eyed Angela knew exactly what to look for. Then he forgot where he kept the baked beans and I betrayed him.

The paramedics picked him up off the crematorium floor and Angela went with him to the hospital as I watched my brother's body roll down the conveyor to the fire and Clare gripped my arm so tight she left fingerprint bruises.

Chapter Ten

The doorways are getting closer together. Some days each one I pass through will take me somewhere new, somewhere old, somewhere grey. And I am getting slower, less able to escape the siren's hum of the doors when they call. I am doubly crippled these days; one arm clamped inside a ridiculous plaster appendage, and the other missing a hand. Some doors lead back to a time of plenty: eight fingers, two thumbs, two hands, two wives, three children. I judge by the sweetness of the air whether it will be a joyful journey or a penance. These days, mostly, it is the latter.

Tonight a slow shuffle through the bathroom doorway leaves me shivering on the other side, standing head-bowed outside a garden shed, thirty years before my prostate nags me to urinate six times a night. For a moment all I can feel is a nameless gut-wrenching guilt before the rest comes into focus, before I properly gauge where I am. Then memory moves my hand to action and I slip the shed key underneath a rhubarb pot so Lydia won't find it. She's not like Heather, who would always defer to me in any situation requiring a spade or power tools. Lydia is far more inclined to just grab a hammer and get stuck in. I know hiding the key is futile but under the pot it goes. My body moves without me willing it, as if I'm not even inside.

I can see my neighbour Graham pulling up leeks next door.

My knees pop as I straighten up and he looks over, calling "Peter." Hearing his voice stops me like a bullet.

I can't help but grin to unnerve him. I let the awkwardness settle before heading for the back door.

"Peter? Do you want some of these?" he says, and I can't stop myself from glancing back to see him hoisting a handful of soily leeks over the fence.

"We're okay, thanks." We are okay. We don't need his leeks.

"I've got a glut. Have some."

My memory says that I refused them with a shake of my head and a backwards wave but this time I am fuelled by thirty-five years of rage and I stop and turn and stare. Graham's face glows pink in the low light. I study his features for a moment, something I never would have done before; I always found it so hard to look him in the eye. My body tries to move but I force it into submission by convincing it that its feet are pegged to the ground. It twitches, conflicted. I tell it to behave or I'll piss myself. I never did make it to the bathroom back in the nursing home.

Graham watches me, arm still outstretched, vegetables dangling flaccidly from his hands. I jog over to take the cold leeks from him and grainy earth tumbles down into my sleeve. "Thank you," I say.

"Not a problem."

I'm stuck again, cradling the leeks in my arms, smiling with no trace of pleasantry at my increasingly disturbed neighbour. He clears his throat. "So… "

"What?"

Graham tries to make it sound nonchalant: "That time of year again."

I pretend I don't know what he means. "November? Yep, it seems to happen every year."

He falters. Makes a new attempt: "Matthew's birthday."

"Saturday."

"Ahh. Five?"

"That's right."

"Five years… " he says, like a wistful grandfather, like he knows what it's like to have an almost five-year-old.

I wait for the rest. His mouth opens and shuts like a faulty trap door. I flick a tiny worm off the end of one of the leeks. Then it comes, in fits and starts: "Have you… ? Heard anything new?"

"About what?"

"About - Well. I mean about your wife. About Heather, I mean. Have you heard anything?"

I laugh. I don't mean to but it just falls out of my mouth. Graham recoils, almost ducks behind the fence. I lean closer, crushing the leeks against the slatted border that separates our little yards. Too close. We've been too close for years, never saying what needed to be said, never looking each other in the face.

"Five years, Graham," I say. "No. I've not heard one bloody thing in five years, and I don't expect to. Ever." I smile again, enjoying the discomfort it causes, and dump the leeks back over his side of the fence. They splay into an awkward fan on his boots. He drops his gardening gloves where he stands and turns to go, and it's my turn to call after him: "But if I do, you'll be the first to know."

#

Two weeks later the house was overrun by sugar-high five-year-olds, chasing the birthday boy, beating him with balloons, fighting over a newspaper-wrapped pass the parcel, collapsing in front of a video of Robin Hood when Lydia could take no more. She'd made him a cake in the shape of a hedgehog. Angela had sensibly opted to go and play at a friend's house rather than suffer the chaos. Alex, who was learning to walk at the time, was knocked over by the whirlwind of children and split his lip on the hearth. I retired to the pub after an hour.

She'd left the day after Matthew was born, but his birthday

forever remained the painful anniversary of Heather's disappearance. And Matthew had begun to ask questions about her. There were children in his class whose parents were divorced, even one girl whose father had died when she was three. But no-one else's mother was a missing person, an invisible memory. Lydia and Alice carefully suggested that until he was a bit older perhaps it was better to tell him the simpler version of events, the one the police insisted on telling me, in which Heather was presumed dead.

I couldn't do it. Even the half-truth was better than that. On the night before his birthday that year, his present from me was an attempt at honesty.

"Mummy is lost," I told him.

"Where?"

"We don't know."

"How did she get lost?"

"She ran away."

"Why don't you go and look for her?"

"I can't. I have to stay here and look after you and Angie and Alex. The police are looking for her."

Matthew's eyebrows lowered into a tense echo of my own. "When are they going to find her?"

"I think, maybe, she doesn't want them to."

"She's hiding?"

"Yes. Sort of."

Matthew's voice became progressively quieter, and the pauses between became longer with each question, as his brain tick-tocked through the reasons for her disappearance.

"Will she come and live with us when she comes back?"

"I don't know. I don't know if she'll ever come back."

"Why not?"

"I don't know. Sometimes people just want to run away and never come back."

"I miss her."

I couldn't stop myself: "But you don't even remember her."

"I still miss her. I want a mummy."

"You have Lydia."

"She's *Alex's* mummy. And Angie's."

"She's yours too. She loves you."

"I want mine."

He wasn't even angry. That came later. At five, he was lost. Just like her.

"I know," I said quietly. "I know."

"I miss her."

"Okay."

"Does she miss me?"

"I bet she does."

He knew I wasn't any good at this. His face crumpled into a sneer of pain. "You're lying."

#

The birthday guests were gone when I returned from the pub. Alex was asleep, Matthew was sitting on the kitchen counter, crying, and Lydia was on the phone. I drop into my younger self again as the front door closes behind me, though just a footstep ago I had been in the garden with Graham. Doorways inside doorways. I lean against the kitchen worktop, ale in my belly, burnt paper and Golden Virginia on my tongue.

"What's going on?" I ask her, even though I know what happens now.

" - I'm so, so sorry. I'll be round in a minute," Lydia says down the phone. She hangs up, pats the receiver a few times, sighs.

"Who was that?"

Lydia puts her arms around Matthew and pulls his face into her chest, speaking in a quiet voice over his head to me. "The kids were in the garden. Matthew says they found the shed key in a flowerbed and went to play 'club house' in it." She adjusts her arms around Matthew's head to cover his ears, and continues. "They found Suki in there."

I made my face blank. Lydia took it for incomprehension,

when really it was cold, sick remorse.

"Suki," she says, "Graham's cat? She must have got locked in. She was dead. Frozen solid."

"Oh."

"I just called next door. I said I'd bring the body over to him. Can you do it? Please?" She jerks her chin at the party paraphernalia still spread across the living room. "I need a drink."

I nod slowly, rub the back of my son's neck and kiss Lydia's temple. There's a pattern in these recollections and there's an uneasiness in my lower intestine that is more than ageing decrepitude. I'm being punished by a ghost of Christmases past that has no intention of allowing me to redeem myself - it wants me to see what I've done before I forget it forever.

#

I stand stooped in the shed with the cat in my arms, its little body stiff and wrapped in a towel. I wonder whether it was the cold or hunger that killed it. I take a spade, too, let myself out of the back gate and in through Graham's. He is waiting for me at the back door, red-eyed.

"I'm sorry. Here," my voice rumbles as I pass over the cold little bundle. Graham doesn't reply, seems to be struggling to withhold whatever he thinks of me. I turn my back on him and look for the patch of soil at the end of the garden where I know there should be a cat-sized grave.

My palms blister as I chip away at the frozen ground. Turning the soil raises the deep scent of peat and chalk - a last embrace for Suki the cat. The winter wind burns my face but the work makes me sweat, and though it takes longer than I remember, I wish I could dig on and on. Room enough for all of us.

Graham goes back inside, reappearing a little while later with two cups of tea. We stand and admire my pathetic handiwork. I wonder if he spat in my mug. "She liked to sleep on the compost bags in there," I say. "In the shed."

"It was an easy mistake to make," Graham replies woodenly, putting his tea down and taking a turn with the spade. He makes quick progress with the warmer dirt beneath the topsoil I broke open. I was irritated, first time around. Now I only watch, straining against the trappings of this younger, stupider, angrier version of myself. I take charge and stumble into a flower bed, scrabbling for a few lengths of tomato stakes which I tie together with bindweed to make a makeshift cross. I lay my tribute next to the towelled corpse and watch my neighbour's wheezing breath dissolve into the air above our heads.

Satisfied with his grave, Graham ceremoniously pours the dregs of his tea into the hole before lowering the cat gently into place. I stand silently, hands clasped behind me in practised funereal manner, waiting to cringe at the feline eulogy I expect to hear. Instead, Graham simply scoops up a spadeful of soil and begins filling in the hole. I help with my hands, eager to warm my blood again after standing in the cold for so long. I wish for the overzealous heat of The Farm House, for heat packs and blankets and biscuits. When the grave is filled in, Graham positions the wooden cross at its head, collects up our mugs and leaves me standing there.

At the back door he pauses and looks back, eyes squinting against the wind. "Tell Matthew happy birthday," he says.

"I will."

"Thank you." He nods, just once, at the grave. "I appreciate your help."

I pick up my spade and swallow the bile that has risen into my gullet. "Okay."

This time it is Graham's smile that lays an ill-at-ease blanket over the garden, and I am not able to return it.

Walking through the garden gate brings me to my knees, into a different pair of knees, inside a different skin, but the guilt remains.

\#

The changes come quicker.

The transitions jar my bones and leave me in a perpetual state of jet lag.

I return to the nursing home. I'm on my knees in my bathroom in trousers soaked with urine, clutching at the shag pile shower mat while waves of gripping aches build and die away in my stomach. The throbbing in my broken arm is the only thing that is new. The past is filling me up and threatening to burst, oozing out of my ears. A nurse appears behind me, tells me to stay put, not to worry, but my bedroom doorway has become frantic again, urging me through and turning the room around me into an unbearable desert that I am forced to flee if I am to breathe, if I am to live. I obey. And I am somewhere worse.

I am staying at my aunt's house while my mother has a nervous breakdown and my father is embalmed at Morleigh the undertaker's, three doors down.

My mother is a war widow even though the war is over. I am partially orphaned. I am six, and embarrassed that my dad did not die in combat. He wanted to be a pilot, but a perforated eardrum made him an engineer instead. A collapsed hangar during an air raid left him half deafened, which is why he did not hear the fire engine that ran him over.

My aunt lives alone, but I have never counted fewer than four people in her house at any time. I'm not sure her door even locks. No-one knocks, and my aunt never shows any surprise when visitors let themselves in. I can hear her in the kitchen below, noisily rolling out dough, telling my not-real-aunties Joyce and Mary about my poor devastated mother who is currently drunk and unconscious in the bedroom next to mine. I sit inside my aunt's wardrobe and stroke her rabbit fur coat, blowing tracks through the black and white hair to reveal the pale dead rabbit skin beneath. My uncle's clothes still hang next to hers, just as my father's still hang next to my mother's at home; dead men's clothes. The stink of mothballs makes me sneeze.

I have toothache and gut ache and brain ache because my breakfast consisted of jam straight from the jar. My aunt believes that letting me do stupid things will encourage me to make the decision not to do them again. My mother believes that shouting and a crack round the head will help. But my mother hasn't spoken to me since they came to tell us about my father. She clings to the bed as though adrift on a rough sea and wipes away her tears with his coat.

The fireman who ran him down brought my father's black coat to our door late Friday night. It's stiff and brittle with dried blood but she won't let my aunt wash it. She rubs it against her face, even when she's not crying, and the salted tears and rough wool leave her skin raw and flaking.

My aunt shouts up the stairs for me to come and help her cut out scones. I wipe my nose on one of my uncle's hanging shirtsleeves. My mother retches in the spare bedroom. Through the half-open door I watch her stumble to the bathroom and lock herself in. I press my teeth with my tongue. They twinge. Maybe I'll just have butter on my scones. Maybe I should go and see my dentist, Alma.

Chapter Eleven

Dad is having a bad day. The nurse put it fondly – "off with the fairies" – when she let me into his room. I'm not sure which fairies he's with, but he is standing at the window pulling long orange threads out of the curtains, somewhere between anxious and content.

Today there is no reaction to Alex's death, even when I turn it into a terrible form of poetry: "Dad. Alex is dead. Alex is dead, Dad. Dad, he died. Alex died, Dad. Alex. Dead. Dad?" And after that I continue on with my list. A reverse confession of sorts. A catalogue of every time Alex was a little shit when we were kids.

"The swimming competition." I say. "I was fifteen."

Dad ignores me, tapping on the glass like he's saying hello to a squirrel or a bird or something. My father: Doctor Dolittle. The man who once threw next door's cat over the fence for pissing on his irises. He fucking hated that cat.

"Swimming, Dad," I say again. I was going to represent the school in front crawl. I had underarm hair and everything. I was starting to get pecs, lose some of the puppy fat. There was a girl. Harriet. She was coming to watch me compete. My dad doesn't know this story. He didn't come.

I sit in his armchair and talk at my knees. "It was summer. You know how hot my room used to get?" It was a south-facing oven, the sun kept at bay by thin polyester curtains. I used to sleep in just my boxers with no duvet. I should have known to watch my back.

Dad turns but doesn't look at me, doesn't seem to even know I'm there. He opens the wardrobe and sifts through his shirts, looking for something - his grasp on reality, the way through to Narnia.

"The night before," I say, "Alex wrote TWAT across my back in black indelible marker while I was asleep."

Dad snorts. My head whips up. Is he laughing at me? His eyes squint and he sneezes loudly into a shirt, wipes his nose with a sleeve and continues his search.

"Yeah, well, as you can imagine, I found it hilarious. Little fucking bastard. And that's why I hit him with that tennis racquet."

I was going to hit him with a chair but thought better of it at the last moment. Alex took advantage of my brief moralising pause to run into the hall. As I followed him, the nearest thing I could grab was Lydia's tennis racquet. I hit him twice. Once on the ribs on his left side, and once on his back as he fell down. He had curved bruises and criss-cross welts for two weeks. When Dad found out, he smacked me round the head so hard I missed a good thirty seconds of his shouting tirade. I tuned back in to " - despicable! He's only eleven! I can't even look at you, get out of my sight!"

I didn't tell him about the skin graffiti. I knew he'd only laugh, and that would be worse than the smack. I shut myself in my room, hooked a chair stacked with heavy books under the door knob and smashed all my swimming awards into little shards of plastic men. Pointless self-destruction as a gut reaction - as if it would temper the punishment I was about to receive.

"I had my first cigarette that day, too," I tell my father's hunched back. "I stole a packet out of Lydia's sock drawer when you took Alex to casualty." Dad was convinced I'd broken the little shit's ribs. I hadn't, lucky for me. Unlucky for Alex, who could only stand two days of a cultivated limp before finding the poor cripple routine too tiring to maintain. "I went down the end of the garden and smoked three in a row. Graham from next door saw me and said he'd heard you shouting." There was always a lot of shouting. Graham would appear on his patio feigning plant-watering or buddleia pruning so that he could peer over into our kitchen window with enlarged, concerned eyes.

Dad has gone stock still, one hand on the door of the wardrobe, the other wrapped around a hanging trouser leg. You could almost believe he was listening, but I know better.

Graham promised he wouldn't tell Dad about the smoking. He seemed to feel sorry for me and didn't laugh when I told him what happened. He stood there afterwards for longer than seemed normal, watched me pretend I knew how to smoke in a cool way, idly scraped dried mud off a trowel. He suggested nail varnish remover to get the ink off, which, incidentally, is a fucking bad idea when applied to scrubbed-raw skin.

"So did you win?" Graham asked.

"Win what?"

"The race. The swimming."

"Oh. No. Third."

"Third? Third is good."

"Yeah, well… "

"Did you get a medal? A trophy?"

"Medal. And a certificate."

"Something to remember it by."

I scoffed. "Good memories."

"You'll laugh one day."

"I think not."

"Well. Laugh now then. You've got your revenge, it's not worth being bitter about."

I thought he was wise. And I felt like an adult talking to him, something that wasn't possible around my dad. I was a perpetual tug on his sleeve. Always an intrusion.

"He said I looked like Mum," I say, louder than is necessary to cross the small room. I want to hurt him. I want a reaction.

My dad sneezes again and wipes his nose on his sleeve. "Five years, and nothing," he says, still facing the wardrobe. "That bastard next door."

"What?"

"That wasn't true. But she never sent *him* any letters."

He's talking about my mum, I know it. His voice changes when he speaks about her, as if he has to put on a different face to do so. My lungs sink into my stomach.

"Who? What letters?" I'm on my feet but I don't remember standing up. He still won't turn and look at me.

"Or maybe she did. Maybe he was laughing at me." He goes very quiet and then starts sniffing. He better not be fucking crying. The fingers poking out of the end of his plaster cast form a gnarled fist.

"Dad?" Just fucking look at me. "Peter?" He controls himself with one extra-loud sniffle. "Peter," I say again. "Did Mum - Did Heather write to you?"

Dad's head jerks up and slightly to the side, as if hearing someone calling his name from another room. The only sound I can hear is the rhythmic suck and groan of the machine wired up to the old lady in the room opposite, and the off-key humming of his neighbour Ingrid. But Dad turns and heads towards the door, oblivious to my presence aside from having to manoeuvre past me, like I'm an inconvenient piece of furniture. I grab him by the shoulder – on his bad arm – and he hisses in pain but looks back at me blankly. There are tears on his face. I let him go.

"Dad?"

"Happy birthday, Matthew," he says, and walks out into the corridor, wiping his eyes with his stump.

#

For a long time I didn't even consider that it might have been hard for my dad. I truly believed, in some way, it was his fault that she'd disappeared. Something he'd done, some dark secret, some violent moment that had driven her away. I was terrified of him at times, not that I really knew why, other than not understanding how he could make his face into an expressionless mask whenever I asked him about my mum.

I lived at Nana Alice's until I was three. He would visit daily after work to have dinner with us and sit in silence while Alice told him about our day. I sat muted, too. Unless she nudged me to add a detail of our thrilling activities: "And what did we pick from the garden for lunch?"

"Broad beans."

"And Matthew podded them all, didn't you little one?"

A nod from me. A nod of acknowledgement from Dad. Nana Alice would continue on, making up for the absent two-thirds of the conversation, talking until she had to stop and sigh in between sentences to catch her breath. Soon after that she'd declare that a cup of tea was needed and we would be gratefully disbanded; me to my room to play, Dad to the sofa to watch the news.

When I moved 'home' to Dad's house I thought it was a punishment. It happened over a bank holiday and I was left to spend three whole days and nights alone with my father - awkward pauses paced between stuttered communication and a lot of TV. His cooking was comparable to Nana Alice's like slurry is to fertiliser. When Nana Alice turned up on Tuesday morning to look after me while Dad went back to work, I hugged her leg so tightly I ripped a ladder in her tights. She set about making Dad's house "a bit more liveable" - emptying the box of toys that had stayed packed away in the corner of my room, laying my mum's favourite knitted blanket on my bed, making sure there was an obligatory crucifix in each room.

Nana Alice had a compulsion for crosses. One in every room, one everywhere you go, even if you had to improvise it out of crossed cutlery, or the sleeves of a shirt, or legs of a toy octopus. That Tuesday she made one out of ice lolly sticks and wool and hung it in the kitchen. She couldn't listen to Jerusalem without joining in, but would always fade out with a lump in her throat by the second verse. A little brass Christ pegged up like bloody washing hung in my room, leering down at me as if asking: "What the fuck did you do this for?" I shut him in my bedside table drawer and used my prayers to beg that he wouldn't free himself during the night and creep across my mattress to stick pins in me while I slept.

When Dad came home to find his house considerably more religious, he rolled his eyes at me and muttered, "Oh bloody… Christ."

Nana Alice made dinner and Dad told me to go and look in the garden - a surprise, he said. The darkness of early evening autumn felt like an endless Halloween and I couldn't bring myself to go out there, couldn't guess what I was being initiated into now that I was the property of my father. I stood at the back door, building up the courage to open it when he appeared behind me with a torch, picked me up in his bony arms and carried me outside. Nana Alice's round face floated like a moon at the kitchen window, sweating over a pot of slowly thickening white sauce. She didn't look up. Perhaps my bedroom was being moved to the shed. The torchlight fell upon what looked like an enormous spider web, then another. "Ta da," Dad said quietly. "What do you think?"

He put me down next to a small green bike and let the torch beam run slowly over it like a game show prize. I stroked the seat and wobbled it from side to side on its stand and fingered the brakes and stared, afraid to tell him I didn't know how to ride a bike.

"Shirley down the road gave it to us. Her boys have grown out of it now, so it's yours," he said. Nana Alice tapped on the window and hooked her thumb backwards to get us to come in.

"Well, well, well!" she laughed. "A *big boy* bike, all for you! Wouldn't your mama be impressed?"

Dad looked at her as if he was going to say something, then cast his eyes down at his dinner.

"Well? Do you like it?" he asked me.

I nodded, but it took the rest of the evening for the warmth to return to my hands and my chest.

#

Angela calls me twice a week now. At first I thought she was just worried about me but really she's hoping for a breakthrough - either that Dad will have suddenly opened up to me, or that Clare will set teenage angst aside and speak to her again. Neither is going to happen. First she uses her nurse tone on me; sympathetic pragmatism to incite me into a self-obsessed rant where I'll admit how shit I'm feeling. "I'm fine," I tell her.

Then comes maternal guilt – she needs someone to help her sort through Dad's stuff at the storage place – she can't do everything for everyone, couldn't I just help her out? I wouldn't even need to see Dad to do it.

I don't bite.

Finally she resorts to shouting and swearing, two things which are usually beneath her - "bullshit excuses" and "selfish bastard" and "total fucker". I accept them all, happy to stay in distanced denial. Angie's voice is different when she asks about Clare; it shrinks away, her okays getting smaller every time Clare refuses to take the phone. But even pity doesn't sway me these days.

Then she hits below the belt:

"Well, don't do it then. I'll call Jamie, see if he'll help me."

"Jamie?" My voice hikes up an octave and Clare's eyes snap to the side to stare at me.

"I can't lift all those boxes, so if you're not going to help me, what other choice do I have?" The "my other brother is dead" subtext is left unsaid, but very much there. Still, Jamie?

I try a laugh. "I don't want him sniffing around Dad's stuff, he'll probably sell half of it," I say.

"Who cares if he does? Look, your Dad's paying something stupid for that storage rental each month and it's not like he needs most of it. He said to get rid of it all. He just wants some books and personal stuff."

A sudden flood of saliva causes me to swallow repeatedly before I can ask: "What *personal stuff?*" Personal stuff like letters from his missing wife? Personal stuff like all the things he'd never tell me in person? Proof that he knows what happened to my mum? Maybe Angie knows. Maybe she's too respectful to look through his stuff herself, but maybe she knows what's in that storage compartment, maybe that's why she's doing such an obvious job of blackmailing me into going. My lack of sleep feeds the paranoia into a hungry beast. "What stuff?"

Angela's sigh rushes down the phone and into my ear. "I don't know, stuff that belonged to his parents I think. Photos. I don't have the time to go down there. If you don't want to do it, just say. I'll pay Jamie to go… "

"You are not paying that fucker anything. I'll do it."

I can hear the self-satisfied manipulative smile in her voice. "Thank you. I'll text you the list of stuff in a minute. Just drop it off when you visit him next week, okay? We can rent a van and clear the whole thing out another time."

The vision of an empty storage compartment makes me nauseous. "He's not dead yet, Angie."

She tuts. "He asked me to do this for him, Matt. I'm just trying to do what he wants."

I mutter an "okay" and Clare pokes me viciously in the left kidney when I put the phone down.

"What have you got against Jamie?" she says.

"He's a dick."

She shrugs, "He's always nice to me. He and Alex bought me my first beer."

"I bet they did."

She narrows her eyes and pokes me harder, bulbous knuckles on skinny fingers like Alex's. "He's a nice guy, I spoke to him at the funeral. He's really fucked up about Alex you know."

"That's because he was Alex's little lapdog. Now he doesn't have anyone to tell him what to do."

"Wow. Bitter much?"

"Yep."

She makes no attempt at hiding the rolling of her eyes. "Anyway… Can I come?"

"Where?"

"To see Grandad's stuff."

"It's a mess in there. Just boxes and furniture piled up."

"Yeah but… " And just like that she transforms herself into a six-year-old with an embarrassed squint, "I bet it smells like his flat. I miss his place."

"Do you remember the house before that? You'd just started school when he moved."

She nods. "The carpet in mum's bedroom looked like it was on fire."

The thought makes me grimace. Hellish sixties swirling orange carpet. Artex on the ceiling that Angie tried to paint with clouds and blue sky. It turned out like a choppy sea. Even after she found her own place the room still felt like it was hers. At Christmas, Dad would squeeze a camp bed in there for Clare, and I would end up on the sofa. Alex took over our little room when I moved out, the twin beds replaced with a double and a desk, so tight up against one another that you could barely open the door. No sign that I had ever lived there but Dad still kept Lydia's glasses on her bedside table. The tortoiseshell case had turned a soft grey with dust.

The year before Dad moved into the flat, Alex and I stayed up to watch *Die Hard 2* on Christmas Eve and he got drunk and told me how he still bought his mum a Christmas present. How he'd hide them in his room until Boxing Day, as if hoping Father Christmas might magic them away to her in the night. I asked him what he did with them afterwards. "Walk into town until I find a skip," he said. Pictures of both our mothers stared down at us from the mantelpiece. A tanned and laughing Lydia, leaning towards the camera with a glass of wine in her hand. And Heather, wishing she could be sucked into the sofa and never be seen again.

"So, can I come?" Clare asks me. "I'll help you."

She doesn't poke me this time, just nudges her shoulder against my ribs. I nod. And I'm sort of glad. I don't want to go in there alone. It might swallow me up.

#

The self-storage place is the kind of yellow that makes you want to pull your eyes out of your skull. Clare and I collect Dad's key code from the front desk and follow brightly-striped industrial floors to his compartment, just like the hospital: green for radiology, blue for paediatrics, grey for whatever floor it was they laid out Alex's dead body.

I haven't been here for a year, not since we dumped Dad's stuff off and dumped him at The Farm House. There are no windows, just echoes; forgotten things and dying people's things and divorced things and unwanted memories that threaten to kill you with guilt if you actually chuck them away. It's the perfect setting for a serial killer movie but I am armed only with a mobile phone and insomniac rage. Fifty metres down from Dad's compartment a guy packs boxes, listening to a comedy podcast on his phone. His laugh resounds around the steel walls.

Clare types in the code and mutters "bam bam baaam" dramatically as the door clicks open. She's right. It smells like him, and rubber floors, and slightly damp cardboard. Automatic lights flutter into life and illuminate Dad's sad stack of possessions. I don't know what Clare was expecting but she looks disappointed.

"I told you, just boxes," I say.

She flips open the nearest one. We're meant to be looking for photo albums, sci-fi novels and a load of sentimental shit Angela tacked onto the list that Dad won't care about. Clare pulls out a crucifix and grimaces - one of Alice's more

104

grotesquely realistic ones. I wonder what the hell it's doing in Dad's stuff.

None of the boxes are labelled, it's all junk we stuffed into cardboard coffins in the hope that we wouldn't need to look at it again. Sabine and I were the ones to clear Dad's house while Angie "settled him in", as if she were putting a toddler to bed. Alex turned up when it was all done, when the father king has been usurped by his meddling children and deposited in his living grave, lined with knitted blankets and pamphlets about coping with dementia. Alex took him out to the pub for the afternoon and Angela and the nurses spoke bright-eyed about how Dad was more like his old self afterwards. Then the prodigal son fucked off back to London and we were left to stack Dad's life into this little metal cell.

Clare comes across a box of photo albums and, just like Sabine did, quickly discovers that there are pretty much no photos of me before the age of four. Dad always said that Nana Alice kept them all, but when she died we found only a handful, sealed inside an envelope with Dad's address on it. I explain this to my niece when she asks and she frowns as if failing to quite comprehend. "Grandad didn't take any?"

"Grandad was in shock for about five years after I was born," I say. "I don't know, maybe Alice had more but we never found them." Maybe she sent them to my mum. Maybe everyone was writing to her and nobody thinks that this information is something I might want to fucking know. The box I'm searching through contains only clothes and random kitchen utensils and I shove it off the stack and kick it into the corner. A stove-top kettle falls out and lands on my foot and even though it didn't hurt, I yell and swipe it up and throw it as hard as I can into the metal wall. Clare smirks for a moment before flipping forward a few pages in the album.

"Grandma took lots though," she says, nodding at the group pictures of Angie and me and baby Alex, my father lurking in the background of some, making it obvious who was behind the camera.

"Lydia? Yeah, she did. She practically papered the dining room in photos."

Clare's eyes lift in a smile, "I remember that. I loved looking at those. Mum says I looked like Alex when I was a kid. Only with blonde hair."

I'd never really thought about it but she did. Sometimes I forget that I'm related to any of them at all. Except I'm not really, am I? Not Angie, not Clare, not Lydia, and not even Alex. Just Dad. "Yeah," I say. "Just the same."

Clare's smile drops and she tosses the photo album at my feet. I never quite know what I've done or said wrong but I know the signs. I'm supposed to say something, I think. "So… "

"What?"

"Are you going to ever talk to your mum again?"

"No."

"Right. That's realistic."

"Shut up."

"Okay."

She pulls out the rest of the photo albums, frisbeeing them carelessly at my shins. "If you want to get rid of me… "

"That's not what I meant." I try to give her a hard, meaningful stare but I don't think it works. She stops throwing things at me, at least. One box and she's already had enough. She sags against the wall and picks at a sticker that says: One man's storage is another man's treasure.

"Of course I'm going to talk to her," she says. "Just not yet. It'll never end, you know? She never stops pushing you. I just want a break before it all hits the fan."

"I know," I tell her. She nods, lets the corners of her mouth flick upwards for a second. She doesn't look nineteen in the same way Alex never looked like a child. Too little fat in the cheeks, too much of Angela's weariness. I don't want her to end up like either of them.

We keep digging in silence. I find a neat little box that Sabine must have packed – stuff from the war, from Dad's father – browned paperwork and army pocketbooks, patches from his uniform, telegrams. And underneath, a soft-focus picture from his parents' wedding day. My dad looks a little bit like both of them; taller than his father but the same hairline; a wider face than his mother but the same nose, same forehead, same tightness of a smile held too long. I throw everything into a carrier bag and open the next box, and the next, but there's nothing secret or dramatic or conspiratorial, nothing that even suggests my mother ever existed. No letters at all, from anyone. Dad was as useless as communicating on paper as he is with his vocal chords.

Clare gets bored, hungry, irritable, and needs to wee. She wanders off to find a toilet and I tell her I'll meet her at the car. There's one more box to look through. I recognise it with the kind of lurch that hits you in the guts when you're about to fall. It's the same faded box that lived at the top of Angie's wardrobe for years - a horrible, pointless, gloating box that I didn't even know existed until Alex told me about it when I was twelve. He'd had a good sift through, not really understanding what the piles of paperwork meant, but knowing that it was something that could hurt me. He showed me where it was and then went and told Dad that I was snooping. I got a fat ear and no pudding and I never saw the box again.

I open it up but I don't bother to read the reports, there are too many and they all say the same thing and nothing at all. Police reports about my mum - red tape and the procedural humouring of a sad little man and his oblivious little baby. If I had a lighter I'd turn the box into kindling - let the whole room go up, scorching the yellow walls black and reducing all this pathetic shit to soot. Paperwork doesn't matter, photos don't matter, letters don't matter. What matters is what my father knows. What he never told the police, or me, or anyone.

#

All I know about my missing mother is that after the birth

107

she needed a lot of stitches – as Nana Alice used to delight in telling me – due to my abnormally large head. And as soon as my mother could walk, albeit wincing, she was gone, leaving me in my little fish tank cot in the maternity ward. No-one thought to stop her while she dressed, packed and limped straight out of the hospital without her baby, and no-one has seen her since. A little boy with a bowling ball for a head was not, apparently, what she had ordered.

Alex took his mum's slender, athletic genes. I was given stocky solidity with a tendency for spilling over my jeans, just like my fat mother. People always imagine that she was some young, thin, beautiful, glamorous thing, and that was why she ran - looking for something better than a grumpy old fucker of a husband and a misshapen kid. People assume that if she were just fat and plain she would have stayed, would have been grateful for what she had, no matter how unhappy it made her. Or people just assume that she was mental, and, by extension, that I might end up the same way too. All I can guess is that she believed disappearing was preferable to my squashed up newborn face, and ran as fast as her thunder thighs would take her.

Alex used to joke that it was a wonder no-one could find her, after all, it couldn't be that hard to miss her. He loved telling people how she ran away, like it said something about me. He stopped after Lydia died, but by then he didn't need to. We'd both lost our mothers, but where he had pathos, I was just unwanted.

I've given three pounds a month to a missing persons charity since I was sixteen, a little fuck-you secret from my dad. I once suggested the idea to him and he looked so lividly lost for words that I blushed and tried to leave the room whispering, "Never mind."

He pulled me back by my sleeve, held me against the door frame, let his voice drop to a rustle, every word a threat. It's the only time I can remember him saying something to my face about my mother's disappearance, right in my face, bitter breath filling my nostrils: "What is the point in looking for someone who doesn't want to be found?"

For my three quid I receive a newsletter every month, pages and pages of lost faces. The problem with taking an active interest in missing people is that you see them everywhere. At the bus stop: Sylvia, thirty-four, missing since December '12. Serving me pints at The Hare and Hound: Ben, twenty-one, missing since July '07. Asking me for spare change outside Starbucks: Gemma, fourteen, missing since October '10. Ethan, twenty-nine, missing since August '04, sold me a digital camera in the January sales. Kathryn, forty-nine, missing since spring '98, gave me her condolences when I bought flowers from her for my brother's funeral.

But never Heather, sixty-five, mousey blonde hair, brown eyes, five foot two inches tall, approximately fourteen stone, missing since November '71, last seen wearing a long black skirt, purple top and blue denim jacket.

I don't bother reading them anymore. Always the same statistics. Most missing people come home within seventy-two hours, but not Mum. Most cases are solved between the police and families and charities, but not Mum's. The longer they're gone, the more likely they are to turn up dead. Or not turn up at all. Like Mum. The ever-present disclaimer; terms and conditions for hopeful relatives.

I spent a lot of time imagining the different ways she might have died. Always tragic, always in the middle of a desperate struggle to get back to her baby. It had all been a terrible mistake. I planned expeditions to find her, to rescue her from kidnappings and torturers, aliens and villains. Even in my daydreams I never got there in time. It was easier if she were dead. I knew that. I just wanted to know how. And why.

I checked under bushes on my way to school, peeked through boarded-up windows, poked at stream beds with sticks. I learned the odds of finding her body in different states of decomposition and wondered if I'd recognise her corpse from the few photos I'd seen. I crept into corners at the library with books on embalming and unexplained murders, making notes on how fast a dead body can decompose. If she'd been buried six feet underground, it would take more than two years - if she'd been embalmed properly and in a coffin, it might take decades. A shallow grave could take just six months. Decomposition of her body would occur twice as fast in the air than under water, and four times as fast as underground. Heat would speed up decay and cold would delay it. I pictured her mummified in a desert, frozen and emulsified halfway up a mountain. Intrepid Heather, one fateful last adventure, destined for tragedy.

I told Sabine all of this, not long after we first met. She seemed the type of person who would not be overly disturbed. She sighed and kissed my cheek. "If you say so, Matt."

I waved away her incredulous expression, pretended the point was moot, "I mean, no matter what happened to her, wherever she died, she'll be a skeleton by now anyway."

"That's all very well," she said. "But what if she's still alive?"

Chapter Twelve

When the police stopped looking for Heather I found someone who would continue the search, albeit with a slightly different approach. No-one knew what Gloria did. I explained her away as an old friend, a colleague of Heather's that I'd kept in touch with. Moral support in a thin disguise. People talked - moving onto the next one so soon after she was gone? But it wasn't anything romantic at first, just desperation. It was only after Alex was born that things became adulterous, but if Lydia ever suspected what I did with Gloria she was only half right. She would have laughed at the real reason for our monthly meetings at Gloria's mousehole of a flat.

I found her number in the Yellow Pages a few weeks after they finished investigating me for bodies under the patio and motives for violence, after they dropped Heather's case like a punctured ball, after the solicitor told me that I could officially mark her down as deceased and cash in on the life insurance. Gloria listened to my garbled explanation on the phone and said, "Come and see me tomorrow."

I fall into tomorrow with a click of the knees and a lightness that reminds me how skinny I became after Heather left, as if my bones might break into little pieces at the slightest knock. I stand outside Gloria's place under a black, wet sky that looks about to collapse. If I hadn't known it was there I might have walked right past it. Her flat barely fits in between a bookies and a laundrette. The building is covered with scaffolding that seemed to have always been part of the structure, though I never saw anyone working on it. Visiting Gloria feels more like coming home than returning to my own ghosted house.

She lets me in by the peeling, warped side door and nods unsmilingly when I tell her who I am, why I'm here. I expected more showmanship. She lacks a certain flamboyance that I thought was a prerequisite; she is almost disturbingly unassuming, standing there in leggings and a cardigan that reaches her knees, neatly brushed hair curling under her chin, the smell of a casserole snaking down the communal stairs behind her. She leads me up to her flat, aiming a gentle nudging kick at a slow old dog attempting to escape the front door, and tells me to wait in the living room while she turns off the cooker. This, at least, is slightly more appropriate: lamps draped with silk scarves, a hazardous amount of candles, a cloud of incense and a red light bulb that smooths the grooves in our skin and dilates our pupils to monstrous size.

I remain standing in the doorway until she pokes me with a knitting needle to move further into the room. I take a seat on the sofa beneath a four-foot fish tank that appears to be empty, but into which she sprinkles a pinch of fish flakes, reaching over my head on bare tiptoes, brushing against the side of my head with her armpit. She lays a ball of wool and her needles on the back of an armchair and settles into it, resting her head on the knitting with a guttural sigh. "Peter," she murmurs, "I don't have much for you, but you want to give me your money anyway, don't you?"

I nod with something that would probably have been a smile if I still had the ability, but this time, this place, this memory is my very own stone age when nothing grows, nothing flourishes, nothing shines - so no, there are no smiles, not even for Gloria. I dig a hand into my pocket and place a small fold of bank notes on the coffee table next to a glassy globe covered in fingerprints and a pack of death-omen cards that she never uses for me.

"She's not dead, Peter. Not yet," Gloria says, eyes lifting from the money to my face, which must look half relieved and half disappointed. "Also, your father is looking for a bus stop, and your mam is looking for a pub."

"They're definitely dead," I say, stupidly, and she humours me with a nod.

"But your wife is not."

"Can you… tell where she is, even if she is still alive?" I ask her, past being embarrassed about something as bizarre as asking a woman I've just met to seek out the aura of my missing wife.

Gloria shakes her head in a distracted way, as if she is trying to shake something out of her ear. "Your dad wants a good roast beef – honestly, that's hardly here nor there." She speaks to the curtained window now, forehead furrowed irritably. "Are you going to say anything relevant, chuck? Or you just going to moan about your stomach? Your lad's heart just got tossed in the fire."

"My mum was a bad cook," I explain.

"But a good drinker, he says."

I nod. My dad's obituary talked about his engineering service, his love of the Isle of Skye where he spent his childhood summers at his grandparents', of his young wife and younger son left behind, of a quiet bookish man who played the piano and wrote limericks for the local paper. My aunt kept the cut-out summary for me but I failed to ally it with the memory of a man who ate like a bird but always gave me any sweet thing he could find, who swore under his breath when someone near him hit a bad note singing hymns on Sundays, who planted sunflowers instead of carrots when rationing began, who would brush his wife's hair and lay her out like a fresh corpse when she passed out drunk, who used to pretend to fall asleep snoring on my chest when he said good night until I'd flounder and flap at him to wake up, semi-seriously concerned about suffocation, giggling in fear that he really had done it this time. He'd grunt and snort and sit up as if he didn't know where he was, then kiss my nose and leave me to sleep, sniggering in the dark.

"Aunt Fern used to save him the end piece of beef," I tell Gloria.

"Yes. The crusty bit. With rosemary and butter parsnips."

"That's it. She's dead too now, long ago."

"He says he'll look out for your lady if she goes his way and he'll let me know."

I give him thanks inside my head.

"He says it's not so bad. He keeps away from your mam mostly, she's still quite cross about him not checking his deaf side twice like she told him. How on earth you could miss a bleedin' fire engine I don't know. But he's glad to have met your boy."

"Matthew?" He is two. There is no Lydia yet, no Angela, no daunting pregnancy and the trappings of a new family. Just me and the boy and the ever-present guilty shadow of Alice. "You mean Matthew?"

"No. The other one. Your littlest. He's angry, doesn't want to talk, but I can see he misses you. Guilt there too."

"My other one?" A bag of nausea drops down my throat as if from a gallows, swinging heavily in my stomach. This isn't how it happened. Doubt blurs my vision of her. She got it wrong. Maybe she was bluffing all along. I look around for a doorway, an escape. This place has a danger to it, suddenly, that makes my lungs close up.

Something aches at me like a full bladder. What am I forgetting? My desperate previous self needs to believe every word Gloria says, needs to know she could find my wife, and resists my probing. But the other me, the one thrashing inside this younger body won't let us be ignorant. What other son? The uncertainty swells in my throat and I gulp down a hard ball of air. I make a conscious decision to open my eyes, even though my body thinks they are open already.

I am still in Gloria's living room, but not quite. An irritating beeping and the rumble of a television in another room join

114

the hum of the fish tank. I blink, carefully. Gloria still sits opposite, smiling sadly at me. She is warm and gentle and doesn't pity me. She lets me forget.

"I don't have any children," I say.

"Right you are."

"I don't, Gloria. I have no children."

"If that's what you say."

"You're wrong."

"No."

"I don't have any children!" I don't, do I? I am on my feet. A blup blup of bubbles escapes the fish tank behind me but I ignore the chance to glance at the elusive resident. Gloria reaches for a knitting needle and uses it to gently slide my money over to her side of the coffee table, tucking it under her left thigh. She taps the needle on her knee and looks back up at me.

"You have a big grey hole in your side," she says, gesturing in a circular motion with the knitting needle at the space to the right of my stomach. "A void. The rest of you is okay - a bit weak, yellows and greens, wavering. That can strengthen in time. But this hole. That's damage. Might not ever close up. Shrink, but not heal."

"I don't have any… "

"Yes, I heard you. No children. Well. I'll see you next month then."

I nod when I don't want to nod. I turn and leave her to the clackering of her knitting and walk into the wet night, wondering if my grey void could get so big that eventually it might engulf me.

The rain somehow isn't wet, although its incessant drumming thuds onto my head, makes it difficult to see. There is no doorway ahead of me but the world closes in like a corridor anyway, so narrow that it scrapes against my shoulders. Someone grasps my arm and my heart skitters against my ribcage. Gloria, come to gloat.

I whirl to face her. To tell her she's wrong.

"Peter… It's me."

"Stop it, Gloria."

"It's Angela."

"Angela?"

"Your daughter." She looks at me as though the words feel strange on her tongue.

"I don't have any children."

"Peter - "

"I don't have any children!"

"Okay."

"So… " I deflate with lack of contradiction. "Good."

"Okay." Gloria looks down at her hands, the same way Angela does when she's trying not to cry. She has the same hair, the same uniform, the same voice. There are no doorways, just the nursing home's long corridors and the sound of my stepdaughter's breath. What on earth is she doing here?

"Angela?"

She exhales as if she's been holding her breath. "Yes?"

"I know what it was," I tell her, conspiratorially.

"What do you mean?"

"In the tank. I know what was in the tank."

Silence.

"A lobster. A blue lobster."

"Right."

"Gloria?"

"It's Angela, Peter."

"It was a lobster."

"Okay, Peter."

#

"Where's my pudding, Skinandbones?" Ingrid yells at me as I walk past her room on my way back from breakfast.

I shrug, trying to remember what I have just eaten, until I realise that you don't have pudding with breakfast. But she's already passed that hurdle and moved on.

116

"How's your little broken wing?" she asks.

I flap my plastered arm once or twice to show her it's okay, wincing involuntarily, causing her to scowl.

"Heard you had a stroke. A baby one. Still, not good, Mr Solemn."

I snort at the thought of my strokes procreating. Little baby ones, frolicking on the squashy expanses of my brain, waiting until they're big enough to tear off a piece of grey matter.

"Does it hurt?"

"Mmm." I rather like it, if I'm honest. A constant reminder that I exist, at least from elbow to wrist, a sign that I am present in this world, feeling something, even if it's pain. I don't take the painkillers they give me. I've amassed quite a collection of tablets and capsules in the box under my bed with my abstinence. When Alma brings me medicine I know it's poison. The pain means her attempts aren't working.

"Before these gave up on me," she says, tapping her legs with a bookmark, "I used to visit the kitchen boys."

I nod, wince, unsure what I am about to hear.

"Self-medication, you understand?"

I don't follow. "With pudding?"

She laughs until she can't speak. When she recovers, her skin glows and her grin is dirty. "No, Mr Solemn. Some very nice marijuana."

A tingling flush creeps up my neck and nestles behind my ears.

"Much better pain relief than anything the nurses give you," Ingrid says. "Chris, I think his name was. Blonde, short hair, smelly little teenager. They have their fag break at about eleven out the back."

She chuckles as I back out of the room, folding my elbow out of the way of the doorframe like a good little bird.

#

On the patio outside the nursing home kitchen stands a shrivelled pergola, held up by the brittle clematis and thick

117

wisteria that have claimed it in loving strangulation. I shrug deeper inside my dressing gown and huddle behind a post, rolling a cigarette with shaky fingers and watching the kitchen doors. An anxious laugh waits in my throat.

A lad shoulders his way out of the back door. He is tall and distinctly unhandsome. Cultivated stubble barely disguises the skin of a terrible diet and probably even worse personal hygiene. He lights a cigarette – angry with it in some way, judging by his roughness – and toes at the gravel. I copy him, slippers muffling the clinking of the stone, and he looks over in surprise, so camouflaged was I against the twist of the helix. Or perhaps I've been assimilated into the pergola, withered and splintered, full of rot and burrowing worms. When I take a step forwards and he realises I'm going to speak to him, the boy lets out an aggravated sigh.

"Chris?" I ask.

He nods, confused.

I start to cough with laughter before I even get the words out and he recoils against the wall like I'm about to offer to buy his soul.

"I'm sorry," I say. I'm out of breath and have to pause. "Hang on."

"What's funny?" he grunts.

He reminds me of Alex, and I imagine my son wheezing with mirth at what I am about to say.

I try to be serious. "I want some drugs, please. Is twenty pounds enough?"

Chris smiles. He half-shrugs, a diagonal sliding of his shoulder that is an unrecognisable gesture but one that I take for affirmative. He takes my money anyway, and slaps me on my good shoulder. "What room are you in?"

"Twenty-seven. I'm Peter."

He shakes my prosthetic hand with distaste and quickly lets go again. "Nice to meet you."

#

118

On my way back inside the conservatory the uPVC doorway flares and melts all around me, plastic lagging on my dressing gown, the stench of burnt rubber drilling down my throat. Choking. Falling. Throwing my arms up to grab onto something as I am sucked through to the other side.

My hands slip on the rungs of the ladder, smearing the notched metal with syrupy blood - my brain cannot understand why my right hand is unable to grasp properly, has not yet caught up with the fact that I am down to one thumb. I make it to the top and haul myself into the roof space, eight feet safe from a dog that cannot climb ladders anyway.

The Dalmatian runs small circles on the landing, sent stupid with conflicted impulses: excitement at such unexpected action, rousing it from its nap; flat-eared fear that causes it to sporadically piss itself, sprinkling the mottled carpet with acrid urine; and carnivorous awakening, the taste of human flesh, hot blood, living bone.

I clutch my wet fist to my chest. The stump of my missing thumb twitches.

"Hank!" the client, Catherine, yells from the kitchen. The kettle pops. A teaspoon is cast down in irritation. "Hank, stop that!" The dog keens and cringes backwards into its bed next to the balustrade. My blood drips from the attic hatch and seeps a crescent shape into the carpet below.

My old soul settles into my younger body and damps down the panic. There is no pain. There won't be, not until we arrive at casualty and a nurse binds up my hand as tight as she can, when it begins to throb. Catherine comes with me, after having a mild panic attack at the top of the stairs when I explain quietly what has happened. She hits the dog, too, the poor little bastard. "Hank, you are the worst dog, the worst. How could you eat the plumber's thumb?" It would have been funny – it was funny – but I didn't think she'd tolerate me laughing so I waited in the attic until she'd shut the dog out in the garden.

It was a beautiful thing, with a happy whipping tail and clean speckled jaws that snapped off my thumb in one neat bite. I'd finished replacing the valve on the cold water tank and dropped down the last few rungs of the ladder, landing on a back paw and startling it from its nap. It yelped, turned, and its jaws clamped briefly over the hand I had outstretched in apology. For a moment it looked surprised to find something in its mouth before appetite took over and it tossed back its head and gulped the digit down.

At the hospital I sit staring at my lap where my hand lies, wrapped in gauze. Catherine's hand is on my knee, blue plastic hospital waiting room chairs beneath, reflecting our faces back at us. Pain now - a deep dull aching, splintered through with undulating sharpness. And guilt that I have not yet called Lydia to tell her what's happened. I feel like stepping out of my body to reject the playback. I am becoming more like a ghost each time I visit these memories; less able to move and unable to influence. More like I did when they happened the first time.

Doorways lead back to Catherine's, to the vet for Hank's last injection. Catherine cries and so do I. She offers to pay me double for the work. I offer to pay for a new landing carpet. We compromise on a bottle of wine and I find out that her breasts aren't real - a post-divorce present to herself, she said, after three kids and twenty wasted years. She kisses like she's drowning.

I want to skip this, speed it up, but I can't. None of the doorways lead back to the nursing home. Not yet. I yearn for my little padded cell and a regular supply of tea, for patronising nurses and the assumption that I am harmless, but the dream will not let me go.

The next doorway takes me two weeks forward into my bathroom. My bandage is loose and there is vomit on the floor. Lydia is a few minutes short of throwing herself at the door to get me to open it. She hammers it with the flats of her hands, calling me things that I know Alex can hear downstairs and will repeat back to me for weeks. I synchronise the shaking of my hands enough to unwind the rest of the dressing and reveal

120

my stinking, gangrenous hand. It smells like fermenting guts and my stomach convulses, emptying itself into the sink and over the side of the bath and onto my bare feet.

I reach behind me and unlock the door so that Lydia won't break it down.

"Jesus," she says, through a throat clenched tight to stop her own puke escaping. "I'm calling an ambulance. You fucking idiot."

I never knew the word 'stump' could have such an effect on a person's masculinity.

Lydia refuses to speak to me from the morning of my amputation to the day I return from the hospital, and even then it is only to tell me to sign on the dole as she dumps a stack of insurance papers in my lap. She kisses me distractedly. She pats rather than hugs, a tense smile struggling to cast off the suspicion that I am punishing myself for something.

Money can't buy you happiness but insurance can pay off a good chunk of your mortgage and soothe your furrowed brow, while you learn how to button a shirt one-handed.

I wasn't sad to give up plumbing, spending my hours elbow deep in other people's waste water, discovering things you wish you hadn't in their pipes. Once you've settled in and they've made you the first cup of tea, you become invisible. Something they step around and leave alone to do its business - an innocuous, impotent intruder. They forget that they have secrets to be seen.

My career was a forced apprenticeship, an arranged marriage, because my aunt said I should learn a trade, because: "Nobody needs English Literature as a qualification. You speak English well enough, don't you?"

One good thing came from it. One shining, stinking nugget at the bottom of all that shit. Deep in the sleep deprivation that comprised the first few months of Alex's life I was called out to a job by a crying, frantic woman who had water streaming through her bedroom ceiling. The man in the flat above let me in with a grumble and pointed me towards the kitchen where two inches of water covering the floor, before vaulting himself back onto the sofa. I played my inconspicuous part – get the job done, get home – and went upstairs to turn off his water. A growling rose as I reached the landing. An Alsatian squared itself up behind a stairgate fitted across a bedroom doorway. Two more dogs roamed behind it. Shit in various stages of freshness pock-marked the bare floorboards. And in between it all: a child. No more than eighteen months old, in a nappy so full it sagged to its knees. A dummy firmly fixed in its mouth. Eyes that showed no sign of fear, no sign of anything much at all.

The dog lowered its rumble as I approached, but the child moved forwards too and pushed the great hound out of its way with chubby little hands. Close up, the smell was acerbic, sweeping over me and lagging at the back of my tongue. The child raised its arms, a universal toddler demand for 'up', and I plucked it out of its cage without a moment's thought, clutching its cool skin close to my face. It didn't make a sound, but the dogs did - harsh, scraping warning barks that did their job well. I lowered the child back onto its feet inside the gate, my shivering turning into spasms of horror and rage as I left it there, taking the stairs in two leaps.

"I need something from the van," I muttered to the bastard on the sofa, stumbling back down to the flat below. The woman with the leaky bedroom listened from the next room as I called social services from her phone and she brought me another cup of tea even though I hadn't asked for one, holding it out to me as gingerly as if it were a handful of broken glass.

And the changes come ever quicker, electronic jolts that leave me breathless and aching. Did I walk here through perdition or did something push me? I stand at iron-wrought gates and watch a six-year-old Matthew come out of school, dread and guilt swelling together like yeast and sugar - a foul, bubbling bitterness that I try to ignore. When Alex started nursery I mourned his absence until it was time to jog up to collect him. Every hour Matthew spent at school was a relief.

Why didn't I miss him in the same way?

The dressings on my handless wrist are still fresh and I recognise this day, the first as a househusband, a stay at home dad, with Lydia back at work and Alex to myself.

He hangs on my remaining hand, five little fingers wrapped around one of mine, and a gush of sorrow swamps me. Fatherhood came so much more naturally with Alex. He was happy or he was screaming and there was nothing in between - simple lines that could be marked with a rule. I could never predict what would send Matthew into a silent fuming implosion. I never knew how to coax him out of it.

Matthew joins us wordlessly and we turn back down the path, the slow journey home to cartoons and milkshakes and Rich Tea biscuits - a routine to keep us safe. I ask Matthew what he did at school and he says he doesn't know. We walk at Alex's pace, jerky sprints and lagging curiosity that incites him to inspect each snail, every garden gate.

Matthew looks over his shoulder at least once a minute, a tic created by my guilty conscience; the overwhelming sense that I am merely his temporary guardian, that Heather will someday return to take over, and that I just need to keep him alive until then. The anticipation builds with every year she is missing until it leeches under his skin and leaves him glancing at the front door and out the lounge window and checking behind curtains when he thinks no-one is watching, forever expecting someone special to appear. Eventually he developed a kind of detachment that required no looking after, a lifelong disappointment that no-one was coming to save him from his father. And then he was an adult, free to leave and hate me forever.

His shoelace flaps around his ankles and I stop him with my spare hand – or what used to be my hand – thumping my stump down on his shoulder, sending a slice of tenderness through blunted nerves. He flinches and looks up at me like he's done something wrong. I kneel down to retie his laces and immediately realise that it's not going to work with only four fingers and one thumb. By the time I look up again, Alex has disappeared around the next corner and the sight nearly gives me a stroke. Or perhaps it does. The first of many unnoticed faults in my foundations. The traffic lights turn and the high street lets loose a tumult of impatient after-school traffic. My baby son is beyond my reach and a double dose of adrenaline floods my system – old and new – even though I know what will happen, even though I know we all survive this.

Matthew's shoe falls right off his foot as I run, practically carrying him along by one wrist, tongue swelling to twice its size and blocking my windpipe, heart bouncing off my ribcage so loudly I can't tell if it is beeping I hear or a child crying.

We round the corner – six feet travelled in what feels like as many hours – to find Alex standing beneath a leaky drainpipe, hands stretched above his head to catch the drips, laughing to himself. I drop Matthew's hand and snatch up my smallest son, hear the air being pushed out of him, close my eyes to the wet little palms that grip my neck in surprise. Matthew is crying, trying to keep his shoeless foot off the damp pavement but unable to keep his balance on one leg.

My shame disregards his age and makes me snap at him, pointing out the difference in importance between a shoe and his brother's life, but I don't need to. He chides himself in his own way: quiet self-loathing and a fruitless check behind him in case his mother is there. His mother, or anyone else preferable to me. Nana Alice would have spoken softly and carried him back to retrieve his shoe. Lydia would have made a joke and challenged him to hop all the way home. Heather would have loved him like I should have. I clumsily and wordlessly tuck his stupid shoelaces back into his shoe with Alex in my arms. Matthew swallows down his wet-socked discomfort and walks home snivelling through his fury.

I have to wait until we reach the house before the front doorway takes me back and I emerge in the dining room of some pansy-scented hotel full of old people. There's a lump in my throat and a pounding of blood in my missing hand.

A woman who looks just like my dentist smiles at me and I politely ask her where I am, but it only seems to make her want to cry.

Chapter Thirteen   Matthew

It's raining and the bus doesn't come. When I clock in late, my manager gives me the look of death and my brain screams against the inside of my skull, but I nod apologetically and shove my stuff in my locker.

They don't know about Alex at work. The funeral was on a Saturday and by the time I walked in on Monday morning it was all over. I don't see the point of milking false sympathy from co-workers I only ever really converse with on Facebook so I say I'm ill, hungover, going through a bad patch with Sabine.

The waiting room is half full. The ticket machine has already fed out twenty-seven tickets - little triangular-nosed pink things, like carnival tokens, except the winner's prize is a heated one-to-one discussion about housing benefit payments. Their payments aren't enough, they're too late, they're being stopped, or the claimant doesn't have the right paperwork, they don't understand the form, they need the money now, for fuck's sake, not next month. The one unifying factor is that it's all my fault. Except it's not. At least in retail the customer is always right - credit notes and refunds and discounts appease an irate public. Here, in the council's offices, the customer doesn't know how lucky they are to get any fucking thing at all.

I yank up the blind on my booth and spend a minute adjusting my chair and blinking and blowing my nose before

I can bring myself to press the button that tells customer number twenty-eight to come to booth number seven. It's a student, probably the same age as Clare, with an A4 envelope in his hands so packed full of paperwork that it has split down the side. He approaches with a smugness that suggests he thinks he's entitled to something he's not - he'd rather fill in another twelve forms than get a bar job.

He asks how long before he gets the money. I take his papers and stare at nothing in particular on them for longer than is comfortable for him. He checks his phone, pulls out headphones from his bag and wraps them round his neck. I hate him for the simple fact that some twat like this is the reason Clare turned up at my door. He rephrases his initial question to prompt me out of my glaring silence. I want to throw the envelope in his face and pepper him with paper cuts.

I tell him that we'll send him a letter once we've processed his claim. I tell him it might take a couple of weeks. I don't tell him that it might take a great deal longer than that when I happen to misplace his file. Judging by the newness of his phone, his parents won't let him starve.

For a moment he seems like he might make a point about the fact that I haven't even glanced at the documents he's given me or really once made eye contact; about how the tone of my voice is on an emotional par with the recorded announcement that brought him to my booth. I count the hangnails on my fingers until he goes away.

My phone buzzes against my leg. I shouldn't answer it, but I do.

Clare says: "I just threw up."

"You're always throwing up."

"I'm lying on the bathroom floor and I can't get up."

"Clare, I'm at work."

"I'm shivering."

"Go to bed with a bucket."

She swallows. Grunts.

"Clare?"

She's crying now, the echoey whines of someone who knows all they can do is wait until the next bout of heaving comes along.

"Clare? I'm at work. Suck on ice cubes if you can't keep water down."

She hangs up.

My eyes feel like they're covered in scales. I knuckle each eyeball until they're filled with static. I jam the student's file into a random pigeonhole below my desk but it immediately slides back out and spreads into a fan on the floor. My phone goes off again and somebody nearby tuts.

"Clare? I'm sorry. Are you okay?"

In a voice all tinny and tiny: "I'm really scared."

"Alright, I'm coming home."

"Sorry Matt."

"Shut up."

I kick the paperwork under my feet into a sort of pile and power-walk to the fire exit. I sit in the dusty stairwell and try not to hyperventilate. The fire escape leads not to safety, but to an enclosed delivery entrance that can only be escaped by dialling the correct code on a rusty old padlock that hangs on the caged retracting door. The code is written on a slip of paper pinned to the notice board two floors above in the back office. The code is wrong. I know because I've tried. If there's a fire, we will all burn with the claim forms.

I haven't got the energy to lie to HR but it's too late to say out loud that my brother is dead. A red snowstorm rages behind my eyelids, collating slowly into blackness until for a moment I can imagine I am a tiny cell inside Alex's body as it shuts down, curiously questioning the numbness, the tiny self-destructive synaptic explosions. Maybe I'm dying. I don't have the risk factor for a dramatic death like Alex's, just my father's wandering path to follow, wading fully clothed into mental breakdown.

I need to go home. I head back up to my locker but my supervisor, Sarah, pokes her head around a doorway, takes my arm and pulls me into the kitchen. "Tea?"

The inappropriate touching makes me shrug for no reason. She's at least five years younger than me but she's my superior, and I harbour entirely un-pornographic fantasies about her that are somehow even worse than just wanting to fuck her. I want to get to the point where we can sit around in our pyjamas taking the piss out of *Dancing on Ice*.

"I was just coming to find you," she says, and the harmless offer of tea drops between us like a deadweight. "Mind if we have a word? In the office?"

I follow her in and finally look at her properly. There are tingles. I'm sort of embarrassed at my own body's reaction to her face.

She swings on her chair and peels at the corner of a sticker on the filing cabinet. "Matt, there's been a complaint about you."

It's probably not a good sign that I can think of several recent instances that might be relevant. I say: "Right." Perhaps they'll fire me. Then I can ask Sarah out.

"It's not serious, but we have to follow it up. Well, you know."

"Right."

"A woman says you sighed at her."

"I sighed?"

"In an impatient way. She was crying, apparently, at the time. You said 'okaaaay' and sighed. She's written to the complaints department."

I don't remember this. Lots of them cry. They can't find the money and we threaten them with bailiffs. Of course they fucking cry. I didn't mean to sigh about it.

"I'm not sleeping very well at the moment, maybe it was a yawn."

Sarah doesn't say anything but also doesn't stop looking at me. She swivels gently on the chair - a few inches left and then right.

"Well. Yawn or sigh, she's upset."

"Sorry."

"Are you okay, Matt? You've been a walking zombie the last couple of weeks."

Her voice doesn't soften, despite her words. She has a curious, wholly indifferent hint of a smirk on her face. She expects me to try to make her laugh, take the piss out of her authority and flirt. Her total lack of concern relaxes me.

The headache presses against my temples from the inside and the brightness of daylight squeezes my face into a scowl. "No. Look, I need to go."

"You just got here."

"Yeah."

She sighs. "What's wrong with you?"

I rehearse it in my head for too long - an accidental dramatic pause. I drag the words out with a shrug and a kind of confrontational edge. "My brother died," I say. "A couple of weeks ago." I can't finalise it with an exact date, even though I know it down to the hour.

"Oh my God."

"And it was probably my fault."

"The one you hated?"

"The only one."

"Shit. Why didn't you say something?"

"It was definitely my fault."

"Matt… You should go home."

"I don't really want to."

"You'd rather work?"

"No, but there's a hole in my living room wall and my niece has gastro or something. She's puking everywhere… "

"Um. Do you want to talk about it?"

She pauses before she offers, like she doesn't mean it, doesn't actually want to claim responsibility for listening to my grief.

I shake my head, push my fists into my eye sockets. "I wouldn't know what to say."

Now she sees it – the whole package – the sunken eyes,

the atrophied smile, the swallow of tears. And she's sold, apparently, on my pathetic, confused soul. She holds my hands over the table and pulses them with little caring squeezes. "Just go home, Matt. Fuck it, go home."

#

By the time I get back to the flat, Clare is asleep in my bed, her right arm curled around a mixing bowl. I call Sabine because I feel bad about Sarah holding my hands. Her phone goes straight to voicemail. I turn on my laptop and open a new document to start writing my letter requesting compassionate leave, like Sarah told me to. I get as far as typing *the death of my brother* and have to turn it off. I try Sabine again. I know she'll see the missed calls from me and roll her eyes but I can't leave her a message and vocalise quite how desperate I am to speak to her.

She loved to tell me how much of a wuss I am. She said I have a timid face. She said that's why she first spoke to me, evidently drawn to someone she could patronise and demoralise at will. I apologise to people who bump into me in the street, I check my invisible watch when someone asks me the time. I thank ATMs.

She has this ability to be honest to the point of rudeness, without seeming offensive at all. She has one of those faces that looks as though it should constantly be backlit against sharp, angular, film-noir set design. I miss her because of and despite the fact that we were totally unsuited as a couple.

I check my answerphone messages to make sure she wasn't calling me back while I was trying to call her the second time. I have two saved messages and one new message, from ten-forty-seven a.m. today, while I was sitting in the kitchen at work with Sarah.

It's Jamie: "Matty. Are you there? I need to talk to you."

I haven't seen him since the funeral where he stood blank-eyed and pale, barely-contained fury rising to the surface

131

of his skin whenever he looked at me. I get it. He and Alex operated with almost supernatural synchronisation when they were kids, allied in the glee they found in treating me like shit. And he blames me.

Dad and Lydia looked on him with a mix of affection and suspicion. I think they secretly hoped that he was some kind of corrupt influence on Alex they could lay blame on. Of course it could never be the case that Alex's antisocial unpleasantness was his own doing. When they were kids they called it the cheekiness of boys. When they were teenagers they called it rebellion. When they were young adults they were simply no longer within parental control.

"Look after your brother," were my daily orders when we left for school, but no-one, apparently, was meant to look after me.

Before I hang up, the saved messages start to play, and even though I know I have plenty of time to avoid the misery that is about to occur, I do nothing to stop it. The first one is from Angie, a few days ago, asking how Clare is and telling her that she has some post to pick up from home. She hopes we're both okay. Beep. I should hang up now. A muscle in my wrist twitches. But still I listen, standing up to the approaching pain with all the likelihood of jumping over a tsunami.

Second saved message: "Alright dick-brain? Are you going to see Dad on Sunday? I need a lift. And I downloaded something for you, I'll give it to you then. Ring me back."

Alex. Immortalised by BT, before he got the letter from his mum, before he drained two bottles of cheap wine and came knocking on my door. Before I killed him. I should be crying but I'm dry. My headache has mutated into throbbing and my jaw will not unclench. I can't feel my fingers around the phone.

I found the birthday gift he'd meant to give me at his flat – a DVD of a new zombie film – still the only real connection we had. That, and the silent agreement to keep our mutual disinterest in football a secret from Dad, who used to demand full, religious concentration whenever Fulham played.

When I was twelve and Alex was eight, Dad took us to a home game. It was the last time he ever held my hand, keeping hold of us among the inescapable mass, the huge symbiotic entity of the crowd, rising and undulating and swearing all together. Indecipherable noise made up of the echo of thousands of voices, all a little late, out of sync, all chanting something that I never quite heard properly but it didn't matter - I could sense the threat in it, the low murderous edge, the bite, the brick. A mob of testosterone. Alex fitted right in. I cowered in my cold plastic seat, clutching a gristly burger, trying to distract myself by counting the pieces of chewing gum on the seat in front of me. Someone had written 'Steve is a penus' on the seat-back – with accompanying illustration – then realised their mistake, crossed out the word 'penus' and replaced it with 'cock'.

I confided in Lydia that I desperately didn't want to go to the next game. And in typical, wonderful Lydia fashion, she had no qualms about lying to my dad, told him I'd been invited to a friend's birthday party that day. Dad took Alex and Jamie instead and never asked me to come along again. Even though Dad couldn't stand the kid, Jamie was a better son than I was.

Why the fuck is he calling me now? Whatever association we had should have died with Alex. What could he possibly want?

I press the phone against my ear until it hurts, the automated voice repeatedly asking me to make a fucking choice or return to the main menu. I hang up and call Sabine again.

"Hi," comes a sigh, rather than a greeting.

I hadn't actually expected her to pick up. Shit. "Hi."

"I'm not going to ask if you're okay. You're not okay. Why are you calling me?"

"I miss you."

"I know you do. I'm working." A long pause, in which

I suspect she is calculating how much straight-talking I can cope with. She acquiesces, uncharacteristically, says softly: "I'll call you later."

"Thank you."

"Okay." She hangs up the way people do in films, without saying goodbye.

I look in the fridge for some lunch, but there is only leftover funeral food.

#

I catch up with Clare that same afternoon, joining her in an alternating puke-fest that has us up for most of the night. It must have been something from the funeral spread - prawns on little blini pancake things probably. We shouldn't have kept the food this long. Frozen, defrosted, hoarded in the fridge, as if it represented the last vestiges of my brother, the body of the fucking antichrist.

When the intervals between toilet visits stretch further and further apart and finally slow to dry heaves, we convene on the sofa, grumbling and watching early morning TV to try to distract from the pain of our stretched, outraged stomachs.

"At least you're used to throwing up," I say.

Clare can't even muster the energy to swear at me, or hit me. It's a nice change.

We doze for an hour or two. She goes off to sit in the bath. Behind closed eyes I listen to a TV medium channel messages from some woman's dead daughter who wants her to move house and make a fresh start, maybe somewhere abroad. The mother says she likes warm weather. And the sea. The daughter was such a good girl, she says. She died of complications following a routine operation. The mother cries. The audience applauds. Someone knocks viciously on my door and the hole in the wall opens like a dark gaping mouth and my stupid brain immediately assumes Alex is back to claim his revenge and my shoulders start shuddering.

I'm hearing things. I'm going mad. Early-onset dementia. A tumour. Schizophrenia. A psychotic episode. A brain aneurysm. I turn up the TV but the knocking gets louder. Has he come to smash my head through the wall? I'm going fucking insane.

A muffled shout comes through the door. "Matty?" It really is him. I'm going to puke again. I lurch off the sofa and lean my forehead against the closed bathroom door. "Clare, let me in, I'm gonna throw up."

"Who's at the door?"

Fuck, it's real then. She can hear it too.

"No-one. Let me in!"

"I'm naked!"

"Clare!"

"Matty!" yells the ghost. Except it's not a ghost. I know that voice. I fall into a crouch and clutch at my guts.

"Matt, get the door," Clare orders, and all at once she's her mother and I have to do as she says.

Jamie looks worse than I do, if that's possible. He has rubbed his eyes red and purple, the bags beneath them are swollen, the skin of his eyelids peels at the edges. His lips are cracked and pale against stubble at least a week old. Doesn't smell like he's washed much in that time either. At odds with the rest of him, his hair has been meticulously waxed into its usual style and he is dressed in a suit, as though stuck in his funereal mourning attire.

"Hi," he says quietly.

"I'm ill," I reply, lamely. "We've both been up all night being sick."

"Oh. Is Clare okay?"

Don't mind me. "Yeah, I think so."

"Oh. Can I - Can I come in?"

"Why?" I didn't mean to say that. He falters. I open the door wider and wave him forward. "Yeah, yeah, come in. Sorry about the smell."

He makes a disgusted face but steps across the threshold.

I have invited the vampire inside my home. He considers the sofa – covered with possibly infected and dribbled upon duvets and pillows, screwed up tissues, and an ice cube tray – but decides against it and leans on the kitchen counter instead.

His eyes fix on the hole in the wall. Mine still sweep by it whenever I look in that direction in a pathetic act of self-preservation. I hear him swallowing down thick spit as he forces his gaze away.

"He just fell over," he says. "He didn't even put his hands out to break the fall. Just keeled over. Like he was dead before he even hit the ground."

I heard the technical story from the doctor but the most I had exchanged with Jamie since the accident was a nod at the crematorium.

"He wasn't though. Dead, I mean," he says, "I checked his pulse. He was still alive but he wasn't there at all. You know? In his eyes."

Shit, he wants to talk about it. All I can do is measure the distance between where I stand and the sink in case I need to throw up again.

"He wouldn't let go of the letter," Jamie says, glaring at me in an awful, wounded way. My stomach flips. We hear the gurgle of the plughole and Clare brushing her teeth.

"I need your help," he says, jaw clenched tight, because clearly I am the last person he would ever choose to help him.

"What?"

"Alex wanted to find his dad. Meet him. His mum had put his name and stuff in the letter. He owns a load of restaurants."

Clare appears in the bathroom doorway wearing my dressing gown and two pairs of socks. She stares at Jamie more vehemently than she's ever looked at me and it's a comfort to know her hate is indiscriminate. She walks tentatively into the kitchen and hangs on my arm. Jamie drops his chin like a reprimanded dog.

"So?" I say. "You want to track him down? Why do you need me?"

Jamie looks like he wants me to collapse on the spot like Alex did. "I don't know, I thought you might want to make amends."

"For what?" I ask slowly.

Jamie shifts his weight away from the counter in a subtly menacing movement. "What do you think? He'd still be alive if it wasn't for his selfish fucking brother," he says quietly, emphasising the last three words as though he were stamping on my face.

Clare, to my deepest horror, doesn't leap to defend me. She stays silent for a telling second before speaking in an unconvincing monotone: "Alex was the one who tried to hit him. It was an accident."

"Well. If I were you I'd feel guilty," Jamie says. "I'd want to do something. His real dad should know he existed."

His passive-aggressive calmness makes me itch. "What the hell would I say? 'Hi, you had a son, but now he's dead. Oh and his mum's dead too. Just thought you should know. See ya!' What is the fucking point?"

Jamie points at the hole in the living room wall but I can't look at it. "Because it was the last wish of your dead brother."

Clare nods slowly beside me. Frustrated anger shoves the nausea aside. I follow Jamie's eyes to my keys lying on the counter. And then it's clear.

"And I'm the only one with a car," I say.

He shrugs. That's settled then. Perfect.

Chapter Fourteen

When the kitchen boy comes by my room I mistake him for Alex at first - he has little grey eyes and a hairline further back than his age should suggest. A flash of my boy for a moment, before my smile weakens and he tosses a small green cling film-wrapped rectangle onto my bed. He nods, closes the door, and leaves me feeling like I've been knifed in the chest. I hold the package in my lap for an hour until the warmth sends a sweet incriminating scent into the air and either I fall asleep or I lose an hour or two on standby, because I wake to my dentist cupping my face with a cold hand asking, "Where did you get this, Peter?" and telling me to hide the weed, pressing it into my palm and closing my fingers around it.

Another leap through time. Her hand is replaced by the frozen slap of a pre-rain wind that stings my cheeks. I am on a bench, oddly positioned halfway up a small bank that leads to a cow field, facing the uninspiring view of the nursing home's conservatory. I find the cellophane package in my pocket but I don't know how much of the stuff to put into my cigarette so I opt for half green, half tobacco. My hands shake as I try to get a decent handle on my lighter. It feels too late to be engaging in a rebellion but as the first draw enters my lungs I can't help but grin through the conservatory window at the loathsome vegetables fused to their armchairs.

I smelt it on Alex and Jamie's clothes when they were teens.

I saw it in their reddened eyeballs and dry lips. I watched them eat a loaf's worth of toast and stretch themselves out on the sofa, playing Uno as though it were the funniest game in the world. I didn't tell Lydia, didn't want to give her the satisfaction that her kid was as wayward as she secretly hoped he'd be. I cornered Matthew instead, assuming or perhaps just deciding that he was responsible. He rebounded my lecture back at me with silent hatred.

I sink lower on the bench, imagining that it is considerably more comfortable than it really is, and watch Paul, my room-neighbour, as he takes a slow, limping stroll round the garden. I smile fixedly at him, knowing that nothing I do will prevent him coming over to talk to me. The other residents have been drawn to me like iron filing slivers to a magnet since the last stroke, since my vocabulary shrank to a variation of grunts and open vowels, occasionally interspersed with short bursts of lucidity. My silence gives them free reign to wax on without interruption, safe in the knowledge I have little inclination to escape their presence and small chance of organising my tongue to interject. Paul creaks his way down next to me and lets out the practised elderly sigh of exhaustion.

"Beautiful day," he says.

The sky to the east is full of billowing black clouds, the air sharp and cold, the grass churned up into a no man's land of mud, cigarette ends and the occasional piece of cat shit.

"Mmmm," I agree.

He sniffs, eyes me sideways. I take another drag.

"Visitors for me, today," he says.

"Hum?"

"Your boy coming later?"

I shrug. I have little concept of what day it is any more. I wouldn't blame Matthew if he took advantage of that fact and never came again.

"Lovely to have your daughter working here, though," he says.

She's not really my daughter, is my unspoken, automatic

139

response. Just as well I can no longer speak these stupid thoughts - I am less hurtful without my voice. I lie with a nod. It's not lovely at all. It's intolerable having a constant witness to my deterioration.

"She's a sweet girl," he says. "So attentive."

I vaguely recall shouting at her – something about seafood – and the way her eyes, which are just the wrong colour to be her mother's eyes, looked back at me as if she were screaming: "I'm *this* close to giving up on you," and then, worse: "But I won't."

My vision begins to pick up colours that previously hadn't appeared to be there. My body swells inside itself and I silently bless Ingrid and the kitchen boy, sinking into the sensation of my shoulders lowering in relaxation despite the wind and the hard back of the bench and the idiot keeping me company. This is what the Tai Chi fella should have given us.

"Not like my Sharon," Paul mutters.

"Hmm?"

"She won't stop moaning about her Franklin. Honestly, if she's going to worry about every little thing, is it any wonder he's such a needy creature?"

I close my eyes and bask in the angry warmth of Paul's shift into phase two of the long march to death: exasperation and disgust and mass disapproval of, well, everything.

Paul expostulates his vast and judgemental opinions about his whining daughter, his saintly son-in-law, their brattish child who he believes has been spoilt beyond all belief through their 'modern parenting', how things were so very different when his daughter was a baby, how Paul wouldn't have put up with half of what she does.

I nod, blow smoke rings, and call him a bastard inside my head. I might have ended up with the same pathetic point of view had Heather been around to raise Matthew, had I not lost my hand and ended up as a househusband while Lydia kept us afloat. I was the teacher, the comforter, the packed lunch maker, the organiser, cleaner, cook, wiper of arses and noses

140

and taxi to appointments and clubs and children's parties. I had to make the multitude of little decisions over how much to praise and how much to refuse and whose fault it was and who deserved what.

I would discuss Alex's potty training with the mums in the playground and they'd lean in and sigh at the tragedy of what they'd heard through the toddler group gossip - such a selfless and contemporary father, utterly devoted to his sons. Didn't they wish their husbands were more like me? Didn't they flirt and flatter and press themselves against me when they laughed? Ruffling the boys' hair as if to ask, "Wouldn't you like me to be your new mother?"

I don't know if I imagined this at the time or am making it up now. It doesn't really matter. Paul eventually tails off his tirade and checks his watch, "Lunch in a bit. I wonder if it's too late to call and tell them not to come today."

I flick my fag end into the bushes behind me and stand in a slow, wonderfully unbalanced way. My voice looses itself from my throat, spontaneously, with a lump of phlegm that I spit between my slippers. I ought to smoke this stuff more often. I turn and press down on his knees with a hand and a stump so my face is too close to his for him to look at me comfortably. "Let them come," I tell him. "Be honest. Tell them what you really think. What can they do?"

A twitching grin rips Paul's face in two and he nods decisively. "I think I will. What can they do?"

I choke down a laugh and meander back to the conservatory, leaving him on the bench to hatch an ungrateful, callous old plan. And maybe I should make one too - tell them all to stop pretending they're not thinking about how my madness is affecting and disturbing and inconveniencing them and ask them how the hell they think I feel about it.

#

I have been staring into space for hours, just breathing.

141

Thinking about not breathing. I think I might have swallowed glass. There must be a very small person sitting on my cheekbones, pushing a sharp stick through the backs of my eyeballs.

I have been deposited in a line-up of comfortable chairs in the common room with the other cast-offs; an army of plastic soldiers made from a Quasimodo mould, stiff and frozen in a variety of unnatural positions. Backs are thrown up into humps by the tectonic plates of our twisted spines; arms wither to bone, loosely-wrapped in flaccid balloon-skin; faces grimace into pain, even when we're smiling.

These are my peers, my contemporaries, and I hate them. We've lived too long, seen too many people die. There are a few here left with souls still intact, hideously jovial creatures who cajole and jolly the rest of us about. They like to check on whether we've had the latest round of tea, they pat our shoulders and call us 'ducks' and try to maintain their parenting instinct, cling to it to keep themselves real and useful and needed.

The rest of us are 'confused', unable to care for ourselves. We make dangerous decisions concerning the use of hobs and seasonal clothing. We speak our minds, except our minds are no longer our own. We sink into the quagmire of things that should already be dead while the young ones watch and pity and forget who we were.

A man in a suit jacket and tracksuit trousers sits across from me, head resting to one side against the wall, hands flickering in his lap. His fingers are so thin that if it weren't for his swollen, arthritic knuckles, the wedding band on his left hand would have flown off long ago. It slides up and down with the undulation of his digits as they tap rhythmically on his thighs. I don't know his name, but I know he used to make a living busking with his saxophone in the town centre. He lived in a caravan by the marina, paid no tax, no rent, made enough money each day to buy himself his daily bread.

After twenty years of living and playing day in and out, he

falls asleep on his pitch - too cold, too slow to make it back to his caravan. He loses most of his toes to frostbite. They section him and find out he has a physiotherapist daughter who happily fronts his weekly rent for The Farm House. He breathes through pursed lips and I can hear a melody there, smell the rot inside him.

A woman called Frances used to sit where I am now, always the green corduroy chair with the silk tassels on the armrest. She made four attempts at escape before I arrived here. She succeeded, twice, but was brought back by staff or police, meek and quiet and thoroughly apologetic - didn't know what had got into her, she said. She was dying before she got here - crippling headaches and a marching band inside her brain playing incessantly, just for her. A holy band of angels guiding her to heaven, she said. She'd been destined for incredible heights but had sacrificed it all for her sickly brother, who died and left her to raise his children. God wanted to reward her, and the marching band told her – or maybe she'd read it somewhere – that if she died in a royal place she'd be eligible for a state funeral; they'd pull out all the stops and the nation would wail for her, just like they did for Diana-lord-let-her-sleep-in-peace. So she took to loitering around the Palace of Westminster, sitting in a lobby chair listening to her auditory hallucinations play *The Saints Go Marching In* on an endless loop, waiting for the day she'd fall asleep forever and watch her good old send off from above. But it was not to be. She was escorted from the premises so many times that eventually social services investigated and found a nice lump sum sitting in her savings account that brought her here instead, where she died three weeks later, sitting in this same armchair watching *Loose Women*.

I gather my bones together and haul myself out of the chair, take a round trip through the circular corridor that leads around the whole ground floor - a never-ending journey for a happy little goldfish. I come to a natural halt at the foyer where an uncomfortable sofa, bookended by dusty plants, faces the receptionist's desk. The Gatekeeper, Ingrid calls her. She frowns at me. I lower myself onto the seat opposite and stare blankly until she looks back down at her paperwork.

Her two bloodhounds languish under the desk at her feet - two more elderly gentlemen, bored out of their tiny brains, here until they die. Their eyelids droop low and their drool stretches to the floor. They smell atrocious but I have an overwhelming urge to join them on the carpet, to rest my head on their flanks, rising and falling so gently. To drape their ears over my hands and see life from a dog's-eye-view.

The receptionist scowls. "It's nearly lunch time, why don't you head down to the dining room?" she barks, too loudly, jarring against my cushioned brain. It's not a bad idea. I am, I realise suddenly, incredibly hungry. I hoist myself to standing and blunder over to her, dropping into an uncomfortable crouch before the dogs.

One raises his dry nose to sniff my outstretched fingers, my nub of a wrist. I wonder if he can sense that one of his brothers was to blame for my maiming. He gives it a lazy lick.

"Good boy."

I rub the spot behind his ears that makes his back legs twitch. I'm almost sure he smiles.

#

I am seventy-four-years-old and I am lying on the carpet behind the reception desk and laughing while the nurses discuss the best way to lift me.

I am thirty-nine and it is a very good year.

I am hugging a dog and I want to cry.

I am flickering like a badly-tuned television set and I need someone to smack me around the ears until I'm sensible again.

I am being lifted by a male care worker and I nuzzle into his chest as he carries me like a baby down a corridor that never ends.

Here's a doorway. I wonder if I will become weightless as

144

we pass through, as my body temporarily loses its soul.

I am standing in a hospital waiting room listening to my wife cry.

When I was thirty-nine, it was a very good year. Heather threw up in a supermarket queue and kept on throwing up every day for a week. She went to the doctor and came back pregnant. Just like that. After ten years of being told that we couldn't have children, and "no, we don't know why" and "no, we can't help you" it had happened out of sheer indifference. Infertility treatments in the sixties weren't like they are now - popping out babies like microwave popcorn, made with a syringe and a Petri dish. The scan produced a little grey ink blot that you squinted at until you pretended to see a limb, or a head, exclaiming, "Amazing!" Nowadays you can find out whose nose your kid will inherit in bizarre orange 3D images, lasered onto little glass paperweights for the grandparents.

The doctors weren't able to tell which one of us was broken, so naturally we blamed ourselves, and secretly, each other. I got angry, she got fat, and we spent ten more years making ourselves enjoy a life without a child. Then Heather came home pale but flushed, shaking and smelling of sick. And pregnant. Alice forced champagne on her nauseous daughter and told her she was eating for two now, even though she had been doing that for several years.

I spent nine terrifying months not mentioning the fact that I expected her to lose it at any moment. I could see she felt the same way, always one hand on her belly. I celebrated my fortieth birthday with an ill and ironic feeling of not being old enough or responsible enough to become a father.

She went into labour at five past six in the morning on the twenty-third of November. I don't know what she went through and I don't want to know and I won't ever know. But I am standing in the hospital waiting room, the same room I have been in – on and off for eighteen hours – listening to her moan and plead and whimper and scream.

The doorways are not an escape; they are torture. A hell

before I get to hell. And I realise now: the doorways were sent by Heather.

I wait there for my eighteen hours and when I am handed my son – a little purple sack of bones with a distended face like a bulldog – Heather lies among bloody sheets, staring at her swollen ankles, and will not meet my eyes.

Chapter Fifteen

I've been driving for an hour so far and Jamie and I have exchanged three words. I found a hard lump behind my ear this morning and I can't stop rubbing it. Maybe it's cancer. Fair enough.

I slept through my alarm this morning, unable to wake to turn it off, tormented in a nightmare of buzzing and bleeping that merged into a crowd of questioning faces all talking at once. Clare grunted and huffed her way through my room – blinded by sleep, kicking aside DVD cases, discarded underwear and crusty crockery – and stabbed the off button as aggressively as possible "Are you fucking deaf? Jamie's going to be here in an hour."

A tight whine forced itself out of my throat. Even with my eyes shut I could hear Clare's eyes roll in disgust. "I'll put the kettle on," she said.

A little envelope flashed at the top of the screen of my phone. A text from Sarah:

HI. HOPE YOU'RE OK. BEEN WORRIED ABOUT YOU. THINK YOU SHOULD TALK ABOUT IT. I CAN COME OVER IF YOU WANT.

Sympathy. I'm not used to that. The very idea of it immediately released a gut-punch of guilt at the thought of feeling anything other than guilt over killing my brother. And horror at the thought of the amount of cleaning I'd need to do for Sarah to step foot in the flat.

A crumpled letter sat next to my phone, as abhorrent as a chainsaw in an orphanage. It contained a list of scribbled details that Jamie had copied down from Lydia's letter, an abridged version that omits all the *my gorgeous boy, please don't be sad, I just wanted you to know that I'm so sorry* filler stuff and focuses on the hard, depressing facts. She was about six weeks pregnant when she met my dad. She'd left Alex's real father – a man named Lee Burnett – a few months before. He was *a good person*. They'd separated amicably. He didn't know about the baby. It just wasn't meant to be, Peter was the one who should have been Alex's father, and she hoped he could still think of him that way, blah, blah, blah, until I start to doubt that it was even written by Lydia. She called things what they were and kept quiet if she couldn't explain it. Lydia was full of clear-cut vinegar; this was positively saccharine.

I sent a hurried reply to Sarah in what I hoped was a nonchalantly stoic tone (THINGS PRETTY SHIT BUT I'M OK) and played down the possibility of a pity date (GOT A FEW THINGS TO DO BUT LET ME KNOW WHEN YOU'RE FREE AND WE'LL WORK SOMETHING OUT).

Jamie didn't bother coming up to knock but let my phone ring twice before hanging up to ensure as little contact as possible. Fine with me. Clare had been relaying messages to him whenever I found something else out about Lee. She'd nod, scowl, then type a text off with furious fingertips. I didn't ask how she knew Jamie's number.

The details on the letter were fairly useless – a phone long ago disconnected – so I spent the week tracking down Lee's employment history. He'd started out in Croydon running a family-friendly American-style restaurant and knocking up Lydia. The month after Alex was born he'd relocated to run a petrol station restaurant in Aberdeen, about as far away as he could get. Then a pizzeria in Stoke-on-Trent, a café-bar called The Starling in Worcester and finally to Bath, where I was told, "Yeah, but he's not in today," when I rang the place he was said to be working, half-cut on boxed wine and not really caring any more whether I got through to anyone.

I swore, apologised, waved frantically at Clare. "Do you know when he'll be in next?" I asked the sighing woman on the phone.

"Tomorrow. Do you want me to tell him you called?"

"No. No. Thanks."

Francis Lane: a contemporary wine bar serving locally sourced, seasonal, organic Tapas. Well done, Lee. Self-important wankiness runs in the blood, clearly.

So: to Bath. And I have no underwear on. After a reply from Sarah to say she could come round after work, I threw all the clothes from my bedroom floor into the washing machine, realising only after I'd put the cycle on that every pair of pants I own were in there. We drive through blue skies into looming grumpy-eyebrowed clouds and the rain appears like a drawn curtain as we hit the motorway.

We'll be there by midday for a friendly chat with the oblivious father of my dead brother and I could be home in time to make dinner for Sarah.

We pass another ten minutes in the comparative silence of the radio until Jamie taps the dash and says, "Alex was so pissed off you got the car."

I shrug. I knew this. When Dad went into the home he didn't need it any more. Angela already had a car, I was next in line, Alex didn't need one in London. I try to shrug it off. "First son and all that. It's a piece of shit anyway."

"You could have put him on the insurance."

So, this is going to be a list of all the things I did to piss off my brother. Okay. If that's my atonement, so be it. But I don't have to agree with him.

"He never asked."

"He loved this car. He learned to drive in it."

"So did I." Oh such joyful memories: Dad thumping his stumped wrist against the gear stick yelling, "Change! Change! Come on, Matthew! Into fourth!"

"Yeah, well. If he'd been able to drive it… If you'd given him a lift that night… "

I turn to glare at him, wrenching the wheel accidentally as I do so, almost veering into the side of a lorry. Jamie shrinks back into his seat, knees pushing against the dashboard. I take a breath. "If I'd given him a lift, he would have charged into a nursing home, wasted, and shouted at my dad. What a lot he would have achieved."

"He'd be alive."

"Would he? Maybe he would have died on the way, or while he was ruining my dad's life, and mine. I thought they said it was inevitable, it was just one of those things."

"Wow. 'Just one of those things'?"

He's smiling. He's enjoying this too much, even though I know it's hurting him to talk about it.

"I can't do this," I say, wondering if honesty works on people made of bile. "I can't drive for two hours with you telling me how it's all my fault. Don't you think I feel guilty enough?"

"Slow down."

We approach a flashing fifty miles per hour sign and an endless stretch of roadworks. I coast to the end of the jam and turn up the radio volume. As we leave one county's radio behind, the static masks most of what the presenter is saying - a quiz on nineties music.

"Cotton-Eyed Joe," Jamie says.

The radio confirms it. I turn up the heater to drown out the music.

I silently rehearse what I'm going to say to Lee like a wedding speech. There's really no easy way to break two deaths to someone in quick succession. Maybe if I say it really fast. Maybe Jamie will help me out. Maybe he loved Alex enough to see this through with me.

The traffic moves several inches forward. We crawl, nose to bumper, for six miles. No sign of a crash, but suddenly we are free, creeping back up to sixty-five as if nothing had happened. I push the scrappy little car up to seventy and it starts shaking - bolts rattle in their housings.

Jamie unbuckles his seatbelt so he can take his jacket off. I visualise braking so suddenly that he flies through the windscreen and ends up stuck through the back window of the camper van in front, legs flailing wildly as the van fishtails across three lanes into the central reservation. Then bursts into flame. One can but dream. "Why are you always in such a foul mood?" Jamie asks me, suddenly, with a grin.

"Maybe it's just when I'm around you."

"Ha. You're funny, Matty."

"Maybe it's because you and Alex spent most of your spare time winding me up and driving me insane."

"You think that's all we did? Don't flatter yourself."

"He's even doing it from the grave," I mutter.

"You. Are. Priceless."

He gives me the same look that has made me cringe with anticipation for nearly thirty years. If we were eight he would have given me a dead leg that bruised brown and purple. If we were twelve he would have spat gum into my hair and pressed it in hard. If we were sixteen he would have flicked a cigarette butt down the back of my shirt. I'm too old for any of this, to be bullied.

"Why are you here?" I ask him. "If you're so convinced that telling Alex's dad the truth is my responsibility, then why do you need to come along, too?"

"To make sure you don't wimp out like usual."

"Right. It's a kind of male posturing thing then."

"Just drive, idiot."

Ninety-four miles to go.

#

I put the coins in the ticket machine slowly and with deliberate irritation while Jamie remains silent on the subject of helping towards the cost of parking. As we walk, I study the Google map I cunningly printed out last night and Jamie stops to buy a packet of Minstrels from a newsagent and doesn't offer me a single one.

The rain has not reached Bath and my blood warms me beneath my open coat. It is twelve-oh-three by my watch, and then twelve-oh-four a few seconds later when I check again. Unsurprisingly, time continues to pass, despite my anxiety at getting back in time to meet Sarah, and I send Clare a text to say please hang my washing on the radiators and maybe wash up those pans that have been in the sink for the three days following her much appreciated spaghetti puttanesca, *please?*

When the bar sign comes into view my blood pressure surges and the clear winter sun becomes a sweltering ball of flame. Jamie is mucking about with his iPhone and carries on walking a shop or two past Francis Lane before he realises that I am stuck to the pavement, as if my feet are made of wax and have melted in all this heat. He stops in front of me and takes the map from my hands, "This it?"

I nod. "What am I supposed to say to him?"

He shrugs, "Not my problem."

If he wasn't such a cunt I'd ask him for a hug. He's already gone, pushed through the double doors into the warm black and red themed wine bar. Buena Vista Social Club plays over the PA. The smell of grilled Mediterranean vegetables and balsamic vinegar makes my stomach clench. There's a waitress behind the bar, also playing with an iPhone.

Jamie stalks the place like a forensic specialist hunting for a fragment of skull bone. "Maybe we should have a drink, first," I mutter in his ear, and take a seat at the bar. The waitress raises eyebrows and makes eye contact for a few seconds before returning to her phone, "Yep?"

"A Becks, please."

Jamie does not sit down, but he still orders a beer and makes no move to remove his wallet from his pocket when she gives us the total to pay. I pay. Of course I do. The waitress takes my money, dumps it in the till and goes to the far end of the bar – as far away as she can get from us – and leans there, alternately flicking pages of a newspaper and tapping the screen of her phone.

"So… " Jamie smiles at me. There's nothing in that smile that should be in a normal smile. His breath stinks of burnt Rizla and ash the same as my dad's always does.

"Just give me a minute."

We sit and listen to the Cubans and their guitars. The waitress picks up a phone call and through the empty bar we can hear every word, "I mean, she's skinny, but she's healthy, she just exercises a lot… Yeah, well, I feel sorry for her and everything, but she *is* a total bitch."

Eventually she rings off. Jamie stares at me for a full song. I take a too-large swig of my beer in an attempt at a manful gesture then try not to choke as some of it slips down my windpipe.

"Excuse me?" I watch the waitress, who can't have failed to hear me, but is still leaning, flicking, phone call finished, tap-tapping again. "Excuse me?"

Jamie sighs, finishes his beer and places it in an unmistakeably final manner on the bar. She looks up, "You guys alright?"

"Excuse me," I say, pointlessly, a third time. "Does Lee work here? Lee Burnett?"

"He's the manager. He's in the office." She points up through the ceiling.

"Can I, we, speak to him?"

She nods, after an uneasy pause, and dials a landline phone that sits by the till. Maybe she thinks we're health and safety inspectors, or mystery diners, or undercover police. She speaks quietly and replaces the handset. "He's coming down now."

"Okay, thanks."

Jamie spins his bottle on its bottom rim, lacking any skill whatsoever, and it clanks onto its side on the bar-top several times, making both the waitress and me wince.

We wait. Two more songs and the CD finishes. The silence

is worse. My brain unhelpfully suggests and rejects a number of different ways in which I can break the news to Lee. Then it starts an imaginary conversation with Sarah in which I'm explaining where I've been today, tweaking things a little to make it sound like it was all my idea, to alleviate some guilt over Alex's death, and how it seemed like the 'right thing to do'. I'm such a twat.

A door marked STAFF ONLY swings outwards and a man steps through into the bar. He has a shaved head, receding hairline clear against the stubble; two small hooped silver earrings in one ear; black-rimmed glasses; plain, unadorned black and grey clothing. He too has an expensive phone cradled in one hand, while he balances a tray with an empty mug and a teapot on the other. The waitress takes the tray from him and nods her head towards us. He takes the bar stool two down from me and smiles, twirling his phone between his fingers and looking a lot like Alex might have looked in thirty years. I'm staring, he's waiting, Jamie is grinning. Shit, it's true, painfully obvious. It's the eyes: dark lower eyelashes, irises rimmed with a thick black line and unnaturally pale grey within. Same lips, same small, neat, square teeth in the same mouth.

"Can I help you?" Alex's older-mouth says.

Jamie elbows me in the gut. "Go on then, Matty."

"Lee Burnett?" I manage.

"Uh huh."

"Lydia Evans." I seem to be speaking in names.

He pauses. Doubt and a heart-flutter pass over his face. "Lydia? I knew her - but thirty-odd years ago."

"She's dead," I say. Well, at least it wasn't another name.

He lets slip a tiny flinch, blows out his cheeks. "Oh. How did it happen?"

"Cancer. She, uh, left her son a letter."

He calculates our ages silently and swallows, waving his hands at us, setting off the music player on his phone, blasting out a Fleetwood Mac chorus. He switches it off, flushing from his ears to the bridge of his nose.

"Hang on, hang on. What are you saying here?"

"Neither of us is your kid," Jamie says tonelessly.

Lee sighs and deflates, making himself half a foot shorter. "Oh. Good."

"But she did say you were the father of her son, Alex." I feel like I'm giving the closing statements to a detective show.

Lee's eyes close and he leans back stiffly, hands tight around the leather-topped seat. He springs off the bar stool, paces behind us and then back again.

"But… " I can't say it. I can't say it out loud. I look at Jamie, he looks hungry in a way that beer won't satisfy. I can't let Jamie tell him. He would be cruel. Suck it up, Matt. "He died too, a few weeks ago. Just after he found out about you. He wanted to meet you, he wanted to - "

Lee stops mid-stride, facing away from us. His shoulders rise and fall, skinny shoulder blades poking triangles through the back of his jumper. He's relieved, I think. I can't really blame him, though it repulses me.

Jamie stands up, buttons his coat, rests a comforting hand on Lee's forearm and turns him around. "He wanted me to give you something."

Lee's miserable eyes lift a miniscule amount. It occurs to me that Alex would have turned out to be pretty good-looking in his old age, and I am struck by just how little he ever looked like my dad. Jamie smiles. "He wanted me to give you this," he says, and his right hand balls into a fist, raises to shoulder height and thuds forward into the left side of Lee's jaw.

"Shit!" The waitress rushes forward a few steps then backtracks and stays safe behind the bar.

Lee sprawls back against the barstools and drops to the floor. I try to help him up but Jamie shoves me away and sticks a boot in his ribs before spinning a theatrical one-eighty and marching out into the street.

I mutter a few sorrys and follow him at a run.

Jamie stands outside a sushi bar, rubbing his knuckles and

staring at his reflection in the window. "What the fuck did you just do?" I say.

His voice is jerky with adrenaline, "Retribution from the grave."

"This was your plan, all along? You couldn't stretch to the train fare and do this alone? You had to be chauffeur-driven? We came all this way just so you could deck him? What did he ever do to Alex? He didn't even know he existed!"

The chef in the middle of the revolving sushi conveyor glares at me. A woman pushing a buggy crosses the road with a frown so she doesn't have to walk past us. Jamie digs furiously in his coat pocket and withdraws a screwed up piece of paper. "Oh it's fucking obvious. He knew about Alex. He must have known, and he didn't give a shit." He shoves the ball of paper into my chest so hard it knocks me off balance.

"So Alex's dying wish was for you to punch his real father? Have you got one for my dad too? You always were a pair of fucking idiots."

"I was more of a brother to him than you ever were," Jamie says. A verbal boot in my ribs to match Lee's. "Just as well you *weren't* his brother. You didn't deserve to be."

We are alone on the pavement; everyone who isn't shouting at the top of their voice is walking quickly along the other side of the road. The sushi chef has stopped slicing up California rolls and holds a phone to his ear, eyeing us with disapproval.

"You deserved each other. Both of you, fucking sociopaths," I say, but it doesn't feel as good as I thought it would.

Jamie shoves me again and I react instinctively even though I've never hit anyone before in my life. I don't punch him, but my fist pulls back and hangs next to my ear while he flinches backwards. I lower my arm. How can anyone consider hitting another person when there are such things as aneurysms in the world? When you can't tell whether even a single strike could be manslaughter. Manslaughter, what a fucking word.

"Make your own way home," I tell him, at normal pitch.

"As if I want to be anywhere near you," he spits back, and

is marching again, halfway down the road before I unclasp the paper in my fist and am able to breathe. I look down at the letter as I cross the road - Lydia's handwriting, Lee's name on about the fifth line. The dead ink of my stepmum hurts more than the fresh wound of my brother's bleeding brain. When I look up again Jamie is gone, and the waitress from Lee's bar has her hands pressed up against the glass frontage, eyes wide and head nodding at me, behind me.

What now? Oh. A bus.

Chapter Sixteen

Across the dining table from me a nurse attempts to shake awake a woman who is so fast asleep, or dead, that her chin clacks against her collarbone with every jostle. I stretch as far as I can out of my chair to look for the sun out the window, wondering if I can work out the time of day by its position. It's wintertime. And the slop in front of me is either lunch or dinner. Rice that begins with an R. A European soupy, cheesy thing, and though I really don't care what the meal should be called it galls me not to be able to recall the word. It doesn't matter what the hell the day is, they're all the same in here.

Paul sits next to me, spooning up his gloop, talking through every single mouthful. He is nothing more than a blur of a jaw and browned teeth moving up and down, making noises I can't translate. I'm not entirely sure how long he's been talking but I have begun to nod in rhythm with his monotonous tone.

I have to wait for my vocal chords to remember their existence. Until then I am stuck reciting inane haiku to the inside of my skull:

Dearest moron Paul
No-one cares about your life
Or what's left of it.

Paul has turned a curious colour. I think he might be choking but then the sound of his outraged shouting slides into focus. Cutlery all along the table stutters into silence like

158

a tiny orchestra faltering to a stop. Little missiles of saliva spurt from his lips like shards of glass.

"Hmm?" I say.

"It's your fault," he says.

I nod. It's always true.

The nurses are watching him but no-one else bothers to look up. "You said to tell her what I really thought. She was hysterical. Crying! She'll never visit again!"

It sounds as if I should agree, and since I can feel my voice hunkering behind my tonsils, I take advantage of it. "No, I expect not."

"You… You callous old bastard!" Paul upends his plate over the tablecloth, his fork and plastic cup of juice dropping into my lap. He turns and stamps as quickly as his furious elderly body will allow from the room while the other diners watch me with a spectrum of incomprehension and amusement and fear. The scrutiny turns my internal thermostat up by ten degrees until my skin begins to bubble under my jumper. I need a doorway. I need an exit. I lurch in the opposite direction to Paul, the utensils in my lap bundled to my chest, wrapped in a cloth napkin. It doesn't matter what I cling to, so long as I hold onto something.

#

When I leave the dining room I fall through a burning doorway that singes the hair on my arms as I pass. It smells like hot iron, like blood. Angela's voice tells me about a dream she had. A dream of her unborn baby. She dreamt it was a boy, a girl, a newborn who could talk, told her its name was Suzie, Kieran, that it wanted a ham sandwich. She dreamt she was chasing her mother through a garden, through gates and over fences and fighting her way into privet bushes that scraped her thighs and whipped her face. Lydia had taken the baby, was meant to look after it just for the day, but she wouldn't give him back no matter how much Angela pleaded.

Four days overdue, she woke me at five-something in the morning, circling her hips by the side of my bed and blowing out her breath like a punctured tyre. Half an hour later I tried to find a way to lift her into the backseat of the car without touching her because every tiny movement made her yelp.

I have no memory of the route we took to the hospital, only the stream of questions that spewed out of me in icy panic. "Do you want the radio on? Off? The fan? Heater? Window open? Am I going too fast? We're about five minutes away. Should I stop and ring the hospital? Angela? Angela?"

I knew she'd be laughing if she weren't in so much pain.

I tried to lag behind when we reached the labour ward and the nurses and the midwife took my place in holding Angela upright while she limped and wailed her way to a little pink room, but Angela's clawed hand held on to my shirtsleeve and dragged me along after, to a place where I was utterly superfluous.

#

"Grandad?"

I can't move. If I try to take a step forward, the rug swirls into a whirlpool and the skirting boards detach from the walls and float down the rapids of the corridor. Two nurses in matching purple approach, bruised uniforms bleeding into the sea, as inescapable as Scylla and Charybdis.

"Grandad? Peter?"

Behind me: a voice, and the water is calmer there. I flounder towards the light - a bay window, the familiar stink of potpourri on a pointless decorative table, and I've never been so glad to see an armchair in my life. The chair consumes me and I tuck my feet up out of the flowing water, a napkin-wrapped parcel pressing into my stomach. Something inside it clinks.

Someone's crying – or trying to cry silently, at least – and I recognise the sniffing. A girl, my girl, little Clare, grown up Clare, still a child really Clare, different Clare. Something wrong. She crouches next to my chair and rests her head on the back of my casted arm.

"Hello," I whisper. I can't be sure she's really there, after all, and the last thing I need is to look like I'm talking to myself.

Her head whips up, hair sticking to her wet face like whiskers. "Grandad."

"Hello, Pickle."

She smiles, a slowly creaking door left on the latch, unsure whether to let this stranger in. "What's my name?" she asks me.

"Scary Clare," I tell her, because she never wanted to be a passive little princess. She knew the dragon got to have more fun.

She nods, twists a bracelet around and around her wrist. I can feel her foot jerking up and down in impatience through the carpet. She doesn't want to be here. Why is she here? Something different in the way she stands. Something new working away behind her eyes.

"I'm scared," she says quietly. "I can't talk to my mum." She looks up and down the corridor. "She's not in today. I checked."

And I see. I know. She has that look on her face – the same look her grandmother had when she was pregnant – a bizarre mix of serenity and unease.

Darling granddaughter,
find a sucker just like me
to help you raise it.

I shake my head. "Just like your mother. And hers. How long do you sirens go back?" She straightens up at my change of tone, disappearing into a distorted silhouette against the hard sunlight behind her and I can see three generations of Sutton women, round-bellied and tired with heaviness, lined up in front of the window, beauteously terrifying and full of power. The light overexposes them, makes me leer, blinking, but there they are, all the same. Lydia with her head to one side, mocking, adoring and ready to give me a slap for being so nostalgic; Angela standing solemn and unblinking, reproving of my self-indulgence; Clare, nervous and furious and wishing she was still small enough to cuddle up and watch *Top Gear* with me, chewing our way through a packet of Liquorice Allsorts.

She would be alright, I knew. Her mother would be shocked, then accepting, then give all the advice I wished I'd had on hand to give Angela nearly twenty years ago. Why do they come to me? What can I possibly offer them?

The three figures bloom into ink blots against the sheer curtains, melting and deforming until they are as twisted and broken as my Mother Whistler. It is their turn to leer. They have come for me, for the things I have hidden. I scramble to stand, treasure clamped to my chest, pushing away the hands that try to grab me as I slip on the wet carpet underfoot. The flood has passed but my feet will sink into the ground if I stay still for too long.

#

I stumble over a threshold into a body drenched in sweat, adrenaline usurping my blood. My hands are white, trembling beyond my control, beyond hiding. Angela didn't have time to suck on the gas canister that they'd wheeled in. I am glad, because the mouthpiece is dimpled with the teeth-marks of other screaming women. She'd barely got inside the room when a flurry of peach-scrubbed staff descended upon her, hands on her head, her belly, between her legs.

Each contraction begins with a fearful and dread-filled curling of her toes, a rolling forward of her shoulders, a bracing of her palms on the bed's side-bars. A noise rises from her like an air raid warning, cyclical and mechanical. She sustains a perfect note for so long I cannot believe she has enough air in her lungs to hold it so steady. Her belly tightens and stands out rigid while she gulps in a breath and the note lifts a few tones, increases its volume, tails off with an upward flick as she tops the peak. What follows is a series of moans too sexual for me to bear to listen to, then a satisfied sigh. I blush every time, even though each one makes me want to cry with pride, with fear, with incomprehension at her strength. How does she know? How can she do this? How can any woman have done this before her?

In my ears her sounds become Heather's terrified pleas, Lydia's low, guttural lowing. Something agonising is yanked out of me with every cry. I force myself to listen to Angela's interpretation, to watch sweat peel from her pores and mingle into a pool between her collarbones. The midwife has a grin on her face now, the nurse too. Angela manages a weak, breathy smile in between contractions, squeezes my hand, nods when the midwife says, "Soon, keep going, honey."

The room descends into a sudden rush of action as Angela's eyes bulge with shock and a stream of negatives spring from her mouth, while the midwife reassures her and everyone sets their eyes on her vagina, except me, who won't even allow myself a prudent glance.

Everyone pulls together – a bloody and agonising Hokey Cokey – while Angela pushes with every vein in her face and holds her breath for longer than is humanly possible. I know this, because I try to hold mine with her, and fail.

"Again!" the midwife yells.

Angela pushes silently. I hear splattering on the floor, a deep exhalation.

"There's the head. Wait. Waaaaait. One more!" My eyes flick automatically to the disembodied little red face protruding from her crotch.

Angela shrieks and a slithering body follows, a boneless thing covered in grey slime, one hand grasping its cord, squeezing rhythmically. It takes a moment to adjust to the cold, bright world, reacts with disappointment and outrage. I smile so hard my cheeks hurt, through eyes full of tears, at the little face which seems to be mostly made up of one huge screaming mouth. The nurses whip a towel around it and place the baby gently onto Angela's chest.

She doesn't speak, the baby doesn't cry. They look at each other. Angela kisses its gunky forehead, streaking blood onto her cheek. As one, the onlookers sway and breathe and swallow the lumps in our throats and the midwife whispers, "Girl."

Angela considers the tiny head rooting for her breasts.

"Clare," she says.

#

I can hear her but I can't see her. Can't find her. Can't breathe. Can't keep going but can't stop moving. Door. Wall. Floor. Something sharp against my ribs. A fork in my fist. And I hear her voice but I see his face. So many times I wanted to hurt him.

"Peter, let me help you," he says.

"Graham," I say.

"Paul," he says. Lies. From the start.

"You," I say. Simpler that way.

My wrist throbs inside its cast. I let him pull me up off the carpet since I don't know how I came to be lying there, and halfway to standing I take my chance. The fork tines pierce his polyester slacks, his fatless thigh, and stick into stringy muscle. He cries out. Falls. And me with him, back down into the ocean again. My head glances off a doorframe and a girl calls my name but this isn't a portal, this is rest.

Chapter Seventeen

I'm only out for a minute or two. I'd sidestepped like a startled
seagull, but not far enough to stop the front right corner of the
bus from barrelling into my left hip ("I just nudged him," the
driver claimed). The impact spun me backwards, perfectly in
line for the wing mirror to crack into the back of my head.
Another 'nudge' that split the plastic.

Sound and vision melt back into my head, taking begrudged
turns as if I am trying to mix oil and water.

"Don't move him!"

"Idiot was in the middle of the road… "

"I'm a witness, I'm a witness. Has someone called the
police?"

"Police? He needs an ambulance, look at his head."

"What's your name?"

I realise my eyes are open and Lee Burnett is looming over
me, a wad of tissues pressed to a fat, split lip, but genuine
concern in his eyes. The buzzing in my brain makes me forget
that it was Alex who got the letter about Dad and not me, and
for a moment the man looking down at me could be my own
alternate father. One who might give a shit if his son got hit
by a bus.

"What's your name?" he says again.

"Matthew."

"Can you move?"

A blush heats my face and I want to cry. My eyes cartwheel, checking that Jamie is not part of the growing crowd. Thank fuck for that.

I grasp blindly for his hands, my depth perception somewhere far off and happy in its ignorance. "I'm so sorry, Lee. I honestly didn't know he was going to hit you."

Lee laughs, throwing his head back like a jovial musketeer, only without the flowing hair. "Don't worry about me. Can you get up? You're still in the road."

A car passes too close, blasting out a baseline that jumps octaves without warning. The beat settles in my stomach and when I sit up I think I'm going to puke.

Lee quickly takes my arm and pulls me, limping, over to the curb so the bus can pull in to the side of the road, letting off a double-deckerload of inquisitive, irritated and irate passengers who take up residence on the opposite side of the street to stare at me.

"Ambulance is coming," the waitress informs us, iPhone to her ear, a strange smile aimed my way.

I count in my head until the siren comes veering around the corner but the numerical order gets lost. I am stuck on seventeen.

Lee dabs at his lip and peers at the tissue to see if his blood has clotted yet.

The paramedic looks us both up and down. "Right, who first?"

In the back of the ambulance they pull at my clothes and ask me why I'm fighting them and I am forced to yell, "No! I'm - I'm - I'm going commando!"

The paramedic pauses, Lee stifles a laugh, the driver says, "What?"

I explain in a whisper, "I had no clean pants this morning."

"Well, we still need to have a look at that leg, mate."

"Please - it's okay, just a bruise. Really."

"I'll close my eyes," Lee says patiently, patting my shoulder. The lump on my head bulges through my hair. It pounds with every heartbeat. Each time I reach up to feel the thick congealed blood, the paramedic tuts at me and slaps my hand away.

Lee shuts his eyes and rests his hands over them. The paramedic lays a sheet of paper towelling over my crotch and cuts away my left jean-leg.

When I was younger I always dreamed about being in some sort of accident - nothing too bad, just enough to warrant a sling, or crutches, or a head bandage. The worst I managed was a sprained ankle when I was twelve, missing a step coming out of a chapel assembly. In fact, shoved by Jamie. Laughed at by Alex. Reluctantly acknowledged by Dad, who only took me to the doctor after it turned black and I couldn't fit my shoe on.

This is not what I dreamed of.

The paramedic's rubber-gloved hands are tacky and drag on my leg-hair. My balls shrink inside my body with shame beneath the pathetic modesty of paper towel.

Hands press my skin. A tongue clicks. My hip is already blotching purple. There's no sweetness of a day-old surface bruise. It's deep. An ache that twists my lower intestine. I don't know what I was expecting.

The paramedic looks up, "Lie back. You need stitches for your head. Maybe an x-ray for this leg."

I nod. No, that was a stupid idea. I shake my head. Equally bad. "I just need to get home," I try. His response is to ping off his gloves.

The ambulance takes a right on a roundabout and I throw up over the side of the gurney, splattering the shoes of Alex's real dad.

#

In A&E I cower in a fold-up wheelchair, clutch my paper towel blanket, and tell Lee repeatedly to go back to his bar, to go home, to leave me here. He ignores me, tells me stories about weird bar customers, the strange things he's found in his restaurant toilets, the idiots he's employed over the years. He manages this for a good hour before he mentions her name, then barrels in with no warning:

"Was Lydia sure Alex was mine?"

I feel like a betrayer to my father even saying it aloud. "She never even talked about it. Alex just got this letter." And I remember I have the very thing – the earth-shattering, equilibrium-destroying object itself – in my pocket. I hold it out to him. "Here."

I can't read it again. I won't. It's actually, bizarrely, pleasantly, none of my business now that Alex is no longer a blood relation of mine. Lee reads it, chewing on his inflamed lip. His Alex-eyes squint at some of the words as if they hurt. When he's finished he sighs long and low, and because you might as well kick someone while they're down, I tell him how his son died. Lee bobs his head rhythmically and empty of expression as he listens. I run out of words when I get to the funeral so he ends it by clearing his throat and trying to pass the letter back. "Keep it," I say, more bitterly than I mean to.

"He was your brother."

He *was* my half-brother. Now I suppose he was my step-brother. Though really, now he's dead, he's nothing to no-one. I nod all the same.

"Who was the other one?" Lee asks, "The one who hit me?"

"Alex's best friend. He's a prick. Sorry."

"Hmm."

"I'm so sorry."

"Stop apologising."

He's too calm. His ability to deal with all this shit is as irritating as it is reassuring. "You've taken all this pretty well," I say.

He sort of smiles, eyes everywhere but my face. "Lydia and I were only together for a few months. Over thirty years ago now. It doesn't really seem real, I suppose."

He can't have known about Alex. Jamie is insane. Lee's a

nice guy. He wouldn't have run if he'd known he had a child. He's looking after me and he's only known me a few hours. I've had a longer conversation with him than I have had with my own father in the last five years.

"When did your brother die?" he asks softly, folding and unfolding the letter in his hands.

"My - " I start to say half/step/non-brother then swallow it down. There is no need to be so pedantic. "About a month ago."

Lee pulls on the handle of my chair so he can look at me straight. "This is the worst part," he says quietly. "But then you'll start feeling guilty for things getting easier. Then angry that people have stopped asking you about it, stopped wondering if you're okay. You'll think they've forgotten. But you'll still think about it all the time. Give it a year. Actually, not spot on a year – that's almost harder than this bit, the anniversary – but give it just over a year and you won't feel so close to it all. It's not going to go away, though. It just gets further away from where it hurts."

But it doesn't hurt. It's just an emptiness. Grief I could work with. I don't know what to do with this void.

"Are you married?" I ask him.

"No."

"Kids?"

He hesitates. "No."

"Oh." The space between us is too quiet. "Do you remember Angela?" I ask.

His face brightens, "Oh, yes, of course. She was such a funny little thing. How is she?"

"She's okay."

He struggles to find the right word, masticates it around his tongue first. "I was… surprised that Lydia had another baby. After Angela. Having her… the birth nearly killed her, you know?"

I didn't. I shake my head. "She had a caesarean with Alex. And blood transfusions after, I think."

He nods. "Does your dad know? About me? The letter?"

169

"No."

"Is he a good dad?" He's asking questions he doesn't want the answers to. It's wounding him to ask them, but he'll probably never see me again so he has to. And I realise that's why he's here: not to look after me but to salve his conscience.

"To Alex? Yeah. He was. Lydia was a good mum to both of us." My fists clench around the scrappy edges of my jeans, holding them tight against my throbbing leg. Every time the automatic doors admit another waiting, bleeding, wheezing A&E patient, goose bumps ripple along my skin. Lee's pale eyes, presumably capable of as much hatred as his son's, peer at me, almost amused. A rush of protective love for Lydia floods me cold. *She chose the right father,* I want to say.

Fuck it, why not? "She chose the right father for Alex."

He blinks, sits back, tucks the letter away inside his jacket. "You're right there."

I edge my wheelchair a few inches back. "You don't have to wait with me."

"It's okay. I'll see you to the doctor, anyway."

"No, really - "

I yank on the wheel to turn away and nearly tip myself out. The spirit level in my head explodes and I have to stuff the paper towel into my mouth to stop myself from being sick again. Instead of leaping away, Lee lays a warm hand on my back and rubs in slow circles. And I, stupidly, start to cry.

Lee sighs, not impatiently, just heavy with air. "I get the feeling you didn't really get on with your brother," he says.

I don't need a pause, "I hated him."

"So why are you so upset?"

"It was my fault."

"Sounds like an accident to me."

I know it does. But I know somehow it wasn't.

A doctor comes through from the treatment rooms and swaps paperwork with a nurse behind the front desk. The waiting inhabitants of the room lean forward expectantly, hoping to hear their name called next.

Lee picks at a jagged thumbnail roughly, "I didn't believe her when she told me. I thought it was just an excuse to make me stay. I was moving to Scotland for a new job and I thought she was just trying to manipulate me."

"Matthew Landrow?" calls the doctor, hiding a yawn behind his clipboard.

"You *knew*?" I whisper.

Lee nods at the doctor, "That's you."

"Why didn't you ever try to find him?"

Lee stands, waves at the doctor and wheels me over to the desk.

"To be honest, Matthew, Lydia was a liar. I didn't want to know if it was true or not. It seemed easier that way." He falters for a moment. "But now I have my karma, don't I?" he pats his pocket where the letter lies.

"Matthew?" the doctor smiles with his mouth but not his eyes. He takes the wheelchair handles from Lee and spins me deftly about and away through the double doors and Lee doesn't say goodbye.

#

I am taken to the underbelly of the hospital, an overflow ward containing what appears to be mostly moaning elderly people. No curtains have been drawn to divide us. After the doctor prods my head and pulls back the paper towel over my crotch without warning, he writes something on my clipboard and leaves again. The nurses at their station refuse to look up in case they make eye contact with someone. It is sweltering but my joints have seized in their sockets and I can't take off my coat.

The man in the cubicle next to me sits on the edge of his bed holding a large paper bag and stares at me. "You here visitin'?" he asks, "Mum or Dad? They dyin'?"

"No… " I say slowly, expecting the dried blood on my face and hands to explain for me.

171

"Check-up for me. And picking up my drugs," he swings the bag at me and hoicks up his left trouser leg, revealing a bloated calf scabbed with black discs and criss-crossed with discoloured veins. "Blood clot," he tells me proudly.

I nod, swallow more saliva than is comfortable. An old man shuffles a painstaking journey from his bed on the right side of the ward to the toilet on the left, drip-stand in tow. He doesn't make it in time. Little pools of urine trail behind him and the stand's wheels leave tracks as he drags them through.

A woman with thinning, greasy red hair makes her rounds from bed to bed. She's not a nurse, clearly – her right eye is half-closed and weepy and she's wearing a purple dressing gown and trainers – but the intent and manner is there. She squeezes blood clot man's shoulders affectionately. "Alright, my darling?" she coos. Her accent is thick and throaty. Her eyes find mine and I try a smile.

"You visiting someone?" she asks. I shake my head, blushing beneath the sweat that gathers on my face under the unnatural heating of the ward.

She scurries around the bed and presses a palm against my forehead, yelling over to the nurse's station, "He is rather hot. He is *very* hot!" then to me, "You're burning up, my darling." And I am. And maybe it's not just the heating. The lump is still there.

The nurses ignore her and she moves onto the old peeing man, just inches away from the toilet door now, and goes to help him in. Finally the nurses move, waving the red-haired woman away and returning the old man to his bed. A porter comes to clean up the piss. A nurse glances at my chart as she passes and returns an hour later with a fucking terrifying curved needle and some catgut or whatever it is.

"You shouldn't really be on this ward," she mutters, as if it's my fault I was brought here.

"Oh," I say.

She shakes her head and when I see the pouches of tiredness beneath her eyes I realise it was meant to be an apology. "Busy afternoon."

"Right."

"Put your head forward."

"Okay."

She stitches up my head with an accompaniment of sighs and a wet cough that she vaguely tries to cover with her forearm. My swollen head throbs around the wound. My jaw aches from clenching. My phone buzzes in my jeans pocket, cut away and hanging over the side of the bed.

"No mobiles allowed in here," she snaps as she cuts the last thread and pulls the knot tight. She smiles like it takes a lot of effort to do so. "I'll try to get a doctor to sign your forms as soon as we can and you can go home."

"Thanks."

She pulls the curtain around my bed as she leaves and I attempt to quietly burst into tears. My phone goes again. It's Sabine. I turn it to silent. Someone else is crying outside my cubicle, a gentle but heartbroken weeping that makes my self-pitying sobs impotent. I wonder if anyone is coming to visit the red-haired wannabe nurse or the pissing man or those blood-clotted legs or anyone else here. I wonder how the fuck Angela maintains any kind of positivity facing this lost battle every day. How Dad doesn't just kill himself outright. I would. Except I wouldn't have the guts. I wonder if it's because of the concussion that I can't remember where I parked the car.

Chapter Eighteen

Peter

It's a hotel room. It's a cell. It's a waiting room. It's my room. Not my room. Not my flat. Not the house. But mine. Temporarily. Connect the dots, you'll get there eventually. Nightness outside. Darkling. A door between me and all the muttering staff people. Spots of blood on the knees of my pyjamas. Not my blood, so that's okay then.

A window, unlatched. Ground floor. I could leave. But nowhere to go. No more doorways. All gone. I think I swallowed my voice.

Don't ask, don't recall
What happened to that damn fork?
No regret, all dark.

Maybe I can pull my voice back up my throat manually. I find the bathroom eventually. It's not where it used to be in my flat - the door opens the wrong way and these are not my towels. Fingers as far back as I can stick them, stroking my epiglottis until bile and mashed vegetables splatter into the toilet bowl but there's no voice to be dragged up. I try again, until nothing is left, until there is blood. Until the retching turns to barking - a flapping seal trapped behind my voice box. My throat is raw but the more I swallow the looser my tongue becomes.

I try softly at first: "My name is Peter Landrow."

It works. A little bit louder. "I am seventy-four-years-old."

It hurts. And I have nothing much else to say. Except sorry. Someone needs a sorry from me. More than one someone. I should find them.

My feet magnetise to the floor and I can only lift them an inch before gravity pulls the soles down again, so I slide instead of walk – ball, shuffle, change – the apology waltz.

The lights are on in the corridor and I pause at the threshold. Mother Whistler's machines hum. I was told to stay in my room but that might have been months ago. I won't go far. If I get lost they'll find me. They always do.

Left, shuffle, tiptoe, stop. Paul's room is empty, bed stripped. Not even the pictures of his family left behind. A sorry belongs to him, I think. A clipboard sits on his bedside table with an inventory checklist and a chewed up biro. I write five apologetic capital letters on the back of it but when I try to read it back it has turned into a scribbled bird's nest. I'm sure he'll know what I meant.

Right and a slide and a one, two, three, one, two, three, stop. Past my dead doorway to Ingrid's. The smell of TCP and oranges. She's busy hacking up a lung. I did not bring her a present or pudding so I pass her the newspaper from her chest of drawers.

"Sit," she says. I fall into her chair. Good dog. It is safe in here.

Ingrid wheezes crossword clues at me in between spluttering spasms. She drags in air through bubbling lungs like a drowning woman.

She has a drip next to her bed now. It wobbles with every cough. She beats her knees with the newspaper and I catch the date. A week until Lydia died, twenty years ago. We put the dust of her into a little concrete box that sits in the gated cremation area at the top of the graveyard on the hill.

"You're no help at all today," Ingrid says. "Do I have to do all the work?"

"Sorry."

"Thinking?"

Nod.

"Well go and do it somewhere else or say it out loud, for Chrissakes."

My muteness falls away but the words still cause harm, "Lydia died - next week."

"Wife?"

"Second."

"What was it?"

"Cancer."

"Ah. Yup. One in three, isn't that what they say? Recently?"

"Long time."

"Still bad. I still get heart pains on the day my mum went. Real pain. Real connection, still, after they're gone. I believe that, anyway."

Nod, nod. Cough, cough.

"You'd better bloody ache when I go," she creaks, about to launch a fresh assault on her ribcage.

"It'll be quieter."

"Ha! I'll miss you, you bugger."

Respite. Just the beeping of old Mother Whistler's monitors across the hall. Ingrid's chest buzzes with fluid.

"She wasn't ready," I say quietly. I didn't mean to say it. For a moment I wonder if I imagined it. Ingrid sits staring at the shoddy brown oil paint landscape that hangs above her dresser.

"None of us are ready. Those who say they are… Lying bastards," she whispers.

"I hated her for it," I say. Lydia convinced us all she'd be okay – no matter what the doctors said – and we wanted to believe her, so we did. Then she was gone and I was solely responsible for three other lives. So many decisions. All that cause and effect, like dominoes falling down. How could they leave me like that? All of them: Heather, Alice, Lydia. They must have known I'd fail. I don't think I say any of that out loud but Ingrid's face drops into a soft sadness.

"You do what you can, Peter. If you made a mess of it, then

176

you made a mess of it. Not much you can do about it now."

"I didn't try hard enough. I didn't do my best."

"Then be a bloody man and blame yourself. God almighty, anyone would think you were the one dying."

She plants her finger on the nurse-call button and yells, "Nurse!" at the top of her scratchy, worn out voice.

"Shhh," I soothe.

"I," she says, "have no regrets."

I smile. "None?"

"Not a single one. They can bury me with glee and no looking back. If I see angels then they can applaud me as I go through the gates. If I see red devils they can feel my wrath. If there's nothing, then I'll just have a good old sleep. But there's no point worrying about it, my love. Who says we have to achieve anything in our lives? Who says we have to find some epiphany? Who says we have to have a clean slate? We're just little particles or something, bouncing around in bits of meat. Eh? Eh?"

Her eyes don't say the same thing as her lips, but I nod, look away so she can wipe the moisture from her cheeks.

"Where's that bloody nurse?"

#

When I was fifty-four, it was a very bad year. It was a very bad year for wives and mothers-in-law and lungs and cancerous cells and old worn out hearts, and I wondered how much death and loss a person could cope with before they no longer felt anything at all.

Alice went first - a 'peaceful' but fatal heart attack that a ticket officer discovered at the end of the line when he tried to wake her so they could clean the train. I sat the children around the dinner table and ruined their appetites. Angela cried into her chips. Alex didn't speak for the rest of the day. Matt ran to his room and wedged a chair underneath the doorknob. She had been a grandmother to all of them. Both

Lydia's parents and mine were dead, but we never seemed to be able to get rid of Alice. The children cheerfully cast off her religious zeal and absorbed her generosity and her inability to give up on difficulty. They cried into each other's shoulders at the funeral and grimaced under the attention of her weird old friends, who insisted on pinching their baby fat and clutching their faces with gnarled hands as if they were juicy peaches to be devoured.

We didn't tell Lydia. She couldn't bear Alice's silent but obvious conviction that Heather would return one day and claim her usurped position as mother hen. But I knew what she would have said: that fate was toying with her, sending her nemesis to the afterlife to keep her company. I let her discover it in her own time, if there was such a thing as time after death. By that point she was flat out on liquid pain relief and a simple conversation exhausted her to the point of unconsciousness.

"I don't want to go," Lydia murmured, a week before she died. "But if it's meant to be… "

I disagreed. Not out loud, but I disagreed. It wasn't meant to happen, not in my plan. I was meant to go first. None of it was meant to happen.

She'd always maintained that fate had played a part in crashing our cars. Some god, some destiny personified, looking down and bringing us together: two damaged hearts in need of one another. A sickening idea, I thought, and told her so, but she didn't mind. No matter what I thought I never told her the whole truth: "No, sorry, you're just a bad driver."

No. It was the next bit that made me take her home and marry her before the pregnancy began to show. She'd said, "If it wasn't for Angela I'd have killed myself by now. And if it wasn't for you I'd still be wishing I'd never had Angela so I could kill myself."

And that I understood. Given that sort of power, how could I walk away?

We gathered again at the dinner table, the day she died. The hospice nurses had known, they must become attuned to the approach of death, like feeling a presence in a room before you turn to see who's there. The kids saw her go. Kissed her. Dropped tears on the bed sheets in little libations. Lydia didn't have enough hands for us all to hold. Angela sacrificed hers for Matthew, and rested her palm on her mother's forehead. I was left with her feet, which I clutched as gently as I could manage, clenching my jaws so hard my fillings throbbed.

It was nothing spectacular. She coughed a lot and the nurse adjusted her drip. There were no final words that any of us remembered afterwards - she wasn't lucid that day, barely awake. Her eyes rolled around in pain beneath her eyelids and her lips were lined with white gunk.

We stood, frozen in a still life, until the nurse gently removed our hands so she could pull the sheets up to Lydia's chin. I didn't remember driving home. When I next blinked we were in front of the house and Angela leaned across my lap to turn off the ignition.

And so we congregated at the dinner table once more and Angela made a pot of tea and poured some squash for Alex.

"I'm sorry," I told them.

No-one told me not to be.

Chapter Nineteen

A taxi takes me to the sushi restaurant, though I don't remember asking it to. The driver found me sitting on a white exit arrow in the underground hospital car park wearing a pair of borrowed tracksuit bottoms from the lost and found. They're too tight and there's some sort of greasy residue inside the pockets and I don't want to know who they used to belong to.

It took me twenty minutes to find a side door out of the maze of the hospital and into an endless series of concrete stairs that led me round and round the car park. I limped up three ramps before my injured leg gave way and my palms slapped down onto damp asphalt, leaving me squeaking out breathless swearwords.

A car revved up the ramp behind me and beeped its fury at my obstruction. I crawled out the way and it swept past me, angry middle fingers bashing against the passenger window.

And then I'm sitting at a conveyor belt with pickled ginger on my tongue and I don't know how many hours I've lost. I try to focus on one particular orange bowl as it revolves around the bar but my headache intensifies the harder I concentrate.

There was a phone call, back in the car park, echoing round the concrete bunker, and Sabine's voice: "You sound like you're in a church."

I didn't tell her where I was. I asked her why she left and

if she was coming back and I don't know what she said but it wasn't good. She said she was sorry. She'd been thinking about it for a while. Leaving me.

Then the beeping and the roaring of a passing car and the warmth of the taxi's fake leather seats and a friendly waitress and sticky rice.

Two teenage girls sit a few stools away to my left. They look about fourteen. One of them is hitting puberty with all cylinders firing, or maybe it's hitting her. Her breasts have been siphoned into an ill-fitting bra and strange bulges protrude out the top and sides of it. The other girl is the same shape as a skinny, awkward boy – like Alex at about that age – all shoulder blades and elbows that need to be tucked into the body to stop them randomly flailing around and taking someone's eye out. I can't see her legs under the table but I know they will be long and brittle and angular. Her skinniness makes me laugh for some reason and I snigger into my plate of noodles, pasting spinach to my chin. The girls stare in disgust.

I think I'm going to throw up. The girls glare, the waitress' smile slips from her mouth, the chef slices squid tentacles. I gag into the sleeve of my coat and limp to the bathroom before my head explodes and wriggling curls of brain and matted hair splatter against the front window.

#

Clare is shouting at me again. And my alarm won't shut off. One or the other. Or both. No. My phone is ringing, and then it's not, and that's when the shouting starts.

"Where the fuck are you? Sarah's here."

I tell her how I got hit by a bus when I wasn't wearing underwear and then I can't stop laughing.

Wait. Sarah's here? I was supposed to cook her dinner and now I'm full of sushi and lying on the floor of a toilet stall. Bollocks.

Clare calls Jamie a dick and a twat and worse when she

hears what he did. He should be scared. I am. She says she's going to find a way to get me home.

Someone knocks on the door. If it's Alex he can fuck right off.

"Excuse me, Sir? Are you okay?"

I didn't lock the door - the polite someone pushes it open and it smacks me in the head. The waitress looks down at me with equal parts concern and trepidation.

"Do you know where I am?" I ask her. Clare is demanding to know. I pass the waitress the phone and close my eyes for just a second.

#

"Don't go to sleep, Matt."

"I'm not."

"Maybe we should stop for some caffeine."

"No, no, I'm fine."

I'm bullshitting, talking in my sleep while I mash pieces of logic and splintered memory together. The hum of my stupid little car's engine struggling to hit sixty-five on the motorway. The whooshing of the heater and the rumble of a passing lorry. Sabine's vanilla perfume. Murmured curses at the sticky fifth gear. Pain in my head and my hip. Soft, old, folded letters.

I can still taste wasabi. I wonder if Sabine can too. I wasn't expecting her. I wasn't expecting the kiss as she clicked my seatbelt in place. Maybe she hadn't meant to do it but I was in no position to stop her and it was really no effort to press my lips against hers when she leaned across.

#

The motorway ends and we segue onto a minor road. Streetlights stream past us into the night. She turns the radio up too loud when she runs out of stimulating conversation to keep me awake. Clouds full of rain lie ahead – bands of grey over plump white, legless sheep – a formation in the middle that looks unnervingly like a human ear. Some god is listening. We stop at a set of lights, its lampposts dressed up in bouquets, old and fresh, rain-soaked notes, cellophane flapping in the wind. I should tape flowers over the hole in my living room wall. It's the done thing.

My stitches keep me sober and aching. I yawn and shift and grumble. Sabine sighs. Guilt and gratitude flood through me. "Thank you," I tell her. And, "I'm so sorry." It pains me to say it out loud, but: "I miss you."

She shrugs. "You're going through some shit," she says.

#

I try to kiss her again when she drops me off but she holds my shoulders still and pushes me backwards until I'm inside my flat and she is the other side of the doorway.

"Not now," she says. She passes over my car keys and shuts the door between us.

Clare is asleep on the sofa. She stirs when I put the kettle on and flaps around me with apologies and swearing insults about what kind of idiot gets hit by a bus. She's been crying, at least.

"Why Sabine?" I ask her.

"I'm sorry," she says. "I didn't know who else to call."

Humiliation that I should have felt a few hours ago saunters in and settles itself down in my stomach. "I bet she was fucking thrilled to come and rescue her damsel in distress…"

Clare twists her face into my eyeline, forces me to look at her. "She wasn't pissed off, Matt. She was worried. As soon as I told her what happened, she said she'd go." She gets no reaction from me. I don't believe her. We watch the kettle come to a boil, shuddering on its base.

"What did you do?" Clare asks. "Why did you break up?"

The kettle's switch pings. Steam douses my face with moisture and my blood pressure drops through the floor. I grip

183

onto the worktop and Clare puts out a hand to steady me.

"What did *I* do?" I snap. "I don't fucking know. Because I'm a bastard. We all are. Every one of us. Don't you know that yet?"

I have out-teenagered her. Her eyes brim. Fuck.

"Yes, you are," she says, a sneer offsetting the tears. "All of you. Bastards and selfish idiots."

"Selfish. Yeah. Not like you, hitching a free ride, ignoring your mum when she's worrying herself fucking sick about you, and my dad, and everyone else, like she always does." Clare tries to cut in but I slap the counter with both palms. "Your mum's brother just died, Clare. Don't you think we all might be trying to deal with something other than you right now?"

She sags: a hunched little girl in her pyjamas in my kitchen. The clock on the microwave says three-oh-nine.

"Go to bed," I tell her. "I'll sleep on the sofa."

She doesn't argue but she stops at the bedroom doorway and stares back at me, her eyes flashing with water. "You know, guilt isn't the same as grief, Matt."

It would have been less painful if she'd slammed the door, but it closes with a soft squeal and all that's left is the grumbling of the cooling kettle.

And I am here, not sleeping, drinking coffee and watching documentaries about fishing in the North Sea, until the birds start freaking out about the dawn and the rising sunlight turns the hole in my living room wall into a grimacing mouth.

184

Chapter Twenty

"You are in so much trouble," Angela hisses, eyes as sharp as open razor blades, ire held back behind her tongue and clamped-shut teeth. I can see the shape of her skull beneath her taut, angry skin. I don't know what she means but I am intrigued. She pauses at the threshold of my room before stamping two steps inside and closing the door behind her.

"I had to have a disciplinary meeting with my manager. I have a *warning* on my file, Peter." She flags a bit. The muscles in her buttocks relax and her whole frame drops a few inches. "Aren't you going to say anything?"

I try. I do. If I could manage it, I'd even attempt to choose my words tactfully, although there is no real way to ask what she's talking about without sounding trite. I shrug instead and stare at my slippers.

She deflates entirely, dropping onto the arm of my chair with a half-groan, half-sigh.

"Do you remember what you did?"

I shake my head.

She pats me gently on the shoulder. I wince as a streak of pain darts down to my wrist. She catches her breath. "I'm sorry. Are you in pain? When did you last have your painkillers?"

I adjust my arm further into my sling like a bird with a damaged wing and flip up a grin in the hope it will make her

185

go away. She and Alma are in cahoots. I know that now. Pills full of poison. A slow, vengeful death.

She grimaces, as if she can draw out my lies with her twisted lips and squinting eyes. "Paul is fine, by the way. In case you care."

I nod. That sounds like a good thing, whoever Paul is.

She shakes her head. "It's my fault. I shouldn't have - I saw you, Peter, talking to that kitchen porter. I was going to report him but he said it might help with the pain. Might... calm you down a bit." She leans in and rests her hands on my knees. "Where did you put it, Peter? If they find it... Please, try to remember."

My shoulders are so used to shrugging I wonder if eventually they'll get stuck up by my ears. I can't help her. I don't even know what's been lost. Angela picks at the loose loops of thread in the arm of the chair and I need to say something to lift her sadness but I don't have any worthwhile words. The sun flashes against the wall, reflecting off a car window as it pulls into the car park. For a second the light filters through her hair and I remember:

"Clare was here."

Angela looks up in confusion. "Last night?"

"Where were you?" I ask. Clare was terrified. I was no help. She needed her mother. "She needed you," I snarl. Regret it immediately. Grasp at her hands in apology.

Angela tries to smile to show it isn't my fault. She blames the strokes, the broken pieces of my psyche, the grumpy old man who has taken possession of my skin. I want her to break, to hate me like the others do, but she knows what I know. She knows what I can't tell Matthew and she still won't desert me.

She takes a long breath in. We blink at each other. She pats my shoulder again and I forget to wince. Then there's a barking gulp from her throat and her shoulders shake as she weeps into her hands.

#

186

"Alice?"

"It's Lauren."

"Alice?"

"My name's Lauren, Peter, you know that."

"Alice?"

A sharp exhalation, halfway to furious, halfway from frustrated. "Whatever," Alice says under her breath.

My eyes can't focus on her; she merely lingers like the ghost of mothers-in-law past by my left shoulder. My right arm is in the hands of another woman, a hospital nurse. She manipulates each finger in turn, flexes and stretches my wrist until it clicks. I turn a whelp of pain into a cough. My sawn-off cast lies disembowelled on the bed next to me. I stroke the strands of gauze that poke out of its belly. Weeks since my last stroke, though I don't remember how I came to fall, and I cannot work out why Alice would be here with me to have my cast removed. She must be at least a hundred by now. The nurse won't let go of my arm and I can't twist around to look at the woman behind me to check who is there. All I can see is her hand impatiently tapping the metal side bar of the bed. It doesn't look like a hundred-year-old hand. It has a silver wedding band and an engagement ring with too many diamonds that I've never seen on Alice before. Did she remarry while I was in the home?

Of course not, her name is Lauren and she's not Heather's mother. But that doesn't stop me asking, "Did you get married again?"

She replies with a petulant and confused, "No."

It isn't Alice's voice either. That proves it. I wonder where Alice is, I could have sworn she was here earlier.

The hospital nurse doesn't speak to me, converses only with someone over my spotted, balding head about physiotherapy and rehabilitation exercises, about monitoring movement and restricted weight-bearing.

Someone has written all over my discarded plaster cast, the same three words in tiny scrawls that I can barely read.

Alex is dead, it says. I think it might be my handwriting but it doesn't make any sense. The letters switch places with each other, mutating and stretching as I watch them: *Alex's head. Alex said. All is ended.*

The nurse gives me a squash ball to squeeze, until the muscles in my forearm contract and scream lactic acid into my bloodstream. Lauren drives me back to the home, switches the radio up to a volume that causes the hairs on the inside of my ears to vibrate.

Alice peers at me in the rear-view mirror. Her eyes are distrustful, irritated and full of tiredness. A phone rings somewhere upon her person. As we stop at a crossroads she peeks at the screen and taps a reply.

"Who was that?" I ask, suddenly aware of the deception in her seated stance.

"Pardon?"

"On the phone, was that her?"

"Who? It's none of your business, Peter."

"You know exactly who I mean, Alice."

"Oh God… I'm not whoever Alice is. That was my son, asking for a lift home from school later, if you must know."

"You lied through your teeth to me, to Matthew, to all of us," I say in a low quiet tone. She shifts in the driver's seat, flicking the indicator with an angry hand, pulling out into a too-small gap and getting beeped as she cuts up a taxi. She knows I know. But she doesn't know about the letters.

"Peter, I don't know what you're talking about. And I'd appreciate it if you stopped raising your voice at me. We'll be back at the home in a minute."

"You knew she was still alive, you never stopped believing. Well, more fool you."

She sits silent, staring ahead at an empty country road as intently as if she were trying to cross four lanes of traffic. Her left foot taps distractedly against the floor mat.

"I knew she never told you, or you wouldn't have been able to keep it a secret. For all your holier-than-thou preaching that we had to keep the faith, she never visited you, did she? Did she?"

"Peter - "

"And now she really is gone, so you can stop holding out for a miracle return, because you're not going to get it. She's at the bottom of the ocean." I can feel a wild grin on my face that disgusts me but protects me from the agony that should be in its place.

There is a long, shuddering pause from her, then: "Peter, I don't know what you're talking about."

I need her to know, to stop believing. I need her to give up, along with me. It's laughable. So I laugh. Lazy, like Ingrid: ha aha, ha.

"She jumped," I tell Alice. "At high tide." She wasn't a swimmer. She called me from the clifftop, from a phone box plastered with numbers for the Samaritans, a box for people just like her. I didn't pick up. All I got was an answerphone message.

Alice blinks like an epileptic doll as we pull into the car park. She sits and breathes in long whistles, hands still on the wheel, shoulders shivering. I roll a cigarette, heave the door open and painstakingly pull myself out of the car. She doesn't move to help me. She can sit and rot there, she's dead after all, been dead a long time. I can't believe I forgot about that.

#

When I was forty-two, it was not a very good year. It was a grey year. Matthew, you were two. Your mother was gone, but not quite gone. Nana Alice posted photos of you through the letter box when I refused to answer the door, until they covered the doormat completely. I started leaving and entering the house through the back door. When I had to pick up the post I'd do so with my eyes closed, feeling blindly across the bristles until my fingertips met matte envelope rather than the gloss of a photograph. She tried to fool me by putting them in

189

envelopes, got her friends to write the address so I wouldn't know they were from her. But I knew. I frisbeed them back onto the doormat, unopened.

A drunken night-spirit, born of several bottles of wine, dared me into action. I swept the pictures up into a rubbish bag with the broom at arm's length, doused them with lighter fluid and left them flaming on that bastard's doorstep. I ran barefoot back to the house, grinding gravel into the soles of my feet, skinning my knee in an elaborate skid as I rounded the corner of my drive.

The wine-spirit was gone when I was safe inside and the lonely terror grasped me by the scruff of my neck. I poured Dettol on my wounds and hissed at the almost full moon. A few days more and I would have made the transition into a beast.

She came in the back, used the spare key that hung behind the birdfeeder. She sat like a Bond villain in darkness, awaiting my return from work, rehearsing her grand reveal.

"Peter," she whispered.

I swore and my heart sucker-punched me in the chest. Heather sat on a kitchen chair, a shaft of moonlight falling in curved lines across her quivering hands which lay on the worktop, quivering.

She'd lost weight. She'd lost the weight of a whole baby and all that went with it. And more. The weight of responsibility and worry and stress and love. Her face was pale and longer than I remembered. Eyes reddened from saltwater rubbed angrily away. She didn't want to cry. She didn't want pity to state her case. She was holding it in with the last of her strength.

I felt less than I thought I would. "He's not here," I told her.

"I know. I've seen him."

"You saw your mother?"

She shook her head, swallowing hard and painful. "I saw him in the garden. He was singing Frère Jacques to the rabbit."

I nodded but couldn't move any closer to her, so strong was

190

the scent that had slowly faded from her left-behind clothes, her pillow, the towel she'd used the night she went into labour. I remembered in a rush of blood all the ways in which I used to hold her; the soft resistance of her skin, the angle of her head against my shoulder, her hot breath leaving condensation on my cheek. Eyelids, lips, tongue, neck, nipples, stomach, hips, buttocks, calves, big toe. Even if she gave them all to me, they no longer belonged. I'd lost her the moment she gave up Matty. I thought that if she smiled she might break me into pieces.

"You got my letters?" she said.

I nodded again. I'd tried to burn them too, on a bonfire at the end of the garden, but my hands wouldn't let go. My fingers disobeyed and stuffed the envelopes into my coat pockets where they sat for months. I had to buy a new coat to avoid contact with them. At last the earth moved around and spring came. I packed away the loaded garment into the top of the wardrobe, out of sight until the following autumn when I somehow found the strength to seal them into a shoebox.

She breathed in bubbles of excess saliva produced by her determination not to cry - countless intakes but no words in exchange. We were almost motionless there together. In three or four strides I could have crossed the vast distance between us, grabbed her by the shoulders and manhandled her into the cupboard under the stairs. I could have kept her in there, fed and watered and safe. I could have dragged the spare room mattress in as well, to make it comfortable for her. I would have slept in the hall. We could have talked through the gap under the door. We would have been close again. We wouldn't have ever had to answer the door.

Her eyes turned dry and enraged, glowering at her bitten-raw fingernails, snapping up to pin me to the wall.

"You would have been happy never to try again. You said: Maybe. It. Just. Wasn't. Meant. To. Be."

"It's my fault?" The words were snatched off my tongue before I could chew them up.

She faltered, rolled her head from side to side, "No. No… I'm sorry, Peter. I'm so sorry."

"Are you coming back?"

"No."

"You don't want me." Not a question.

She didn't reply.

"You don't want your son." Not a question.

No reply.

"Do you want - " I can't say his name, " - Him?"

"No. No!"

"What are you going to do?"

"What's left?"

And that was the point at which I should have gathered her up into my arms and kissed her, stroked her hair behind her ears, pressed her against my chest and held her tight and all those clichés that mean nothing when you've been carved out and left echoing. She'd shrunk into someone I didn't know, perched miserably on her chair like a pigeon in the pouring rain. It wasn't that I didn't love her. It wasn't that I didn't want her to stay. It wasn't that I wanted her dead. I don't know what it was. Pride, perhaps? Stubbornness. Lydia's idea of fate, come to punish me? So I did nothing. Said nothing. I might have even nodded, validating the unspoken implication. It was my fault.

"Why are you here?" I asked her.

She rounded her shoulders and her bottom lip curled down over itself in a grin which possessed no joy at all. Her eyes squinted into lines and out came the tears. Still, she tried to prevent them, gritting her teeth so her voice came through the gaps in a squeak, "I don't know."

I turned around and ripped off a few sheets of kitchen roll, tossing them onto the counter in front of her. "Thank you," she whispered.

I sat down opposite her. "You didn't have to tell me," I said softly.

"I know."

"You could have pretended."

"I know."

"I would have loved him anyway."

She looked up and the resolution behind her eyes terrified me. "I wouldn't have," she said. "I can't."

She left again and I didn't stop her. I didn't watch her disappear down the road. She might never have been there at all but for the crumpled up kitchen paper that had blown onto the floor with the breeze of the front door closing.

Chapter Twenty-One

I must have passed out on the sofa. I wake at midday and Clare is gone and my flat is a shithole and my phone is full of messages.

Sarah: asking if I want to meet up after work later for a drink, which I was not expecting at all after standing her up for a concussion last night.

Clare: telling me to go fuck myself, which I was definitely expecting and probably deserve. I should go fuck myself and she's moving out.

Third one's the charm.

Angela: half begging, half demanding that I visit my dad this morning because he's gone and done something really fucking stupid.

I drive one-handed, picking chunks of congealed blood out of the back of my head to keep myself awake. The B-roads run through tree-lined tunnels and on a clear day the sun strobes through the branches. I always miss the turning. A sign in the shape of a chicken, hidden in a hedge, is the only indication that a narrow dirt road veers off round a blind corner. I take the turn too sharply and my tyres freewheel on the gravel. The car park is half empty, half full, depending on how depressed you are.

The receptionist non-smiles politely as I push through the double doors. I nod, pointing towards my dad's corridor with questioning eyebrows. She shakes her head and jerks a thumb in the direction of the common room.

The residents cluster around the telly like it's a cold fire. Grey rain batters against the windows - an all-consuming white noise that puts me slightly off balance. No-one looks up when I walk through the doorway. A glossy gold paper chain flutters down from the mantelpiece without a single reaction. A nurse squeezes past me with a fresh catheter bag, followed by a porter in rubber gloves carrying a bucket of soapy water. They are ignored too.

And there in the corner I spy, with my tired, jealous eyes, a father who is asleep. Well, at least I won't have to talk to him.

"There you are!" Every shoulder in the room twitches but this one's for me. It's the duty manager for Dad's corridor. Hannah? Helen? No, something odder. I meet her halfway across the room. She continues to shout, even though we're standing a foot apart. Her name badge reads 'Honour'.

"I've been looking for you!"

"My dad's asleep. Is Angela around? She asked me to come in."

Honour lies with no attempt at grace, "Angela's busy with a resident at the moment. I just need to have a quick word with you if you don't mind." She looks me up and down, taking note of the abrasions on my face, the awkward stance that keeps me off my sore leg. She doesn't look impressed.

Honour heads off towards Dad's room and I follow with sickly anticipation. Why the hell does she want to talk to me? The staff either pity me or flick disdainful glances at me for not visiting my dad enough. I'm just the idiot son. Angela knows all the technical stuff and the money stuff and the medical stuff and the emotional stuff. All I do is come in once a week to tell Dad that Alex is dead. The one thing Angela can't do.

"It's not like an old death," Angie told me. She's had enough of them. She's been ready for Dad to die since the moment she co-signed the home's application form with me. Her face slipped for a second and then recalibrated into something more solid than before - a face beyond her face that could not be touched by what was inside.

"With Alex… When it happens like that, with no warning. It's like being shaken." Her face was not controlled, then. She sat across from me in the hospital canteen and her eyes twitched, squinting like she was looking into the sun. The tightness of her mouth pushed new lines into her skin. Her hands would not leave her alone, scratching at imaginary itches, pulling on strands of hair until they snapped out of her skull, rubbing across her eyelids until lashes came away on her fingertips. At the funeral her expression contorted into a cry with no sound, no breath. And now there's just the flinching. Every mention of her little brother's name is an open-handed strike. Thinking of Dad's predictable death must feel like a relief.

The woman in the room across from Dad sits so upright it looks unnatural. I watch her until the door closes behind me and I can be sure she's not about to leap out of bed, baring fangs. Honour lowers her voice once we're safely inside Dad's room, now that there is no-one to overhear.

"There was an incident yesterday," she says. "I don't know if Angela told you."

It's happening again. Another stroke. He's been losing the power of sensible speech for months. My lungs tense to half their capacity. "What happened?"

"Well. As far as we can tell, Peter got hold of something he shouldn't have."

Shit. He tried to top himself. What with? A knife? Pills? Shoelaces? The thought weighs like stones in my stomach. My voice becomes paper thin, creeping up high, past the massive swelling that has suddenly appeared in my throat. "What happened?"

"Another resident believes he may have been… on some sort of non-prescription drugs."

"What?" Seriously? I'm smiling and I can't help it.

She pauses disapprovingly. "Recreational drugs, I mean.

196

Marijuana, maybe."

"Where did he get it from?"

She looks at me predominantly with her left eye, as if it is the more judgemental of the two.

I laugh. "I have not given my dad any weed." I have to sit down. Honour is glaring. "And neither has Angela." My face is stuck in a rictus grin. I am not helping, I can tell.

"That isn't the only incident that occurred yesterday," she continues, and it gets better. I don't mean to laugh, I mean, I really don't. She tells me about Paul and the fork and Dad falling sweetly asleep afterwards and not remembering a thing. I bite the insides of my cheeks until the flesh makes a crunching sound. They're worried about sudden deterioration, a stroke gone unnoticed, severe changes in personality, violence, aggression, depression, drug abuse. But oh my God my dad got stoned and stabbed an old man with a fork.

Honour folds her hands into her apron. "We haven't found any evidence. Yet. But I need to let you know that we take possession of illegal drugs very seriously. If we were to come across any proof, we would have to ask him to leave."

I force my face into a frown. "Yes, of course."

"But because your sister - "

"Stepsister." God, shut up, shut up, you moron.

"Because your stepsister is a member of staff, I am willing to let you… have a little check yourself, before we search his room thoroughly." The left eye is protruding again, this time accompanied by a bouncing eyebrow. She's trying to be subtle. I nod slowly to let her know I'm in on the game.

"Thank you."

"Let's just hope it doesn't happen again."

"It won't, I promise."

She gives a curt nod in reply and swishes from the room. I close the door behind her and rest my head against the lacquered wood. His bed looks the type that would swallow you whole with its orthopaedic mattress and layers and layers of bedding. I could lie down – for just a moment – if I don't sleep soon I might go on a forking rampage of my own. My jaw is so tense I cannot unclench it. Ulcers have sprouted all along my gum line.

Fuck, it's hot in here. I swing the window open and try to focus. I need to sweep my way through his room before he wakes up. I don't want to get caught up in that confrontation. Right. Wardrobe: clean. Chest of drawers: clean. Miscellaneous boxes of photos and my grandfather's military insignia: clean. Shoes: clean. I consider my dad's level of sneakiness and check the hems of his curtains and the top of his wardrobe: clean. Drawers under the bed: clean. Ah. *Behind* the drawers under the bed: a shoebox. It rattles and shuffles when shaken. I pull it out amidst a wave of dust-sneezes. Inside: pills. Pills? Has he been hiding his meds? A dusty little bag of skunk. I pocket it. It's sweet and plump and strong. Dad, you cheeky bastard.

But my smile reverses when I see what lies at the bottom of the box.

Letters. Signed *Heather*.

\#

I'm gone before Angela's finished dealing with her patient, before Dad wakes up, before I put my head through a wall. I'm gone without the letters and I'm driving without really focusing my eyes properly.

My phone has been ringing since I left but I shut it into the glove compartment and let it buzz itself stupid. It's almost three o'clock. Sarah gets off early on a Friday. She wants to meet in the park by the council offices. The sky looks like snow gone to slush - a dirty wash over the sun, flat and unromantic. There are no shadows. In the park, people jog along the paths leaving no trace on the ground, the trees are just trees, the pavement just grey.

I wait on a wet bench and the cold seeps into my damaged hip, my knee, the back of my head where the stitches pull tight as the skin knits together. Behind closed eyes, my mother's signature has been burned onto my retinas. My dad's lies. The dates on the envelopes spread over weeks, months after she left. No wonder he wants to die. Then he can leave all his confessions in a neat little letter of his own. Like my mother. Like Lydia.

And there's the difference. Alex had his letter and he was going to do something about it. I finally reach my pot of gold and I put it back where I found it. I've spent so many years burying her inside soft, glutinous guilt, fabricating solutions and justifications that would explain thirty-five years of silence, I can't risk finding out that she just didn't want me. Alex watched his mother die, internalising it into night terrors - cold, tormented feet kicking me awake whenever he crawled into my bed. Fighting something, or trying to get away, but always clinging, hanging on my pyjama sleeves for dear life. Sometimes I'd kick him back. His mother was dying and I'd kick him out of the bed onto the floor where he'd thrash until the chilled air woke him with a whimper.

When Lydia was ill, our job was to stay quiet in the house and help with the housework. When she moved into the hospital the same rules applied: be quiet, clean and tidy. Smile. Don't talk too much.

Alex was ten when she died. Her absence trapped him like a rat in a box, running a loop of mad, frantic terror; wound so tight that when it gets free all it can do is go straight for your face. I can barely remember him before.

The sun dips below the terraced houses at the edge of the park. There's a police depot on the west side. A high slanted chain-link fence guards a fleet of police cars parked in neat, toyish lines. Alex would have climbed it, just to say he'd been inside. He was the friend I wished I'd had. Before I went off to uni he'd creep in after his curfew and sit on the floor next to my bed, swaying with adrenaline and whatever cocktail of drugs and alcohol he had in his belly. He'd tell me all the things he and Jamie had done: exploring the derelict petrol station, climbing up the high rise fire escapes and getting drunk on the roof, chasing girls into the churchyard and getting groped for their trouble. "You should've been there," he would whisper breathlessly.

And I would roll my eyes at him. I would make him feel stupid. I would make him hate me. He was my Frankenstein's monster.

I can't wait for Sarah. I haul myself off the bench, stiff and limping worse than ever, down towards the bleeding sunset sky, towards the fence that I'm going to fucking climb because it's there and it's staring at me and it's what I should have done years ago with my little shit of a brother.

#

My feet are too big to fit safely into the diamond holes of the wire fence. My hands grip onto the chains like determined claws, but halfway up my hip starts to throb, and I realise my muscles, atrophied by laziness, will be tired out before I reach the top of the fence.

"Matt?"

I look down and almost slip. Sarah watches me from the darkness of the park. I can't see her face clearly but I see now she's far too young, too likely to pity me and think it's love.

"What are you doing? Get down!" She adds a laugh but it's not genuine.

I ignore her, haul myself up over the swaying fence top, legs dangling free for a moment, twelve feet off the ground.

"Fucking hell, be careful."

"Shhhhhh," I hiss back, craning over my shoulder into the floodlit depot but there's no-one there. I imagine letting go, dropping down to the concrete, hearing my ankles crack on impact. I take the descent too fast, arms screeching with my weight, leaping down in an ungainly abseil, a few feet at a time. The wire shakes and rattles, far too loud, and my skin flushes with low-standard pride.

"Seriously, Matt, what are you doing?" Sarah whispers, pressing herself up against the other side of the fence.

When I reach the ground it feels as if it is swaying. "I have no idea," I tell her. She beckons me over and draws breath over her teeth when she sees my bruised face.

"Poor baby."

Maybe she's not too young. Maybe I'm not too old. I just climbed a fucking fence, didn't I?

For a second, Sarah looks like she wants to kiss me. Then her eyes flick to something behind me and a woman's voice yells, "Oi!"

A policewoman crosses the car park at a run and Sarah yelps. I jump at the fence and start to climb, scared clumsiness making it twice as difficult this time. The policewoman reaches me in slow motion and grabs the back of my jeans, jerking me backwards and off the fence. I land on her legs and she grunts. I am too sleep-deprived to operate on anything but adrenaline and I twist around to pin her flat against the ground.

Sarah mutters "oh shit" over and over in an endless stream of ineffectual anxiety.

The policewoman's eyes give away a moment of uncertainty before her training surges to the surface with indignant embarrassment. Her knee shoots up into my nuts and she shoves me sideways, reversing our positions and kneeling on my chest, grinding my wrists into gravel as she holds my arms down.

"What do you think you're doing?" the policewoman barks, a blush sweeping from the bridge of her nose to the tips of her ears.

"Arrest me, please," I say. I had hoped it would have sounded more forceful than it did. I probably should have left off the 'please'.

She wasn't expecting that. "Why? What have you done, besides trespassing and being an idiot?"

"For murder," I say. "Or manslaughter at least."

She doesn't move but her fingers dig into my forearms.

"Are you serious?"

I nod. We are speaking too quietly for Sarah to hear, even with her face pressed against the fence.

The policewoman shifts on my chest, knees pushing a little closer to my throat. "If you want me to arrest you, then you're going to cooperate when I let you up, alright? You're going to walk nicely with me into the station so I can ask you some questions. Right?"

"I promise."

"Okay?"

"Okay."

"Let's go then."

Sarah starts shouting after us but I don't bother to look back.

Chapter Twenty-Two

I listen to the gentle breathing that drifts down the phone line for several minutes before I realise it is my own.

"Hello?"

There are cracks in my voice that weren't there a few years ago, a few months ago. I am pleading but nobody's listening.

"No answer?" the receptionist asks, taking the receiver out of my hands.

She had to dial Matthew's number for me because I couldn't work out the keypad, even though of course I know how to use a bloody goddamned stupid phone. Except the numbers keep changing, and the tones make discordant music, and there was someone down the line talking to me but it wasn't my son. Or not the right one. I can't remember which one I was trying to call.

I need to talk to Alex. The doorways have gone quiet. My voice is back, temporarily. The pressure in my head clamps tighter, squeezing me out of existence. I need to talk to Matthew. There's something I need to tell him. Something I need to ask. Something about Alex.

I push myself away from the receptionist desk - a badly orchestrated series of manoeuvres that results in a tottering stumble into the opposite wall. She moves to help but I growl at her, causing the bloodhounds at her feet to raise their heads.

"Where's Angela?" I demand.

The receptionist tilts her face away and flares her nostrils as if she is a posturing bird. "You saw her this morning, Peter."

"I know I did. Where is she now?"

She smiles slowly and returns to her all-knowing book of schedules, shift patterns and emergency contact numbers. "Angelaaaah," she drawls, licking a finger and flicking over a page. "She'll be pretty busy with dinner until six-thirty, Peter," she explains with fake regret. "And then she'll be going home. I can page her if you waaaant… " Her whining vowels imply that I would be incomprehensibly selfish to insist on such a thing. Not that I want to bother her anyway. I don't want to see her cry again.

"Matthew?" I ask.

She sighs and that's always a bad sign. "Peter. He's been and gone."

I want my son. I can't wait until next week. I try to nod, clench back tears. "Yes, of course."

"I can call him again for you if you like."

"No, no." Then, quietly, tentatively: "Alex?" It's worth a try.

Her eyes squint with pity. "I'm sorry, Peter."

Back to my room then. Perhaps Matthew will be waiting there. Maybe he's been there all along, wondering where I've got to.

"Ah, finally!" The receptionist exclaims, rolling her eyes at something behind me through the double doors that are ever so slightly too heavy for the average old person to push their way through without assistance; a clever security measure disguised as an open invitation to leave at any time. The country roads stretch for miles in every direction with no bus service and no pavements. A mid-Sussex Gulag. Nowhere to run, not that any of us can run any more.

A hearse pulls into the car park and two funeral directors unhurriedly climb out. I shuffle faster. I don't want to witness their jovial exchange with the receptionist. I don't want them to eye me over, nodding politely, marking me down as an inevitable client - visions of death in satin-lined jackets.

I tense for verbal abuse as I pass Ingrid's half-closed door, for a screeching "Hey, Mr Solemn!" but there is nothing. Not even a cough. I push her door fully open and my guts make origami folds inside me. Her bed is fully reclined. Her face is grey and still. The rasping white noise that has served as her breathing for the last few weeks is oddly absent. My throat contracts behind my Adam's apple, unsure whether I am trying to swallow, take in breath, or make noise. A singular low note of meditation escapes it.

Yesterday's crossword lies on her bedside table, annotated and smudged by unsteady fingers. Her hands have clawed themselves into fists. Her drip no longer drips, has been disconnected from her cannula, tubes and leads neatly coiled and hung from the hook. Her catheter is gone, her sheets smoothed around her body, tucked in tight. Night night, Ingrid, sleep well, sleep long, forever.

I drop into a slow, creaky crouch, like an elderly frog, holding onto the edge of her bed for fear of drowning. The sheets are cold. She was not a small woman but her body appears to have shrunk, devoid of its spirit, its brashness. The only sound in the room is the ticking of wood panelled walls, tortured by central heating.

"Excuse me, Sir." A warm hand clamps under my armpit. One of the funeral directors gets down on one knee next to me. "Need a hand getting up?"

I do, but I don't want one. He pulls me to my feet anyway.

"What are you doing in here?" The receptionist barks shrilly, like her bloodhounds.

"When did she go?" I ask.

"This morning," she says, with only a little softening of her voice.

There's nothing really more to say. I shake my arm to dislodge the grip of the funeral director who peers into my face to see if there are tears. I smile and turn, swiping the audio book box set of *The Lord of the Rings* from her dresser on my way.

I burst through the swinging kitchen doors like a cowboy into a saloon, though with considerably less balance. The staff startle but no-one steps forward to take the responsibility of removing me. A tall porter with bad skin grimaces and hurries towards the side door when I catch his eye. "Alex!" I call after him, following at my own pace, knocking aside the half-hearted attempts to stop me.

There is moisture in the air outside that promises rain within the next half an hour but I have nowhere to go, no appointments to keep, no plans to be ruined by the weather. Alex waits, defeated, by the back wall. I thrust the box set into his hands.

"What's this?" he says.

"For you. Payment. I need some more."

The boy stares incredulously. "They confiscated it, mate. They thought one of your kids brought it in. Thank fuck. Look. You can't talk to me anymore, I don't want to get fired for this."

My kids. My baby boy. Alex tries to pass the box back to me but I hold his hands still. "Why don't you visit me?"

He pauses. "I don't know you, mate. Sorry."

Confusion feels like drunkenness. He's right but I can't work out how. "You... But you visited Ingrid."

"Not really. It's just a bit of weed."

"She died," I say, and still the tears don't come.

He falters. "Sorry," the boy says. "She was cool."

"She was."

Cool like Lydia. Women who said exactly what was on their minds, regardless of who they were speaking to; who frightened me as much as they amused me. Women who died as if they'd been turned inside out, turned into a reversal of their living selves: weak and terrified and uncertain. Unwomaned. Terrordied.

My last conversation with Ingrid had been painful and sporadic:

"I should have had children," she'd said. "Some nice, clean girls. No, maybe not girls. Boys have that mumsy attachment that make them feel guilty enough to look after you to the bitter end. Haven't you seen? The men visit more than the women. Don't roll their eyes quite so much. You're lucky you've got boys."

I sat at her bedside, knuckling pins and needles out of my legs.

"Oh I've got friends, but who wants to come all the way out here? No bus, too expensive for a taxi. I don't blame them."

I folded my legs under the chair, folded my hands in my lap, folded my lips into well-worn grooves and listened to her choke on her own breath. "Your sister?"

"Yvonne? She'd be too busy, I think. She's got one of those posh phones now - does everything. Has all her appointments in it and a camera and a radio. But she'll be busy. I don't want to bother her. Had enough of those calls myself, pain in the bloody arse. I don't want to be a boil on the arse of life, if that's the last thing I can be."

There were tears in her voice, and fear, even though her eyes stayed fierce. "Nope. I'll leave all that crap to the home. I hope I shit myself while they're cleaning me up. Dead bodies do that, you know. All our sins come out in the end, the body lets it all go, relaxes for once. You know, being so uptight makes you hold it all in, Peter, you should think about that, think about not being so constipated all the time. Are you listening to me?"

"Yes, Ingrid."

"Have a good old poo."

"Okay."

"Don't let them dress me like a trussed up turkey with my hair all curled, covered in lipstick, will you? I don't want to look like one of those drag women. Men. You know. No-one would recognise me."

"I'll try."

"Are you coming to the funeral? Please do, I'd love you to be there, if they let you out. Get your girl to take you. Your little Angela. Sweet girl."

I nodded slowly.

"I'd feel better if you were there. I won't be so nervous. Nerve-wracking, lying up there in front of all those people, talking about me, looking at me, feeling sorry for me."

I won't be there, I knew, silently.

"They wouldn't even let me mow my own bloody lawn, Peter! Next door's Freya nagged and nagged that her husband could do it. Well, I said, he *could* do it, I said, but I know the contours of the ground... "

#

The wind throws spatters of rain into my face, stinging my eyes, which still refuse to cry for my only friend. A young man stands beside me, smoking, and he looks something like Alex.

"Where is he?" I ask, but he doesn't know. "Where's Alex?" I ask, but he doesn't know who I mean.

I look for something that will hurt. The brittle bones of my fist click when they make contact with my temple. I shake my head and try again, the other arm this time, battering my stump against my forehead. I pull at my remaining hair, ripping it out at the roots. Greasy tufts poke through the gaps in my fingers. I punch again at my crown, finding a rhythm, using the pointiest part of my knuckles to cause the most pain.

"Dude... " the boy says. "Stop it. What are you doing?"

He grabs my forearms and holds them still. He is strong and I am old. I throw my head back against the pebble-dashed wall instead.

"Stop it! It's okay," he says, in a soft voice that is strangely reassuring. He gently releases my arms. "You want Alex?"

I nod vehemently. And now the crying begins.

"Come with me. He's waiting in your room. Let's go back to your room."

He wraps an arm awkwardly around my shoulders and guides me out of the rain, into the stinking steam of the kitchen where they are cooking spaghetti for dinner.

Chapter Twenty-Three

"Look, Sir," the policewoman says, "I still don't see how your brother's death was your fault."

Why is she calling me Sir? Her tired sarcasm is beginning to grate. I don't know how else to tell it.

"I hated him and he died." So many times I'd told him the same thing: I hate you and I want you to die. Fuck off and die. Just go and die in a hole. Because he was annoying and a bully and my dad loved him more than me. What kind of person thinks that about their own brother?

The sergeant blinks a few times, stifles a yawn. "He tried to hit you. He was drunk. You moved out of the way. He fell." She glances down to her notes, not that she needs to, "Is that all correct?"

I nod. Shake my head. It's not that simple. "It's not that simple," I say.

"You pushed him then?"

"No."

"You deliberately lured him to a position where he'd hit his head?"

"No, but - "

"You bashed your voodoo doll against the wall the night before?"

I start to answer 'no' before I realise it wasn't a valid question. Her eyes widen with the realisation that she said

209

that out loud.

"Sorry. I'm sorry, it's been a really long day, Mr Landrow." She gestures at my scabby face. "Looks like you've had a rough time of it too. I think you should go home and think about this overnight."

She finishes up the paperwork and asks me to fill in my details. I read back the address I've written twice before I realise why it's wrong - it's the house I grew up in, conjured up by my confession. I don't amend it.

She stands. I don't. She sighs. "Look. Your statement's down. I can see if I can get a copy of the coroner's report for your half-brother if you think it might help. But I would really recommend that you get some rest, go see your GP, and find some help." She tries a smile. "We'll call you if we find anything we can charge you with. Please stop beating yourself up and take your girlfriend home."

She got the half-brother bit right. Probably the first person in months to do so. I almost go to correct her. I have to say something to fill the gap: "She's not my girlfriend."

I can see the silhouette of Sarah's messy ponytail through the safety glass set into the door. She's been sitting in the waiting room this whole time. I don't want to go home with her. I don't want to go home.

"I used to tease him that he had long eyelashes," I blurt out.

"What?"

"Alex. Cow eyelashes. Girl's eyelashes. I convinced him to cut them. He cut his eyelashes off because of me. It was meant to be just a trim but he went too far. Do you know how long it takes to grow eyelashes? How weird you look without them?"

"No," she replies.

"A long time. And weird."

The sergeant holds her arm out towards the door, "Well. Shall we?"

I can't move. She's going to have to physically pick me up if she wants me to leave. "I didn't pass on the message that

210

Angie had got into university because I didn't want her to leave me alone with *them*."

"Right."

They called her back. It was fine. But I left her stressing about whether she'd got in or not for a whole week. "She was the peacemaker. Lydia was dead and it would have been just us three left. Alex, Dad and me."

"I see."

"I persuaded Jenna Rowbray to drink half a bottle of vodka so I could get her drunk enough to… I don't know… do something, anything with me. But she snogged Kieran Hadley instead. Then when she puked all over herself I called her mum to pick her up and told her Jenna had bought us the vodka.

"I stole a Mars bar from the corner shop every Friday after school for a whole year. I accidentally snapped Angie's dreamcatcher thing she'd made on a school trip and blamed Alex. I smoked all of Lydia's secret stash of fags and she never asked who did it. I never told Nana Alice that I loved her."

I never told Nana Alice that I loved her. Not once. I'd roll my eyes when she hugged me, squirm out of the way, grunt responses like a stupid little teenager, when she was the only one to really, genuinely mother me.

My voice grows higher and higher and is laden with squeaks - the boulder in my throat making it difficult for sound to squeeze past it. Maybe it's throat cancer. I swallow and it hurts. The policewoman nods absently and stares at the floor.

"I only visit my dad because I have to. I hate it. I hate that place. I feel like I'm going to have a panic attack when I pull into the drive. I don't want to talk to him, I don't care if he's there or not. When he dies it will be a weight off my shoulders and that's a fucking awful thing to say, isn't it? I'm just waiting for him to die because it's really inconvenient and annoying for me to have to visit him every single fucking week, visit a Dad that doesn't give a shit about me, has never been proud - never once looked at me and been proud of me. I'm a horrible person."

I'm trying to think of more confessions and trying not to cry at the same time. "I told Alex he had cow eyes."

She sits on the edge of the desk, her whole body sinking into a silent sigh. "I can see that you're feeling a lot of guilt," she says, very quietly. "But you don't seem like a bad person to me. I think you should talk to someone professional, or someone close to you, about all of this."

I glance out the door again. "Can't you put me in a cell, just for tonight?"

Another grimace of pity. "No."

I remember what's in my pocket and lay Dad's confiscated bag of weed on the table between us.

"Please?" I bargain.

"Really?" The sergeant almost laughs but stops herself. She slides the drugs over to her side and shakes her head. "You're not getting in a cell for that."

"It's not mine, anyway," I tell her, and an uninvited grin stamps itself onto my mouth. "It's my fucking dad's."

She licks her lips, chews the bottom one, lets it slide free of her teeth and ping out again. "Is there no-one you can talk to about all of this?"

I sniff, excuse myself, say "Sabine?" Like she would know who that is, like she could magically make her appear, make Sarah disappear, make everything go away.

The sergeant says she'll tell Sarah to go if I promise not to drive home. She leaves me in a little back office with some tissues and a polystyrene cup of thin tea and I cry for a bit, while she goes and dumps my non-girlfriend-supervisor for me.

When the policewoman returns she makes me promise again – no driving – and I say of course not. I don't say what I really think which is that if I got on a bus right now I think I'll start punching people. She shakes my hand and looks sorry. I limp out of the station and along the dark path through the park to my car.

"What was that all about?"

Sarah sits on the back bumper with a six pack of beer in

her lap. The sun is gone, faded behind cardboard cut-outs of suburbia. It's been raining but I can't feel the cold and I couldn't care less. I feel drunk, though I'm not, so I reckon I should probably tie up the sensation with some hard proof and take the drink Sarah offers me.

She points with her own beer back towards the police station. "Did they charge you with anything?"

"No. Told me to get my head checked."

"Good plan."

"Should probably do that, yeah."

I drink. She drinks. And I say a silent toast for my confessions.

Sarah says, "Are you going to go completely mental or is this just a little breakdown?"

"I don't know."

The beer is grainy and pissy but it quells the feeling of looseness that has been making me trip over my feet. The warmth nestles into my chest and gets sucked through the appropriate channels under my skin, to spread to my groin and my throat and my hands. It starts to rain again but I'm sweating and it's a relief.

"Do you want me to drop you home?" I ask her. It's probably too late for an apology.

"No," she says, dumping the rest of the beers into my arms and turning back towards the park. "Just... Sort yourself out before you come back to work. If you're coming back. And if you ever feel better, you can ask me out properly."

#

I park outside my house, the one on the police form, the one we grew up in, Alex and Angela and me. And Dad, alone with three kids, in way over his head.

The house looks too small to have contained us all: a martyr, a runaway, a tyrant, a demon and the rest. They've double glazed the windows and put on a porch. They've got

213

venetian blinds and a Honda Civic.

My glovebox rings. I leave it shut, standing like a stalker on the grass verge, watching for lights to go on, for someone to come out and shout at me.

"Matthew?"

A thin, doddery man pauses halfway up the path next door dragging a wheelie bin behind him, gripping onto the handle as if it's the only think keeping him upright. "Matthew? Matt?"

Shit, is he still living there? "Graham?"

He beckons me over, laughing breathlessly at something that really isn't funny.

"I thought it was you," he says, patting me awkwardly on the arms, then the shoulders, almost instigating a hug but restraining himself to a palm on my cheek - apparently still unconvinced that I'm real. I am on my second beer and my concussion is loving it. When he stops touching me I am left swaying.

"Matt. It's been… It's good to see you. What happened to your head? Do you want to come in for a bit?"

I shrug. I think I might start crying again. The rain is getting heavier and the cold has started to seep through my numbness. "I brought some beer," I say, and follow him up the path.

Chapter Twenty-Four

There must have been some sort of photographic explosion. Pictures carpet the floor of my room - a spectrum of sepia and greyscale, the orange tinge of the seventies and the unreal brightness of digital image. My parents and my parents' parents sit stiffly with uneasy smiles - babies trussed up in ruffled collars and hard leather shoes, young women in shift dresses and gloves. Men in uniform, men in lines like sports teams; front row down on one knee, the next with fists in laps, the last standing awkwardly behind. I find one of my father and his peers. My aunt has neatly marked a date of death for each face on the reverse.

There are pictures of Lydia's ancestors too, people I never knew, and I will never now know their names or deeds and misdeeds. Uncontrollably curly hair stands out from heads down the generations: cherubs in infancy, a Pears' soap advert in youth, tempered styling in adulthood.

Most of Heather's photos are gone. I couldn't look at them. I found a way to ignore the one that sat, unageing, on the mantelpiece, even when I was facing it, even when I dusted the very wood beneath it. It was easier to be widowed. There's peace in a lover being dead and cold, to watch their coffin slide into the furnace, to know you will never touch them again, to have to be satisfied with the memories you still hold onto and the warming remnants of the ones you don't. Losing

Heather left behind the gut-yanking nausea of realising the hob has been left burning, of getting onto a plane without your luggage, of losing grip on a child's hand in a crowd.

I drag the rest of the albums down from the top of the wardrobe and start to pull pictures out of their little crackled sheaths. The floor is covered in faces. I sit amongst them and they watch soundlessly as I fall apart. The children are here in various stages of youth and happiness. Little protruding bellies and chubby wrists, lengthening limbs, braces on teeth, growing out fringes and the odd scraped knee. Posing with bikes, outside tents, next to snowmen, up trees, in sacks in races, trying to avoid the camera's eye with adolescent rage. And little Clare, surrounded by toys – my favourite picture of them all – a Christmas day. Angela tired and serene, Clare barely six months, sitting wobbly in a circle of cushions, Alex offering her a stuffed panda, Matthew watching behind with proud affection in his eyes.

Blood spatters across Matthew's face. I blink. Another drip explodes in a blossom of crimson on the glossy surface of the picture. Blink. Think. I check beneath my nose but I can't feel my fingers. My hand is missing. Blood dribbles down my forearm. It doesn't hurt but it won't stop bleeding and I should be worried, shouldn't I?

I peel a photo of Lydia's father off the carpet and crumple it around my wrist as a rudimentary bandage. I drop to my knees and crawl through the faces and holidays and family gatherings to find my missing hand. It's got to be here somewhere. It can't have got far.

#

Ding dong merrily on high, in heaven my wife is cursing.

Ding dong goes the porter's page, they're coming to stop me singing.

Glooooooooooooooooooooooooooooooria!

My mystic in exchange, please?

Glooooooooooooooooooooooooooooria...

"Peter. Stop, please."

"What's wrong with Christmas carols?"

"Just stop, Peter."

"Bugger it."

"Peter."

"WHAT?" I roar.

I couldn't escape through the doorway if I tried. It glows angrily but two nurses and a porter wearing a Father Christmas hat block my way out of the bedroom. I am floating on an ocean of false smiles and I have lost something important.

"Where the hell is Gloria when you need her?"

"Gloria? You mean Angela?"

"No, I mean Gloria."

"Who's Gloria?"

"Never mind, she's probably dead now."

"Angela's in a meeting - "

"Are you deaf? I want Gloria!"

"Please don't shout, Peter."

"I'll shout if I bloody well want to." I straighten up and my head meets the overhanging corner of the chest of drawers. The nurses hiss in a communal wincing breath. The porter takes a step forward but I sweep my hand through the photographs like kicking up autumn leaves and a flurry of pictures rains down between us. Alice and Matthew sitting on a pair of swings. Lydia heavily pregnant, shading her eyes from the sun. Angela sitting on my lap, pretending to drive the car. Alex swaddled up tight in a Moses basket. My eyes are full of water. "Gloria can talk to the dead," I tell his image. "She talked to you."

The staff exchange glances. "Peter, let us tidy all this up," a nurse says softly. The porter pulls the Christmas hat from his head and picks at the white woolly bobble.

Alex and Matthew made up a game: goldfish in a bowl. They'd flap their fins and run circles round the living room, chanting, "One, two, three, blip!" changing direction as their memories reset. They'd feign interest in a piece of furniture, a pattern on the carpet, a juice cup, then lose their minds after a count of three and see the world anew again.

I close my eyes and count to three but the memory doesn't disappear. The porter pulls me to my feet and rests me down in the armchair. One of the nurses stacks the photographs into a box. My knees are scuffed and sore from the carpet, my wrist throbs but is not bleeding. It was never bleeding. The blotches of blood I'd seen soaking into the carpet are gone. I pull back my sleeve to find my stump as it always was: pinched and sealed, slightly pinker than the rest of my arm. But I can still smell the iron tinge of blood, feel the slick greasiness on my skin, the deep ache where canine teeth tore through flesh.

I spread my remaining hand flat on my knee, palm facing upwards. Gloria said no two hands are the same, that the lines differ from left to right. The dominant takes on life's genuine path while the other shows the potential you are born with. I am left with the left, full of hypotheticals. Lifeline: longer than I desired, fragmented along its entirety. Loveline: forking and curved, intersecting the lifeline at its tip. Feather-light lines on the side of my hand beneath the little finger: three little lives I inherited as my own.

I can hear the nurses discussing me in low tones, wisps of whispers that fall into my ears. They think my off switch has been flicked. "God, it's heartbreaking, really."

"Why doesn't Angela tell him?"

"She has, he doesn't remember."

"She should tell him the truth."

"Would you? Again and again?"

"I just can't believe he doesn't know."

It is as if I am lying in the wreck of a car, listening to the battered radio spew out travel reports about how my twisted body is holding up the evening commute by so many miles of gridlocked traffic. I am paralysed by the sight of my hand. How much would the other have diverged in the mapping of my existence? What might have been and what was. What does a missing hand signify? What else am I missing? I swallow down thick mucus with a thud and realise it's the other way around: what did I never have in the first place?

Chapter Twenty-Five — Matthew

Third beer. Concussion is winning. Graham is skinny and shrunken and unfamiliar. He watches me across the kitchen worktop until I break the anti-social spell. "My brother died," I say. I can say it now, without feeling like I've been kicked in the nuts.

He nods. "I heard. I'm so sorry."

Graham's kitchen is a mirror image of how ours used to be, back to front, but the same orange-lacquer on the cabinet fronts, the same fake marble lino. Memories of my childhood home slide into place, overlaid with someone else's possessions. "My brother died." This time it makes me cry. I've cried more this afternoon than I've done since I was a whining nine-year-old being bullied by my five-year-old brother.

Graham pats the worktop in a gentle rhythm and it's strangely soothing. When it becomes evident I'm not going to stop sniffling he turns to stuff a new liner into the bin and washes his hands, slow and thorough, staring out into the darkness of the garden. He's probably a decade younger than my dad, but looks as if he would snap if you high-fived him. He takes down a couple of tumblers from a cupboard and polishes them with a tea towel before clinking them together and nodding at the beer.

"Enough left for a toast?" he says.

I scrub my wet face on my wet sleeve. "What for?"

He shrugs. "To Alex."

I slide the remaining cans over the counter. Let's be civilised about this. Why the fuck not?

Graham sips the cheap beer, grimaces, and puts his glass down purposefully. "I heard about Peter." Then: "Your dad," like I wouldn't know who he meant.

"What about him?"

"That he's losing it."

I nod. That's about it.

We drink. It's comfortably uncomfortable, somehow. There are no questions of what I am doing with my life, about Angela or Clare or any details of my brother's death or why I had been standing outside his house. He wipes away something invisible on the counter and exhales more air than could possibly be in his lungs with one long whistling stream.

"Peter did the same as you a few years ago," he gestured to my left, to the front door. "Staring up at his old house, drinking on the curb. I didn't invite him in though." Graham shakes his head as if he's forgotten what he meant to say. "I should have moved. I should have left. But… " he swept his arms loosely around the dark kitchen. "This is home."

I don't know what he means. Was living next to us so awful? "Dad wasn't a very good neighbour," I try a smile. "Don't take it personally. He hates everyone." But that's not quite true. He reserved a special flavour of loathing for some people. The first time I heard Dad swear was about Graham. "That bastard next door." It became an epithet - forged so long before my comprehension that I never really questioned it, though it seemed at odds with how Graham was to me and the other kids. He'd looked after us a few times after Lydia went into hospital. He had no children of his own but he brought a box of Lego and an Atari down from the attic and we gawped and punched the air with hissing yeses before ignoring him completely for the rest of the evening. Contended and ungrateful. He tried to send us home with the toys but my Dad left them on his doorstep and muttered about pity and charity and not accepting anything from that bastard next door.

"He had his reasons to be angry," Graham says. I don't get it. The alcohol flares up some suppressed ember of hatred and I can't stop shaking my head. My dad has been a monolith of fear and resentment and uncertainty my whole life and I haven't stopped trying to gain his approval even though it should mean nothing. He doesn't deserve to approve of me.

"Why should he be allowed to be such an arsehole when we all have to try to be decent people? Why is he the exception?" I go to pour out the rest of my can but it's empty. Graham slides his glass into my hand.

"I thought maybe he'd died when I saw you out there," he mutters. Chance would be a fine fucking thing. The words settle behind my tongue, unsaid, but I fail to feel any guilt. Instead I say, "Not yet."

"Did you ever…?" Graham stops, falters, twists his face around the question and finishes with a grimace. "Ever hear from your mother? Ever find out what happened to her?"

The question is a slap on drunken cheeks. "No." But Dad did. My voice resolves into an edge. "Why?"

Graham tries not to look at me but can't help taking little nibbling glances while he waits for me to stop staring threateningly back. "I just wondered. It was all just so sad," he says. There are no tears from him but I can tell they're there, behind puckered old eyelids and circular glasses and I can't tell why my mum's disappearance can still make him want to cry, when all I have is fury.

"You knew her, you tell me why she left," I hear myself say - words I've wanted to scream in my father's face, a question I've not asked since I was a child.

Graham bares his teeth in an odd, restrained expression - holding back, holding in, holding onto something. "Your father knows, I'm sure."

"You think? He can't even remember that Alex is dead."

"Matthew. I'm almost as old as he is and there are plenty

222

of things I've forgotten. Your mother - she's not one of them. Your father can't have forgotten either."

I was wrong, he looks older than my dad. Sadder. Sorrier. Knocked down and reversed over again. I down the rest of my drink. He smiles a pathetic smile at me and I feel like I owe him something. "She sent him letters," I say, and his eyes snap up to drill into mine.

"What did you say?" he whispers.

"I found a stack of them, in Dad's room." Before he asks the inevitable, I tell him: "I don't know what they said. But it means he's lied to me my whole fucking life."

There is water in his eyes now. His chin trembles and saliva stretches between his lips as he lets out a strangled sort of cry. He reaches across the counter to hold my hands and his skin is warmer than I think it's going to be. Not a zombie. Softer. Infinitely more human in the last few minutes than my Dad has been in years.

"Matthew, I'm sorry," he says, taking two steps around the counter and sliding his arms around my neck. "I'm so sorry." He pulls me into his chest with more strength than he should possess, and he is crying the way I should be able to about Alex. About my mother. About my dying, demented dad. I hug him back and he smells like all the things that were lost when Dad moved into the home.

\#

I am as drunk as I am tired and I shouldn't be driving. I take the backstreets, stay below twenty and lean into the windscreen as though it might help my eyes to focus. There is a plastic bag on the passenger seat that makes me cry every time it catches my peripheral vision. Inside the bag is a collection of envelopes. Inside the envelopes are pictures. And inside the photos are images of me as a baby, as a toddler, as a preschooler. All the ones missing from Dad's albums. Ones he threw away. Tried to burn. Pictures Graham found on the street, apparently, and squirrelled away in place of a family of his own. He pressed the bag into my chest when I left.

"I meant to write to you when you moved out," he said quietly, as if worried that my Dad would still be able to hear him. "I thought you might want them." He didn't finish his thought – explain why he never followed through – and I didn't ask.

#

I have thirty-six missed calls. For about a mile I was convinced the car was going to explode until I realised it wasn't the engine rattling but an angry phone locked in a glovebox. Clare, Sarah, Angela, Sabine, the nursing home and round and round again, backed up with answerphone messages that I don't listen to and texts that I don't look at.

If the drive sobered me at all, the cold walk to my flat sends a fresh flow of heaviness into my blood. I need to sleep and forget everything.

A couple stand arguing outside the entrance to my block of flats but instead of ignoring me and carrying on as I weave around the corner, they both stop mid-sentence and take an aggressively synchronised step towards me. It's fine, they can mug me, beat me, whatever. I don't care anymore.

"Matt?" the man says.

"Where have you been?" the woman says.

I know their voices, I don't need to look out from under my hood to see their faces.

"Fuck off," I reply.

Sabine shoves her palms into my shoulders. "Matt, where the fuck have you been?"

"We've been trying to call," Jamie says. He doesn't shove me but his stance tells me he wants to.

"Fuck. Off."

I try to push past them to the stairs but Sabine pulls at my coat and Jamie blocks my way. "Have you heard from Clare?"

Sabine asks.

"She's not answering her phone either," Jamie says.

"Matt?"

"Have you seen her?"

"Not since this morning," I say, watching them both shrink a few inches. My hands are still in my pockets and my fingers close around my phone in reflexive memory. "She's been calling me though… "

"For fuck's sake, Matt!" Jamie's voice is hoarse and I can't collate the reasons for urgency together with my soft, diluted brain.

"Call her back," Sabine demands.

"Why do you care where my niece is?" I ask them both, emphasising the possession.

Jamie sort of collapses forwards with his elbows against the wall, his hands clawing at his face. "She came over to mine this morning and we had a fight. She left and now she won't answer her phone."

"She fucking *what*?"

He avoids my eyes but I grab one of his hands and tear it away from his face. "Why was Clare at yours?"

Sabine pries the phone from my fist and presses redial on Clare's number.

Jamie doesn't reply but I still have him by the wrist and I smack him in the forehead with his own hand like we're at school again, chanting: *stop hitting yourself, stop hitting yourself.* "What the fuck is going on with you two?"

He sort of growls. I make him hit himself again. A few more times. He hunches back against the wall and for the first time in our lives I am the fucking alpha, but instead of feeling satisfied I am just exhausted.

Sabine pokes the screen of my phone angrily. "She's not picking up."

Jamie's hand isn't hitting hard enough. I lift my free fist and he slides down a few inches. "It's mine," he says. "The baby's mine."

Sabine's mouth freezes half open.

"Jesus," I say. "That's just fucking perfect."

"She's nineteen!" Sabine shouts at him, then turns on me, gesturing viciously with my phone, "Did you know she was pregnant?"

I nod. Jamie gives me a loathing look. I send him one back. "I've been looking after her. What the fuck have you been doing? Punching random old men in the face. Getting teenagers pregnant. What the *fuck*, Jamie? When did it happen?"

He rubs at his forehead, readjusts his hair absent-mindedly. "I was starting my PhD. She was in her second year. It wasn't a one-off," he says quietly, then remembers to glare at me. "She didn't want to tell you because you hate me."

"Yeah, I do," It's too late for guilt trips. "What did you fight about? Where did she go?"

He returns to the face clawing. "I said I was going to tell her mum about it. She went mental at me and stormed out. You need to get hold of her, see if she's okay. Please?"

Sabine strides towards me and thrusts my phone into my stomach and I enjoy Jamie's flinch as she passes him. "Listen to your messages," she says.

Chapter Twenty-Six

Whistler died today. I watched her fold in two from across the hall. For once the machines didn't beep.

Something has sprung a leak. Water seeps beneath my closed door with a head of dirty foam. The bubbles burst lazily as they reach the foot of my armchair, leaving white scum across my toes. Every so often the shingle turns over an empty mussel shell, a tiny crab fighting its way to the surface of the carpet, a faded old crisp packet. Outside my window, seagulls fight over scraps, beaks tipped with red, eyes wild and piercing.

She knocks on my door and I nod my acquiescence. She waits for the seventh wave to build, the largest in the pattern, before she gently pushes her way in. The water soaks me up to my knees and trickles down between my legs to pool in my crotch. A flurry of seaweed rushes in behind her – the kind made of smooth rubbery pustules with fronds like a Celtic tattoo – and it settles itself in eye-watering complexity on top of the already over-designed carpet.

"Morning, lover," Heather says. Her mouth is full of sand. She's never spoken to me like that before. I nod again. She's beautiful. I must have forgotten quite how beautiful she always was. She hears my thoughts and smiles, grit stuck between her teeth.

"I miss you," is my counter-offer.

"No, you don't," she says, laughing, but not amused, "you're confused."

A nurse passes my doorway but doesn't glance in. The taint of sewage hangs in the air; a pipe set too near the shore. I used to let the kids swim here.

"I still have your letters," I tell her, hoping they're safe from the seawater in their shoebox under the bed.

"Burn them," Heather says. She is the deity of wrath and I am afraid. "I don't want Matthew to see them."

"I've kept enough from him."

"They're dangerous, Peter. A letter killed your other son."

The wind picks up and the spray becomes tiny splinters of glass, flying sideways, embedding themselves deep into my skin. She takes a step forward. Seaweed capsules pop under her feet.

"Burn them," she orders.

"You blame me, don't you?" I say, and can't keep the aggression out of my voice, can't help the injustice making me turn a plum purple, holding my breath like a petulant child until she answers.

"You don't think I should?"

I splutter, spitting out empty exclamations of "Puh! Puh! Buh!" until I feel a rubber band snap in my head. Snowstorm static invades my vision and my face begins to melt.

Heather's vein-riddled hands reach up to her frozen, eternal face. Her skin has turned translucent from the fluid beneath. She blinks once, twice, then takes out her eyes – pops them clean out of their sockets – and holds out her hand to me. They lie moist and shining in her palm and I forget how to breathe and a seventh stroke runs its way down the right side of my body and urine runs down my right leg.

She leans forward and places her eyeballs in my hand.

"Try seeing things from my perspective," she says.

#

228

My brain starts shutting doors, closing up for the night - switching off appliances and lights and rolling down the shutters. My body shivers like a furious Jack Russell.

Heather sees her demand through. She sits on the bed and rolls me cigarette after cigarette using the browning letters she sent me thirty-something years ago. They burn faster than Rizla, taste like dirt and coal fires, make my eyes water until I can't tell if I'm weeping or bleeding. Her eyeballs rest in my lap, watching me smoke away the proof. I run out of tobacco the letter before last, toking down the word 'Heather' in one painful breath. And then she is gone.

I cough until I vomit - bloody and thick with mucus. I stumble through the seaweed to shut the door behind her, to seal the doorway for good, sobbing into the little plastic sign that tells me where to find my nearest fire exit. There is salt on my fingertips, grimy tidelines on the furniture, but the water has disappeared.

There's something in my pocket, in my fist. My palm spasms open and I feel paper wrinkle itself outwards again, like a time-lapse flower in bloom. I smooth out the final letter, tracing the indents of her pen, the confession I wished she'd never posted.

Through the door I can hear the nurses clattering around Mother Whistler as they disconnect her robot counterparts and I have to force myself not to charge out and stop them, from gathering the old skeleton up in my arms and singing her a lullaby. Poor Whistler. Poor Ingrid. Poor Alex.

The shoebox sits on the bed, malicious and innocuous. I'm certain I didn't put it there. It's only three paces away – only two medium steps to reach my little box of palpitations – but it takes at least twenty to get there. The shoebox is empty of paper but full of tablets.

The letter in my pocket is the last test. It holds all the answers to Matthew's incessant questions and Angela's do-gooder prodding and Alice's chirpy Christian mourning. The anger I've tended to all these years flames into guilt and tastes like chalk on my dry tongue.

I unfold the soft paper. Age has turned it to the texture of brushed cotton. I read the lines one more time and tear it into eight neat pieces along the well-folded edges. It dissolves in my mouth like sugar-paper. The pulp soothes my scorched throat as it goes down, pushing the lump of grief along with it. I manipulate Heather's eyeballs in my palm like Chinese meditation balls.

When I have swallowed down her dirty little secret I reach for the shoebox and its jumble of pills, to take my headache and my hallucinations and the stickiness of my palms far away.

Three will do it. I carry the box to the bathroom and drink from the tap until my stomach swells. I drop the eyeballs down the toilet but they refuse to flush. The pills in my hand are gone too, though I don't remember taking them. Never mind, there are plenty more.

Chapter Twenty-Seven　Matthew

Message one. Angela: "Matt, why didn't you wait for me at work this morning? I really need to talk to you about your dad. Did you find anything in his room? Call me back."

Message four. Clare: "You're absolutely right you're all bastards, you stupid bastard."

Message nine. Sabine: "I'm at your flat but I don't have a key anymore. Are you here? Are you ignoring me? Fucking hell, Matt."

Message sixteen. The Farm House: "Mr Landrow, we're calling about your father. Angela says she's been trying to get hold of you too but if you get this message please call the main number on - "

Message twenty-one. Clare crying.

Message twenty-five. Angela crying.

Message thirty-two. Jamie: "Matty. Please."

Message thirty-four. Angela: "Matthew. Sabine just called me about Clare, what the hell is going on? Matt, please, please, answer your phone."

Clare's number goes straight to answerphone, no matter how many times I yell at it.

My mobile slides up and down my lap on speakerphone as I drive into the rain and through the university campus, back to Angela's flat and Jamie's place, to Clare's friend Becca's. No-one's in. Angie isn't picking up her phone either. I can't go back to my flat. If Jamie's still there I'll put his head through the wall on purpose.

I get stuck in the one-way system on my second circle of the high street when Clare finally calls. I throw the steering wheel over to the left and almost get hit by a taxi as I pull into a bus stop.

"Clare? Where are you?"

I can't understand a fucking word she's saying through the choking and the screeching of her hysterics.

I've got used to the tiredness, the flashes of homicidal rage and insatiable hunger pretty easily – she wasn't much different before she'd got pregnant – but I've not seen her cry so much since she was two. Now she'll cry at adverts, at the prospect of an essay deadline, at the ending of a particularly emotional episode of EastEnders.

From the moment she showed me the secret little thing wrapped up in tissue, the positive pregnancy test, I was at her mercy. She begged me not to tell her mum. She wasn't even twelve weeks gone.

I tell her to breathe and the snorting and the sniffing eventually dies down.

"I'm okay, I'm okay. I just - " I catch, before she's off again. Then she hangs up.

I sit and wait, rubbing the lump on the back of my neck, pressing it until it hurts, knuckling my thighs until they bruise. Two minutes later she calls back.

"Where are you?" I shout at her. "We've been worrying out of our fucking minds."

I can actually hear her 'fuck you' expression down the line. "I started bleeding. I've been calling you all day, Matt."

"Oh my God, Clare - " and now I'm choking up, "I'm so sorry. Is the baby…? Are you okay? Where *are* you?"

"At the hospital. They just discharged me." Her voice falls back into squeaks and sniffs and she can't make sense anymore.

And? Did my niece just miscarry while I was getting

232

arrested and feeling sorry for my stupid fucking self?

"Clare, please, is everything okay?"

A huge shuddering breath and the longest moment of my life, then: "Yes, yeah, it's fine. They gave me a scan. Baby's there. Fuck, Matt, there was loads of blood. Where were you?"

Her last three words echo against my eardrum and drown out the irate beeping of the bus trying to pull in behind me. Clare's voice swamps every single stupid thing that I have packed inside my stupid head and grateful tears pour down my face. "I'm coming to get you. Wait there."

#

When Clare gets in the car we sit in the A&E drop-off bay staring at the dashboard when we should be hugging.

"You're really okay?" I ask her.

She nods, just once. Her face is red, blotched and drawn downwards as if she has gained a decade in an afternoon.

"What do you want to do?"

"Just go home."

"To your mum's?"

"No!"

"Clare, she's not going to be angry. She'll want to look after you."

"She fucking hates me right now." Clare's usual fury has dissipated into resignation. She really believes Angela wouldn't care. Did she get that from me? Clare winds a tissue around her index finger and stares at the smokers huddled around the hospital entrance. "She'll say I'm just making the same mistakes she did, like her mum did."

"Shit," I say.

She looks sideways at me. "On your birthday, I told her I was going to drop out of uni. She went mental - well, you probably heard. Said how she'd had to work twice as hard after I was born. Like, basically, she shouldn't have had me. She was too young."

233

A whining sob compresses Clare's voice into her throat. "How could I fucking tell her after all of that?"

And then she's crying again and the only thing I can think to do is lay my hand on her belly. It takes a moment for the warmth of my palms to travel through her t-shirt and she stops mid-sob. There's no little bump yet but her stomach is rigid and hot under my hand. Her breathing slows, but not because she's winding up her energy to knock me out – I've never dared to touch her in any other way than awkward patting or playful headlocks for several years now – because I look up and she's smiling crookedly.

"But this little thing is okay? That's what matters. Not your mum."

Clare gives an involuntary, shaky inhalation as her tears leave her body. She taps my hands away and starts brushing tissue flecks off her jeans. She'll be a wonderful, harsh, hilarious, terrifying, loving mother.

And we are not going to become our parents.

I start the car, swing it out of the car park and start speeding out of town.

"Where are we going?" Clare asks.

"To see my dad. To tell your mum. To tell them everything." Angela will be shocked, then she'll sort everything out, and Clare will be okay. And Dad can die knowing about Lydia, about Alex, Lee, all of it. I don't care if it breaks him. And then he's going to tell me about my mother. He has to. It's all I've got. My last bargaining chip.

She's quiet. It's dark, raining; a silent kidnapping. Clare doesn't try to dissuade me. I tell her about the letters. I tell her that I won't be able to read them when Dad's gone. I tell her how I need to hear it from him. I need to know what he did to make her leave me. I need to know that he thinks I'm worth knowing whatever it is he's stored up my whole life. I tell her some cliché like life's too short and things can be gone in an instant and I tune in and out to the sound of my own voice not even sure what I'm telling her but craving her reassurance, ending each sentence with, "You know? You understand?"

She nods, but she's not listening.

The car aquaplanes on the tighter corners. Clare clutches at the door handle every time it happens and I hope she can't smell the beer on my breath. I wind down my window to stop my tired vision from sliding into the middle distance. The rain is touching upon hail and every drop that strikes my face feels thick and almost solidified. It helps me concentrate - it is taking all my effort not to focus on each singular little bead of water streaming defiantly up the windscreen. I wonder where they came from; which ocean, which river, which puddle of piss outside a kebab shop. The downpour melts the snow piled at the side of the road revealing the green beneath. This winter has lasted for years. So much grey that I had forgotten colour exists.

There is water on my face - both warm and cold. Clare looks over at me in quiet curiosity and I swipe the tears and rain away.

She touches her stomach and says, "You should be its dad."

I swear at her because I am trying to watch the road and I misunderstand her with a flush of panic.

"I don't mean like that," she says quickly. "Not that we're blood-related or anything. But I didn't mean it like that, you twat."

"What do you mean then?" I snap. "I thought you were with Jamie."

She is finding it hard to speak in articulate sentences because of the speed we are travelling. Her eyes clack from side to side, trying to keep up with the flashing foliage as it passes by.

"I am. I mean, I want to be. I know you think he's - "

"A fucking arsehole?"

"Yeah. But he's not. And I don't even know if it's going to work, so why not you? You're responsible, you're nice, you like kids. I'm already living with you."

"Clare, you can't just decide that I should be a father figure to your kid, that's just... What about Sabine? What about your mum? Jamie? What the fuck are you thinking?"

Her jaw clenches and creates a hollow at the base of her cheek - it is all I can see when I glance over, losing my accuracy between the white lines and whirring over cat's eyes for a few seconds.

"I just thought... " she murmurs, not wistfully, not wounded, but vicious. "I didn't mean like a father. Just a guy that my kid can look up to."

I grip the steering wheel so tight I can't feel my fingers. "I'm not nice, or responsible, I'm a moron." Just like my father before me. "You think you're following in your mum's footsteps? Lydia's? Try wearing my dad's shoes." Have I got that to look forward to? "You don't want me, Clare, think about it. No-one wants me."

She doesn't disagree. Too busy swallowing tears that I will no doubt pay for later.

I didn't mean to make her cry again. I didn't even mean what I said.

"Clare, I'm sorry."

"Fuck you, Matt."

Chapter Twenty-Eight   Peter

We make a crooked family tree. Twisted and diseased, marked with an X for destruction. I can feel the roots in my forehead - gnarled old veins sticking out like embodiments of bitterness. I take two pills for the pain.

I could have moved house. Part of me worried that if I left, Heather wouldn't be able to find me when, or if she returned, as if telephones and electoral rolls and in-laws didn't exist.

I didn't move. I wanted to show that bastard next door that I was not ashamed, even though I was. I wanted to prove that Matthew was my son, no matter where he came from. It wasn't some mindless alpha male competition. I hated Graham. I wanted to rip his lungs from his chest, but I loved my son, his boy, my son. Even if I found it hard to even look at Matthew's little face for a long time.

I take two pills for the pain.

His little face and his little ears. The result of two recessive genes - earlobes attached to the side of his head and not 'free', detached, hanging low like a regimental soldier. Heather said it was the last piece of proof. She remembered it from the first year of her biology degree, before she dropped out, knew the moment she saw him. She went to see a woman called Gloria who could read palms and tell the future and talk to the dead and she told my wife that I couldn't have children and Heather believed her. It's all in the letter, the one in my belly, how she knew he wasn't mine.

My ears hang low. Freckled, hairy and detached. Heather's didn't. And neither did Graham's. This piece of ridiculous sleuth work was her logic, what sent her packing. She wasn't well. She was depressed, I know that, and possibly somewhere beyond that, into a place where earlobes and a psychic were enough to send her off the edge. Right off the edge, into the ocean.

I take a handful of pills for the pain.

She wrote to me, a week after she disappeared, saying Matthew was Graham's son. Ten years of trying and that bastard next door succeeded where I couldn't. Graham must have known – perhaps he got his own batch of letters – and so I made sure he had to watch that boy grow up from the other side of a garden fence. My boy. Because she left him with me. I had that, at the very least.

My head is splitting open. I know I have painkillers here somewhere. A handy boxful sits in my lap, in fact - sweet shells like M&Ms, chalky within. I crunch them between crumbling molars, two at a time. The animals went in two by two before the rains came and the whole world got washed away. Washed clean. Noah even took the cockroaches with him and it is the cockroaches, not the meek, who shall inherit the earth.

The rain pours unrepentantly, gathering in the top edge of the open window, streaming quietly into the potpourri on the sill. I choke, silently, on an oblong tablet I shove into my gullet without waiting for the others to go down. This could be how it ends. I look for the nurse call button but something shifts. Tired old tissue slackens and allows the pill to slither a little way down, settling on the inside ledge of my sternum.

I briefly consider arranging the remaining tablets into a tableau of apology for whoever finds my body: I'm sorry I was useless; I didn't mean to be so pathetic; I realise now that I was quite unpleasant to many people; please use my organs for research on self-destruction.

The box is empty. At least that's something I've followed through. No more proof, no more secrets. And the ones I'd forgotten are clear. Alex is dead. My baby is dead. My son and not my son, just like his brother who was not his brother. I loved Lydia enough to let her think that I didn't know her well-intended deception, but now my littlest boy – the one I managed to love so easily – he's gone, and I missed it. A blink that lasted weeks.

Matthew tried to tell me. He was just here, sitting beside me on the bed, trying to find the words to make me remember. Just a minute ago, I'm sure. He could still be nearby. I could catch him. Not on foot, not following behind, but I could cut him off in the car park. I could catch him and keep him and stroke spots of rain off his shoulders and send him loose to find his real father. This needn't be the end for him. I can give him that truth. He deserves it.

The window slides fully open with the aid of my shoulder. I climb out stiffly, slippers sliding in the mulch of the flower beds. My one hand grabs clumsily at the ledge and a rusty hinge slices a jagged lifeline across my palm.

The wet car park steams in the night, all but empty. Matthew's car has gone. How can the sun have dropped so suddenly? The failing motor in my head ticks off-beat. It forces me forward through an asphalt plain, peppered with fat little water crowns, appearing and disappearing on impact, as if the raindrops are an inch wide. No more doorways, no more portals, just a road.

He can't have got far. I can catch him if I hurry.

Chapter Twenty-Nine   **Matthew**

I might die tonight, a mangled mess indistinguishable from the twisted frame of my car. The rain sprints down, throwing itself like arrows at the windscreen, so heavy the wipers can only sweep brief lines through the deluge. The headlights barely cut through a square metre in front of the car, and beyond lies the darkness of nine-nine-nine calls and the afterlife. But I am unable to ease off the accelerator, the conclusion to this endless day careering forward like a stampeding animal driven into blind panic.

The raindrops on the windscreen, like blinking stars, distract me from what is behind them.

It's only when Clare goes quiet that I take notice of her. She swallows, like she's forgotten how, and stares out through the darkness ahead with squinted, pained eyes. Her hands rise from the sides of her seat, fixed in a clawed grasp, levitating up to chest height as if she is trying to point but can't seem to straighten her index fingers.

I'm entranced by her slow motion, drained of the heat that has driven me this far. I could fall asleep without any effort right this second. And then I realise I have been watching her instead of the road, and I should already be braking. I see what she sees too late: a man in the road. He wears a dressing gown and slippers, weighed down with the rain. And though we're moving too fast to see his face, I could swear blind that

I catch the pale streak of a smile under hooded eyes.

#

Angela says she heard splashing from the hallway outside dad's door. She saw the open window first, the sodden carpet, then blood on the sill - finger smears left there for balance. Finally: the shoebox. And one overlooked tablet on the floor.

She climbed out the same way he had gone, slid in the flowerbed and fell into the dirt on her side. She says she began crying then, long before she heard the harsh attack of brakes and bumper plastic crunching.

Her fall dislodged the crocus bulbs attempting their way through into the spring air and they lay in disarray around her legs. She carefully returned them to their homes, tucked the slippery soil around them, clambered to her feet and started screaming for Dad. Not Peter, she said. Dad. And just the word on her tongue makes her cry even harder.

#

The car finishes its pirouette and snuggles beneath the awning of overhanging trees, facing the opposite way to which it had been travelling. The rain sieves through the leaves and each dink on the bonnet sounds like an atom bomb.

A hundred metre sprint away is a pile of clothing which barely contains a man. But the dawn of the aftermath has not yet broken and so no-one is sprinting yet. The consistency of time is still Newtonian - solidifying against pressure, melting away when left alone.

The ringing and the white noise begins to fade, too. And then the birds call out for morning.

Chapter Thirty

A part of me rips free from the cluster of my soul. The furious possessiveness that created spite for one son and desperate adoration for the other does not reverse itself, but splits in two and distributes itself evenly between them. Hatred and sorrow never dissipate, but divided, they can weigh less.

The road is black and half-covered with water. I realise that I am days and weeks and years too late to catch Matthew, and a bubble of self-pity belches from my throat, along with a handful of pathetic fallacy tears, for once supporting the rain instead of the other way around.

Memories closest to the surface are the first to go – I grasp at the vague image of a box of clattering pills before it flashes out of existence – along with the logic of why the inside of my head has been replaced with pillow. My pulse judders, frightened of its own beat, and my mouth is dry and yet flooding with saliva until my drool adds to the pool around me. Though I know I should be cold there is heat in my hands and my throat and behind my ears, and I know the lights I see aren't the same as the one we are told to follow to salvation, or perhaps they are and there's a final choice. Maybe existence is just pot luck.

Pinwheels of streaking white light linger in between raindrops as one of Alice's devils roars a claiming circle around me. I fall into pieces but the ground is soft and smells of windy autumn days. Damp grass and bonfires.

There was no collision. Even the cushioned shunt into the undergrowth was an afterthought to the anticlimactic bump against the curb. Our necks were not impressed, but the worst physical occurrence was the stalling of the car.

Clare breathes with a careful precision, her arms folded over her stomach - a calmness at terrible odds with her terrified eyes. I count the rectangles of coloured light in her irises, trapped in the thick moment before everything comes rushing back to speed.

Time lets go of us and we collapse the few inches back into our seats.

There was a man. We both remember. She lets out a choke and forgets what to do with her hands – simultaneously trying to cover her mouth and make an exclaiming gesture – slapping herself in the face by mistake.

I could laugh but I'm already falling out of the open door and receiving my own slapping from the frozen rain. The light from the headlamps disguises the depth of the water on the tarmac surface and I find myself wading rather than running towards the crumpled shape ahead of me.

I know we didn't hit him. But he's not moving and it's my fault. And before I even reach the sodden curled up pile of rags, I know what I am about to see. I curse him with words he has never heard me dare to say, apologising and swearing and by the time I get there I am empty. There's a square of solidified bone where my heart used to be and it hurts like nothing I've ever fucking imagined, like what Alex's death should have felt like, more than a zombie bite, more than anything.

Peter

I see the silhouette of Matthew's face. His ears stick out against the white cloud above him. And though his features are not mine, the years have moulded his expressions into a parody of my own; his frown, his confusion, his sorrow. He looks down on me and my eyes adjust to the light and I realise he is not frowning but in pain, trying to memorise my face.

Just as suddenly, Alex's face emerges from somewhere in between us, and though he smiles, I can see just how little he looks like me.

Still. You are my boys. Mine. You belonged to me.

I will keep talking to Gloria and hope you find your way to her one day.

Matthew

I knelt in the wet road and watched my father's back judder up and down as he tried to breathe. I didn't know it until we reached the hospital – after they removed a creamy globule of papier mâché from his throat – that he'd been choking. The doctor rolled the ball over a few times with the end of his pen.

"Do you know what this is? What he'd been eating?"

"Pills," Angela said.

"Oh my God," Clare said.

"Letters," I said.

Angela had joined me in the road, under the ceaseless, uncaring rain. She stopped the same exact distance away from Dad, as if there were a glass box around his body. She leaned against my shoulder and clenched her teeth and pushed her nails into her knees.

Dad's hand was on his stomach when I turned him over. And on his face: a contented look, as if he had died savouring something delicious.

Acknowledgements

To my husband - thank you for never doubting, always believing, and forever improving my work (and life) with honesty and love. You're the spark that keeps my writing alight and a thousand more cheesy metaphors... And to my babies - you may not sleep, but you make up for it with pure joy. Although it would be nice to be slightly less sleep-deprived for the next book, okay?

To my friends and family - you always said I would, and now I have! Thank you for being there and proving yourselves right. Hugs, high fives and chest-bumps all round.

To my imaginary online buddies and fellow writers - thank you for the excitement, the critiques, the advice, the late night hysterics, the editing and the endless sources of procrastination.

And one final enormous dose of gratitude to the team at Legend Press, and to Elaine and the rest of Luke Bitmead's family - thank you for the most gobsmacking evening of my life, and for the wonderful generosity, support and encouragement you've given me since then.

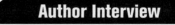
Author Interview

When and why did you start writing?

I can remember the precise moment I realised writing could be magical. I was ten, and had just discovered what a thesaurus was for. Suddenly a story didn't simply have to tell you the practical events of 'this' then 'that'; words could be chosen for their beauty, or their rhythm, or their texture. But instead of pursuing poetry, I proceeded to knock-off my favourite films and books, writing predictable ghost stories, tragic westerns, and a science fiction epic that bore an uncanny resemblance to Star Wars.

By the time I got to secondary school, writing was my lifeboat, and I wrote hundreds of thousands of words in an attempt to exist somewhere other than inside a depressed and bullied teenager. From that point to this there's a trail of unfinished novels, screenplays and short stories, because sometimes the act of writing is more important than knowing where you're going. And then along came *White Lies*.

As for the 'why' of it all, without being too dramatic (although, to be fair, being dramatic is an integral part of storytelling), writing is a compulsion. Fiction is as much of an escape for a writer as it is for a reader. And often it's simply a case of having a story rattling around my head that would really rather be out of it.

The novel approaches sensitive subjects including dementia and end of life care. How important was it to you that these topics were covered accurately?

When I started writing the book, I realised there were two red flags to watch out for. First: I didn't want to perpetuate any damaging stereotypes or myths about elderly care. And second: I didn't want the story to be completely from an 'outside-looking-in' perspective. Peter's voice had to be central, since he is the one actually going through the experience of dementia. Understandably, the majority of personal stories about dementia I found during my research were from the view of family members, but I also managed to find a few sources written by people actually living with dementia, which offered incredibly vivid and touching glimpses into their world. And that's what I tried to recreate for *White Lies*.

Ultimately, the book is about individuals and how they react to a rising heap of impossible situations. Peter's state of mind is just one facet of that journey. My aim was to focus on the details. I remember visiting relatives in nursing homes when I was younger: the smell, the oppressive heat, the frustration and fury and paranoia. A sense of loss nudged up against intense camaraderie. One of my last memories of my grandmother is seeing her throw her zimmer frame down the hall because she couldn't get it over a lump in the carpet - a hilariously tragic moment that was so utterly *her*, just as she was starting to fade away.

How do you feel mental illness is portrayed by society?

I think there's a strange dichotomy surrounding the whole issue. On one hand, media and fiction have a tendency to glorify dark, brooding characters and sociopathic heroes who in reality would be crippled with depression or at the very least be a danger to themselves. And then, on the other hand, we have real life, where mental illness is something people feel incredibly uncomfortable talking about. It's grossly misunderstood, and yet so prevalent - ignoring it isn't going to make it go away.

We live in a big, weird, complex world and not everyone's brain is going to react the same way to all the stimuli and pressure and stress we're exposed to. There's a huge amount of social anxiety over 'fixing' mental illness, rather than acknowledging it. The human brain is incredible - we can adapt and symptoms can often be alleviated, but the solution is not always about trying to make these problems disappear. What often gets forgotten is the fact that there's a person behind the condition who needs to be seen and heard before anything can change.

Your novel is about family secrets, how has having children changed your perception of family relationships?

I think having kids makes you realise the challenges your parents faced and helps you to understand the choices they've made - whether you agree with them or not. We all have good relationships and bad family relationships, but most of them are anchored in childhood - those little flashes of memory are what your siblings and your parents are formed of. And then you're all adults together and sometimes you need to completely rewrite your relationships to accommodate the fact that those familial connections aren't quite so simple any more.

White Lies *explores the milestones of life - from childhood and parenthood to old age. How did you go about researching the novel and creating your characters?*

I actually found Peter easier to write than Matthew, despite him being so far away in age from me. Perhaps deep down I'm just an angry old man. With both characters, I started with a premise and they grew from there. For Matthew it was the difficulty of dealing with the death of someone he hated. How do you deal with that situation? Especially when everyone's looking to you for help? For Peter it was a case of fear and denial: he sees ageing as a sort of disgrace and he doesn't want to face up to what he's leaving behind. Neither of them knows what they want, but they're determined to blame someone else for their situation.

The novel had its own milestones, too. I started writing it soon after my first son was born, and finished the first draft just before my second son was born. When you become a parent, there's suddenly this new awareness of the million little things that contribute to your child's personality - how you affect your child's view of the world, how they are shaped by their experiences and their relationships, how easy it is to get it wrong. It's an overwhelming responsibility at times. And you start to see the trace of family in everyone – what made them that way, what they're going to pass onto their own kids, what's nature and what's nurture. And in case you're asking what I think you're asking: no, neither my parents nor my children are depicted in any way in *White Lies*.

Who are your favourite writers?

I have an enormous space in my heart for Kurt Vonnegut. He has a way of finding humanity and humour in the deepest darkness. Then there's Joseph Heller, Amy Hempel, Gabriel Garcia Marquez, Shakespeare, Cormac McCarthy, Margaret Atwood, Ali Smith… Too many to mention. I read a lot of short fiction and non-fiction, too.

What did it mean to you to win the Luke Bitmead Bursary?

Winning the bursary felt like being very, very drunk without actually having had anything to drink. It was a big, lucky leapfrog into the publishing world and I am so grateful to Legend Press and Luke Bitmead's family for making it happen. It's inspiring to work with a group of people who are so generous in their support of new writers, and who have such an admirable goal of raising awareness of the truths of mental illness. And I feel proud for *White Lies* to be a part of that.

White Lies was the Winner of the
2013 Luke Bitmead Bursary

The award was set up shortly after Luke's death in 2006 by his family to support and encourage the work of fledgling novel writers. The top prize is a publishing contract with Legend Press, as well as a cash bursary.

We are delighted to be working with Luke's family to ensure that Luke's name and memory lives on – not only through his work, but through this wonderful memorial bursary too. For those of you lucky enough to have met Luke you will know that he was hugely compassionate and would love the idea of another struggling talented writer being supported on the arduous road to securing their first publishing deal.

We will ensure that, as with all our authors, we give the winner of the bursary as much support as we can, and offer them the most effective creative platform from which to showcase their talent. We can't wait to start reading and judging the submissions.

We are pleased to be continuing this brilliant bursary for a seventh year, and hope to follow in the success of our previous winners Andrew Blackman (*On the Holloway Road*, February 2009), Ruth Dugdall (*The Woman Before Me*, August 2010), Sophie Duffy (*The Generation Game*, August 2011), J.R. Crook (*Sleeping Patterns*, July 2012), Joanne Graham (*Lacey's House,* May 2013), and Jo Gatford (*White Lies,* July 2014).

For more information on the bursary and all
Legend Press titles visit:
www.legendpress.co.uk
Follow us @legend_press